RISE OF
THE WATCHERS

'PROOF' The Sequel

RISE OF THE WATCHERS

TED D. BERNER

GRIGORI
Publishing

First edition from Grigori Publishing, October 2021

Published in the United States by Grigori Publishing LLC
Box 966, Lincoln, MT 59639

Cover design by: JH Illustration
Editing by: The Editorial Department; Renni Browne, John Robert Marlow and Doug Wagner
Book Design by: Maureen Cutajar, www.gopublished.com

ISBN: 978-0-9964156-3-7

www.proofthesequel.com

Printed in the United States of America

ACKNOWLEDGMENTS

First and foremost I'd like to thank my readers. To be able to share the fruits of my labor with all of you makes the countless hours spent investigating the past a most rewarding experience. I'd also like to thank the ancients for leaving us the telltale signs of their lost knowledge. The clues left behind have driven me to research their legends and weave them into a fictitious story that may explain the inexplicable.

*"If you want to find the secrets of the universe,
think in terms of energy, frequency and vibration."*

NIKOLA TESLA

PROLOGUE

The myths, legends and locations mentioned in this book are real, or as real as they ever were. None have been fabricated by the author.

ACTUAL EVENT
DECEMBER 9, 1965
KECKSBERG, PENNSYLVANIA

In the early evening hours of December 9, 1965, just outside Kecksberg, numerous witnesses reported seeing a fireball streak through the sky. It made two sharp turns before it crashed into a wooded ravine with a thud.

Not long after impact, witnesses saw a blue glow coming from the area where the object had landed. About fifteen minutes later, a state trooper arrived at a nearby farmhouse with two plainclothes officials. One was seen carrying a Geiger counter as they disappeared into the woods.

The local volunteer fire department was called out to look for a possible airplane crash in the area. What they found was a line of broken treetops leading to a long furrow in the ground. At the end of the trench was a metallic object the size of a VW and shaped like an acorn. They all saw a ring around the bottom that was covered with markings resembling Egyptian hieroglyphics. The object was still hissing as it slowly cooled when men wearing trench coats arrived. They told the locals the area had been quarantined and ordered the onlookers to leave.

Hundreds of spectators gathered in the distance to see what was going on. Some reported an odd odor—similar to sulfur—in the air. Shortly after the spectators arrived, armed military personnel flooded the outlying area and ordered everyone out of that area as well.

Within three hours of the crash, several military men came to town and set up a command center at the Kecksberg fire station. The military even invaded a farmhouse close to the site to use as a base.

Men dressed in hazmat clothing with NASA insignias arrived carrying a five-foot-square box with protruding rods to hold it by—eerily similar to the method used to transport the biblical Ark of the Covenant. They disappeared into the woods carrying the box.

Soon after, a military convoy arrived with several Army jeeps escorting a large flatbed truck. After the object had been loaded on the flatbed, somehow a carload of teens were able to get close enough to see the truck's payload before it was covered with a tarp. They, too, corroborated the previous descriptions of the strange object: a metallic, acorn-shaped device with Egyptian hieroglyphics around a ring at the base.

Later that night, several more witnesses saw the flatbed truck leave the scene carrying an object the size of a VW bug covered with a tarp. The truck driver was in such a hurry that witnesses were sure that if anyone got in the way, "they would have had to scrape them up with a putty knife."

Word that the object had been transported to Wright-Patterson Air Force Base surfaced and a local truck driver inadvertently saw the object in a nearby facility the next day. Again, his description matched the rest.

NASA had no record of space debris that should have been in the area at the time. The government initially said that nothing was found but later said it was a meteorite. Everyone who saw the device said the same thing: it was an acorn shaped, metallic object, with Egyptian like hieroglyphics on the side around its base. The only other description of the object was that it was the shape of a bell …

APRIL 1945
WALTER MINE SHAFT
BENEATH THE OWL MOUNTAINS, POLAND

Blasting can be heard as bombs trounce the ground above an old mine shaft. The percussion reverberates through the earth as rocks break free from between the support beams. Soldiers scurry about, gathering up equipment. Several men wearing lab coats are lined up and being shot in the head where they stand by soldiers wearing swastika armbands.

A young boy darts out from the shadows and runs away unnoticed, then disappears into an alcove through a small hole in the rocks. It caves in seconds later.

As the blasting from above continues, a large copper-colored object is hastily moved through the tunnel on a forklift. Then, almost out of nowhere, an old man wearing a red hat and carrying a handbag runs in to the mine shaft from which the object has just been removed. He grabs several tube-shaped canisters and turns to run back into another corridor when a soldier notices him.

"Halt! Halt where you are!" the Nazi shouts, but the old man keeps running.

The Nazi raises his weapon and fires. Bullets ricochet off the tunnel walls, and one strikes the old man in the back of the head just as he ducks into an offshoot.

Another large blast shakes the earth even more. Boulders plummet from the roof of the mine shaft until the offshoot is completely blocked, sealing the cave from the rest of the tunnel.

The forklift continues down the open mine shaft with its odd payload and turns at a junction, exposing the object one last time. On its side is a swastika and strange markings around the base. The object bears a striking resemblance to a large bell.

RISE OF THE WATCHERS

CHAPTER 1

THE LIMOUSINE RIDE WAS relatively smooth over the pothole-pocked road in the run-down, sparsely lit neighborhood. The aging man in the backseat despised America and all it stood for. The depressed sight out his window repulsed him. It was the first time Rudolf Himmler—one of Heinrich Himmler's forgotten illegitimate sons—had been to the United Sates, and he hoped it would be the last.

Of all the places in the country, why did it have to be the poverty-stricken bowels of New Orleans where he would, at long last, find the one who could make his father's lifelong dream of a super-soldier a reality? Only he was going to take it a step further and clone a Watcher. One of the biblical fallen angels mentioned in many legends across the globe. With the unimaginable power possessed by these long-lost spiritual beings at his beck and call, he would be unstoppable. Avenging his father's death would be his first order of business.

If she's the real thing, it will be well worth putting up with the filth of this offensive place and the wretched smell of impoverished America. He stared out the window. A bit of joy shared space with the hatred seething through his eyes.

He'd known for some time of the existence of a recycled soul from the time of the first giant hunters centuries ago, and this one was supposedly very special. So much so that Himmler was sure he could help him track down a living descendent of the ancient giants also known as the Nephilim. One whose DNA would still have traces of the elusive God gene from the fallen angels also known as the Watchers. That was all he needed to fulfill his dream.

The car came to a stop. The large man with a small scar across his left eye in the driver's seat turned to face his boss in the back. "I do believe this is it, sir. Would you like me to accompany you?"

Himmler stared out the window for a moment. "No need," he said in his thick German accent as he got out of the car. "It will not take long to see if this one is real or just another fraud."

Even though there was a steady rain beating down on the city, the old man's hopefulness overshadowed any unpleasantness that may have otherwise made his trip more distasteful. As he walked closer to the small house tucked into the tightly packed neighborhood, he couldn't help but think of how pleased his father would have been to see his plan coming to a possible head.

A cat snarled and ran out of the bushes just as Himmler was about to knock on the door. He heard the doorknob unlatch, followed by the raspy voice of an old woman.

"It's open. I've been expecting you."

Impressive ... She just might be the one after all.

He opened the door, unveiling the sight of the elderly woman dressed in a long flowing garment like a gypsy from the old country. The woman's home resembled a museum, decorated with relics from a lost era.

He gazed about the room and tried to hide his accent. "Very nice place you and your husband have here, ma'am. Thank you for allowing me into your humble abode unannounced … although it seems as though you knew of my arrival." His eyes stopped on the old woman. "Which brings me to ask: how *did* you know of my coming?"

"Ah … but isn't that why you have sought me out? To ask a question? I do have a gift, sir, but it only shows me bits and pieces and it comes when it comes … That I cannot control."

"So then, if you are for real, do I even need to ask?"

"As I said, it shows itself at its choosing. Come, sit and give me your hands … Touching sometimes seems to help with answers."

He did as she asked and stared into her eyes while he sat. It was obvious from the décor of the room that the old woman lived alone—that was good. He remained silent as she squeezed his hands. Her eyelids instantly began to flutter as though her soul had slipped into another realm.

"The one you are looking for is one of the *first* …" She seemed to fall into a trance-like-state. "There is *only* one here now, but he has not yet awakened to his true purpose or who he once was."

Her body shuddered, and more of the past began to flow. "He has been here before and the proof of his being still exists even to this day, but his mission is not over. His infatuation with the men of renown is no accident." She paused and cocked her head. "I see … I see another being from long ago. One who humans fear, but even he is afraid of the one you seek. He has the face … the face of a serpent."

Himmler spoke softly. "Can you see his name? Do you know where he is?"

Her head tilted back slightly as her eyelids continued their hypnotic flutter. "He is close … very close, and in this time … he has been drawn to …"—she seemed to slip further away from the present—"drawn to the same area as the co-creator of the oldest structure on the banks of the great river … the one once known as Ra-Ta."

The old man didn't like riddles, but he could sense he was close to the end of his long quest.

She continued in broken dialogue as if she were reading off a blurry cue card. "He is now just a stone's throw from where Ra-Ta made his last appearance in this realm … A student … a student in Virginia … Alexandria, Virginia."

"But a name." He was calm, but his patience was growing thin. "What is his name?"

"His current name is …" It seemed as if something was trying to block her vision.

"What? What is it?"

"Larson … The boy's family name is now Larson, but it's who he *was* that is so—"

"What about his first name? What does he go by now?" *Larson at a school in Alexandria, Virginia. Is that enough to find him? Probably, but she must know more.*

It still seemed as if someone or *something* was impeding her sight. "I … I can't tell, but … I can see his father … He goes by Grant." She appeared to be struggling. "Yes, and he is also close to the boy."

He'd heard enough and didn't care who the Larson boy was in a past life. It might take a little to track him down, but he knew this was enough. The old woman still seemed to be lost in another dimension far away when he got up and went for the door.

Finally, at long last I will be able to finish what my father started years ago.

He pulled the door almost closed but made sure to leave it unlatched as he left. The rain was still beating down on the world around him, but with his goal now closer than ever before, getting wet was the last thing on his mind.

The driver looked in his mirror at Himmler as he shut the door and got settled in his seat. "Did you find what you're looking for, sir?"

Himmler nodded while looking into the mirror at the chauffeur's reflection. "I did indeed. Now we must cover our tracks, my friend."

The driver nodded and got out of the car into the rain and went toward the house.

A MANGY CAT RAN from the back room of the small house. It raced past the old woman, who was still in a deep trance. The cat let out a yowl and threw itself against the front door that had been left ajar, latching it shut, which jarred the woman back to life.

"Thank you, my feline friend, but your valiant attempt will only buy me a minute or two."

She stood and turned away from the door and picked up the old rotary phone on the small table next to her chair. An external force guided her fingers to the numbers. She put the phone to her ear. It only rang once before someone answered on the other end miles away.

"I don't have much time, so listen carefully."

There was a firm knock on the door. The old woman paused for a moment before proceeding to talk to the stranger on the other end. "There's something I must tell you. ... Never mind who I am, but know that I have an important message. I am a seer, but unfortunately my ... *gift* is not controlled by me."

The knocking on the door grew louder.

"Please open the door, ma'am," she heard from the other side. "My boss would like to pay you for your time."

"There is a soul whom you seek," she continued, "but you are not alone. Unfortunately, I believe I have disclosed his current identity to someone I should not have … Never mind who I am. My time in this plane is short and I must try to make right from my gaffe. The entity now goes by the name of Larson, son of Grant Larson, but he is unaware of who he is, although I can assure you he is one of the *originals* … How do you know you can trust me?"

The old woman turned to the door to see the scarred face of her reaper come crashing through. In her crackly voice, she uttered her last words.

"I knew to call you, didn't I?"

PRESENT DAY
ANDES MOUNTAINS, ARGENTINA

"NO!" DAN YELLED AS he and Selena watched Himmler's fortress explode in a bright blue flash in the distance.

"What in the name of God?" Selena froze as she watched the Nazi's lair, which Grant and Ty had just infiltrated, disappear before their eyes.

They had been waiting from their safe vantage point several hundred yards away after smuggling Grant and Ty into the complex. Grant and Ty were going to sabotage the six generators, which had just recently been bumped up to full capacity to power what they thought was Himmler's attempt at creating a super-soldier of some kind.

"It's gone … completely gone!" Dan was in a state of shock.

"We saw them get caught, so I don't understand. Do you think they did something to those generators to cause that?"

Dan shook his head. "They weren't there long enough before they were nabbed. What they were planning to do was going to take enough time that they would be able to get out the same way they got in—in the trunk of your car in the morning. I just don't get it."

The ominous glow that had lit up the sky slowly faded to black.

UNITED FLIGHT 3882
WASHINGTON, D.C., TO BUENOS AIRES, ARGENTINA

SO FAR, THE FLIGHT to Buenos Aires, Argentina had been smooth. It had only been ten hours since Butch Colton had received the strange text from his silent associate, Grant. And in that time, it had become apparent that the rather large and *odd* explosion reported at the base of the Andes outside the small town of Oran, Argentina, was connected to Grant and his son's disappearance.

Butch and Grant had crossed paths in the border patrol some thirty years ago. It was shortly after that when Grant had bailed Butch out of a sticky situation that most assuredly would have cost him his life or, at the very least, a life sentence in a foreign prison. Since that time, he knew that everything good in life that he'd had since was because of Grant's unselfish action. Butch vowed to repay him every chance he got.

Butch had received only a portion of the text for help from Grant before the signal was interrupted. *Help … Himmler … Watcher.* He wasn't quite sure what it meant yet, but with their shared text app, Butch was able to get a latitude and longitude fix from where the message originated. With the enormous blast from the same location as the origination of Grant's call for help, he could only hope he wasn't too late.

Butch had been helping Grant try to find out who had been following his son, Ty, for several days, only to finally hear the wildest story he'd ever heard in all his years in the espionage business.

This had been the first time he'd heard of Genesis 6:4 and the fallen angels taking human women for wives and having children, which were the giants known as the Nephilim. But when they found out from Ty's classmate Tom Bruiner that the aging Nazi Rudolf Himmler—illegitimate son of Heinrich Himmler—was using Ty as a bloodhound to track down a living descendant of the Nephilim, the story got even more bizarre.

Between the secret group that Bruiner was with, known as S.O.J., which had been trying to eliminate anyone with Nephilim blood in their veins since the great flood and Himmler trying to find one so he could create a super-being to help restore the power of the Third Reich, Butch just didn't know what to believe. Was it possible the Nazi had actually created even something more than the Bruiner kid had told them about? Butch had trouble digesting the super-soldier story they dragged out of the kid, but a Watcher, an actual spiritual being—was that even possible?

And what about the connection to the ancient mysterious megalithic stone structures scattered across the planet, such as the Great Pyramid? Could this biblical civilization really have been involved in their construction? Grant's son Ty certainly seemed to think so.

Then there was the mystery of Mount Hermon. Why would there be a UN outpost on the exact spot where the fallen angels first appeared on the planet? Butch knew Ty had been intrigued by that coincidence, and it sure struck him as extremely odd.

He was staring out the window of the Boeing 777 as it started its final descent when the voice of the attractive flight attendant interrupted his train of thought.

"We're preparing for landing now, sir. You'll have to raise your seat back, please."

Butch was annoyed by the interruption and leisurely turned his head until he made eye contact with the lowly airline employee. "Don't worry about it, little girl. It'll be up be before we land."

The flight attendant paused, then took a step back. She seemed to be processing what he had just said. It was apparent she wasn't used to that kind of response. The look he gave her must have been enough to make her decide that moving on and leaving him alone was in everyone's best interest.

Butch never did well with taking orders, which was one reason he had left the CIA. This parting also opened up several other lucrative business opportunities that would have been ignored by someone with higher ethics. His moral code had always been an easy one: whatever benefited him the most at the time was going to happen.

There had been several people over the years who had found out the hard way that he was anything but a gentle giant. Although he was a very large man, he never gave the appearance of being gentle. He had a rugged face, with cold dark brown eyes, and always wore his hair as if he were in the Marine Corps, although learning how to march wasn't something he'd ever been willing to do. A five o'clock shadow wasn't enough to hide a long scar on his left cheek. With hands like a gorilla's, he rarely needed a weapon to defend himself but almost always had at least one. Grant was the only person on earth Butch would actually drop everything he was doing in order to help out. He liked not having to answer to anyone.

The flight attendant sheepishly continued to walk down the aisle, finally taking her eyes off Butch to carry on with her duties. He turned his head back to face the window. Thoughts of what may have taken place to have Grant send for him started to race through his mind. The information they had extracted from Tom Bruiner a few days before had seemed so absurd to him that he had a hard time believing it. The only thing he knew for certain was that Mr. Bruiner believed it. The truth serum Butch had injected into his bloodstream made him sure of that.

Butch had always thought the Bible was nothing more than a big fairy tale, so stories of an aging Nazi extremist's aspiration to somehow resurrect one of the Nephilim had to be nothing more than another fantasy. Nonetheless, something strange had taken place in the remote area of South America. Something that had all the world's secret agencies swarming like ants to a picnic basket.

The airliner planted on the runway with a hard thump and roared as it decelerated while the blast from the thrust reversers reverberated throughout the fuselage. As it exited the runway and slowed to taxi speed, Butch could see something wasn't right. Airplanes were parked on almost every square inch of the ramp space. But the oddest thing was the subconscious feeling he had as he stared out the window, a feeling he couldn't quite put a finger on.

Clearing customs was a much longer and more painful experience than he'd had to endure since the days right after the terrorist attacks of September 11. The terminal was crawling with reporters, and there were several men with matching dark blue suits and black ties who looked as if they'd all come from the same cookie cutter. Had he not acted as soon as Grant's call for help came, he most likely would have had to get a car the old-fashioned way, as there were sold out signs posted at all the car rental agencies at the airport.

Having several fake IDs, he'd chosen that of a freelance traveling journalist from the United States to help squelch any questions as to why he was there.

"The midsize SUV you requested is ready for you Mr. Spartan, but may I suggest an upgrade to something a little roomier?" The rental agent's programmed spiel came without looking up as he filled in the empty fields on his computer screen.

"If I had wanted something else, you'd already know it, because that's what I would've ordered." Butch's response was gruff and coarse enough to cause the agent to look up from his computer and into Butch's eyes. "Any more questions?"

The agent quickly looked back to his screen. "No … no, sir. Your choice of vehicles is most wise for this area." He handed Butch the keys and pointed him to the parking garage where his car was waiting.

Once he was in his rental and out of the garage, his first stop was to acquire some essentials he'd been unable to bring with him on such short notice. Not only that, but transporting weapons of any kind might draw the kind of attention he liked to stay away from.

The SUV was anything but a smooth ride because of the rugged suspension he had requested. But as he made his way to his connection—which was about to set him up with a small arsenal—the lack of comfort was the last thing on his mind. What could possibly have happened to cause the blast that was most likely the reason Grant seemed to have fallen off the edge of the earth?

Butch's thoughts were brought back to his current mission as he approached the house of the gun dealer who was going to set him up with the tools of his trade. He felt naked not having anything other than his fists for defense, but that was about to change.

He drove past his destination in the rather modest neighborhood on the outskirts of the metropolitan area. All the homes were adjoined and looked alike, with a tan stucco exterior. It looked like any wind at all would take some of Spanish tiles on the roofs for a ride. The mostly vacant street was narrow, with just enough room to park and let one lane of traffic pass.

He came to a stop a few buildings beyond the one he would soon enter. He lit a cigarette and waited several minutes while he watched the area in his rearview mirror. It didn't take long to see he was not in anyone's sights. Being cautious was a trait that had kept him out of many a precarious situation.

With his cigarette burned almost to the butt, he scanned the area one more time. He opened the door, pinched the last of the life from the ember and flicked the remains into the debris along the street. From the backseat, he retrieved two large empty duffel bags. It was a slight uphill walk back to where he would meet his contact. Even though he was dressed modestly, his massive frame under the long trench coat made him stand out from the few locals who were going about their business.

When he got to the front of the building, he carefully scanned the area before proceeding into the narrow alleyway leading to the back of the building, just as he had been instructed. He'd been given the address by one of his trusted contacts he'd met years ago.

It was the third door down, number 3A. He only had to knock once and the door opened to reveal a man of small stature but with somewhat of a grisly face.

"Yes, Señor, may I help you?" The man's English was surprisingly good, which didn't matter to Butch, as he was fluent in several languages, Spanish being one of them.

"I'm in the market for some local flare," Butch said as he looked the little man over. "Juan mentioned you could steer me in the right direction." He paused and looked up at the blue sky. "Looks like rain in the air."

The unshaven, sun-worn little man didn't bother to look as he opened the door wide.

"Come in, Señor ... We do business now."

CHAPTER 2

VICTOR BLACKWELL'S
DELMARVA PENINSULA, VIRGINIA

IT HAD BEEN ONLY a couple of months since Victor Blackwell's young late-night guest had made his surprise visit. The fact that the Larson boy had been drawn to his most prized possession had caught him off guard but was an event that had been foretold. Victor walked over to the display and picked up the old dagger in admiration but also with an air of puzzlement. Ty Larson just didn't seem like he could possibly be one of the *originals*.

The letters *S.O.J.* had been etched into the handle in relatively recent years, but the ancient markings on the other side were a different story. He turned the artifact over to reveal what might be the oldest written language on the planet. Even older than the Sumerian cuneiform text found on the clay tablets in Mesopotamia. This was the written word of the people before the great flood and was saved by the survivors on the ark. The blade had been forged from a metal-like material of an unknown source.

S. O. J.: The Sons of Jared. If only the original giant hunters knew their undertaking would be needed throughout the millennia. Victor turned his attention back to the artifact.

Rumors were that Sir Charles Warren had found the dagger on Mount Hermon in 1869. It had been close to the temple where he found the mysterious stone inscription of an oath taken by the two hundred fallen angels: "According to the command of the greatest and Holy God, those who take an oath proceed from here."

Victor had made a special trip to the British Museum to see the stone with the mysterious inscription when he first heard of its existence many years ago. That was the trip where he met the strange man who told him of the secret dagger and helped him eventually acquire it. According to legend, it was forged from the same material as the missing capstone of the great pyramid itself—a material unlike anything ever found on the planet. Some thought the strange material must have come from the outer reaches of the universe in the form of a meteor. If anyone knew for sure, they never unveiled the secret.

Victor had witnessed how the boy gravitated to the dagger. *Was it possible he had once used this ancient tool for its true purpose?* Victor knew the information he received was always accurate and never asked the Organizer where it came from.

He placed the relic back in its case. The invigorating feeling he had every time he touched the object flowed through his body like a drug of limitless power. He could only pray its services would never again be needed, although he feared that the outcome of the latest events would be what everyone in the movement had been trying so desperately to avoid for millennia.

BASE OF THE ANDES MOUNTAINS
ARGENTINA

BUTCH HAD BEEN ON the road for several hours and was almost

to his destination. While he was driving through the small town of Oran, it had been obvious that something of great magnitude had taken place, as most of the national TV networks had a presence. He knew it was only going to get worse.

With no news from Grant, Butch had to get to ground zero. Going in through the front door wasn't an option, which is why he chose the vehicle he was driving. The SUV had a higher suspension than just about anything else available and was built to traverse the primitive road he was now on.

After several miles of rough traveling, he finally made it as far as he could drive. From here he would have to walk. The surrounding area with the towering Andes looming over the wooded foothills was a beautiful sight to behold. Besides his two bags of black-market goodies, he had purchased a large backpack and other survival supplies that he'd methodically packed for the fifteen-mile hike he was about to embark on.

He'd been on several jobs that required a backdoor visit to add to the element of surprise, but he truly had no idea what he'd find at the end of this offbeat jaunt. The fact that he was loaded for just about anything that might try to get in his way added several pounds to carry across the rugged terrain. He'd always kept his body in the best possible physical shape to aid his efforts to stay alive with unforeseen dangerous obstacles lurking on the horizon, which were common in the life of a mercenary.

Butch moved across the landscape like a machine. Mile after mile he trudged through the wilderness while wondering what could possibly have happened to his longtime friend. Could the story of the fallen angels' taking human women for wives be true? And what about their giant offspring—might that actually be true as well? Butch had never believed the Bible or mythology to be true, but now he wasn't quite so sure.

The night-vision goggles he brought were a must to have as the sun descended over the tops of the high mountains. With the goggles, his GPS, plenty of water and an occasional protein bar, his sleep-deprived body would be able to continue to Grant's last known location—only a few miles away now.

Butch's body was wearing down, but he was getting close and the sun had just started peeking over the horizon. He topped one last hill and an odd feeling came over him—the air itself felt strange. Then, as he came through the trees at the top of the rise, he saw it.

The gaping hole in the landscape before him must have been at least as big as two football fields, only perfectly round and about half as deep. What was even more amazing was that the hole was a perfect half sphere.

Butch crouched next to a large rock under one of the last trees at the apex of the ridgeline and took out his binoculars to get a better look. On the opposite side of the hollow he could see the local authorities scurrying about on the edge. There must have been close to a hundred military personnel, along with numerous armored personnel carriers and even a couple of tanks.

He scanned the area again to make sure he was alone. From his vantage point, he was invisible to everyone at the scene below.

Focusing again on the newly formed void, he was still puzzled by the sight. It was the oddest thing he'd ever seen. What the hell could have caused it? A meteorite? *No … it's just too perfect.*

Suddenly, something even stranger jumped out at him. At first, he was so taken in by the enormous hole in front of him that he hadn't noticed it. But it wasn't what was there that was odd—it was what *wasn't* there. There was absolutely no debris anywhere to be seen.

CHAPTER 3

ETHAN ALDRIDGE, ALSO KNOWN as the Organizer, was a tall middle-aged man. He was well-groomed and wore a relaxed-fit custom Armani three-piece suit. And although his shoes were very high-end, they were most definitely built for comfort.

He paced the grand room of his upper Manhattan apartment contemplating the possible strategies to be used if what he feared was actually on the horizon. Although the event had happened a continent away, Ethan knew all too well that it was only a matter of time before the effects would be felt globally. There was a chance the explosion had snuffed out the madman's dream, but he was afraid it only signified the beginning of something he'd been trying to prevent his entire adult life. Thousands of years ago, the Creator took drastic action to clean up a mess of epic proportions. His concern now was that same situation might be unfolding once more.

Could the rise of the Nephilim actually be about to be unleashed on humanity again? And what if—God forbid—the Watchers were freed from their earthly prison? The thought was hard to come to terms with. His organization's quest to extinguish the Nephilim bloodline had been a valiant effort by many of his comrades around the world for millennia but might have been in vain after all.

With the mysterious call from the old woman several months back, he thought they'd have an inside track to derail ODESSA—the infamous group that had helped smuggle Nazis out of Germany after the war—but it didn't appear so now. It had been just in the last week that he'd heard from an informant inside the Nazi's lair that what the madman was really trying to create was not one of the Nephilim but a Watcher, one of the fallen angels themselves. Or maybe something even greater. Then what? Ethan didn't want to rule anything out. If the crazy man's lab experiment was a success, it might only be a matter of time before history would repeat itself.

Hopefully, the explosion annihilated everything before the creature was complete. Or maybe the creation's soul will be that of pureness and not of lust and greed. Both were happy thoughts, but neither seemed likely. If the creation of a spiritual being had actually taken place, how could it be destroyed by a mere physical explosion? A spiritual being would surely have to be a pure form of energy, and wouldn't that just facilitate the process? The fact that there had been no reports of any strange creatures seen in the area after the explosion was a bit puzzling, though.

He stopped pacing to look at the globe on the mantel. He spun it a few degrees and stared at the spot on the planet where the Creator had imprisoned the most dangerous Watcher. His confinement was secure, but if another of their kind had been born, would it not eventually seek out its equals? And if Azazyel—the evil one—was released, surely his first agenda would be to release the remainder of the two hundred. The thought sent chills up Ethan's spine.

He reached for the old rotary phone and dialed. It didn't take long for his old friend to answer.

"Blackwell, we need to talk."

TWENTY-FOUR HOURS LATER
BASE OF THE ANDES MOUNTAINS
ARGENTINA

"SELENA," DAN WHISPERED TO the attractive woman in the crowd. "We're going to have to tell someone at the agency about this."

She turned her head, making eye contact with Dan, then turned away to face the crowd. "I know, but what are we going to say happened?"

"I have absolutely no idea." Dan stared off into the distance. "But we need to make a plan."

"For Christ's sake, I don't even know where to begin. This whole thing was unbelievable from the start. And that explosion—that was the strangest thing I've ever seen!"

He nodded and motioned toward a more secluded spot at the edge of the onlookers. "Do you think it's even remotely possible Grant and Ty got out?"

"I don't see how they could have. I don't know how anything could have. Unless they somehow slipped out the back and got far enough away before the explosion happened, but we saw them get caught, so …" She shook her head. "I hate to think the worst, but—"

"I know." Dan put his hand on her shoulder. "It doesn't look good, but there's always a chance. But that blast—it was like something I've never seen before. Almost like a blue plasma erupted into a miniature supernova or something."

"I wonder what the hell could have caused it? Maybe something they did to those generators?"

"I don't know." Dan lowered his voice as a group of reporters walked past. "But it's the weirdest thing I've ever seen. And why isn't there any rubble anywhere?"

"Could everything just have vaporized somehow?"

"Not sure," Dan said as he shrugged his shoulders. "Nothing about this makes any sense."

"And not to sound insensitive"—Selena raised her eyes to meet his—"but what's going to happen to us when we come forward and tell the boss what we were doing without authorization?"

"I don't know, Selena. Hopefully he'll cut us some slack. But as far as Grant and Ty go, we have to hope for the best, which is they got out. And if they did, they're probably going to need help. We can't abandon them … not now."

"You're right." Selena turned away. "We can't do that, but I'd still rather try on our own to find them before we rat ourselves out for trying to take down Himmler without approval from the agency."

Just then, Dan noticed a rather large man wearing a trench coat and a well-worn fedora watching them. No sooner than their eyes met did the stranger look away.

"Don't be obvious, but glance over to your right at the big guy in the trench coat."

"The big bruiser? What about him?"

"So, you don't recognize him? He was watching us a second ago and I just happened to catch him, so he knows I saw him."

The man was now wandering away and taking pictures of the area with an expensive-looking camera.

"It looks to me as though he's some kind of a reporter or photographer," Selena said out of the corner of her mouth. "One I wouldn't want to meet in a dark alley."

Dan nodded. "Maybe … I don't think we should trust anyone right now, though." He scanned the crowd. "It's possible some of those Nazis or whoever they were weren't in there when the complex blew. Somebody around here must know more about the whole thing, and I think we should find them."

"So, what do you propose? Should we pose as journalists, or just concerned tourists maybe?" Selena looked the crowd over as she spoke. "Some kind of a reporter might get more response from any-one we need to talk to. How about we take a geological viewpoint and go with that for our questioning?"

"Sounds good to me." Dan said as he looked around for the man in the trench coat. He was nowhere to be seen. "We'd better get to town and dress the part."

GIZA PLATEAU, EGYPT

DEEP UNDERGROUND, DIRECTLY UNDER the right front paw of the Sphinx of Giza, was a cavity that had been sealed off from humanity for several thousand years. A lot had happened to the face of the planet in that time, but the contents of the dark room were somewhere in the far recesses of mankind's memories, just out of reach.

Then there was the sound of metal slamming into a rock. Then another and another until a thin ray of light came streaming in. A noise grew louder and the ray of light grew even larger. A greenish hue filled the room with an ominous glow as a shovel came crashing through.

CHAPTER 4

ORAN, ARGENTINA

DAN AND SELENA HAD been posing as writers for a geological magazine. After two days of questioning anyone they thought might be able to help, they'd come up empty. They knew no more than they did before the event, and that wasn't much. There were a few people who seemed to know of Germans who had been in the area for several years. There had also been an occasional sighting of none other than Adolf Hitler himself in years past, but nobody seemed to know anything concrete. At least now they were operating under the banner of the CIA, as they had both contacted their superiors. Of course, they left out anything that would hang themselves.

As they sat at a local coffee house discussing the situation, they were at a loss as to how to proceed.

"How much longer are we going to keep digging up nothing but dead ends?" Selena aimlessly swirled her spoon in her coffee. "We're going to have to get a look at that hole in the ground close up, but it's going to be hard to get past the Argentine army."

Dan nodded. "Yeah, that's going to be a bit of a problem. You got any contacts down here to help with that?"

She stared into her coffee for a bit and was about to say something when a slight breeze swept through the room. It was enough to make them both turn around to see the same large man they had seen a few days ago in the crowd of people shortly after the explosion. This time, though, he didn't look away when they made eye contact. In fact, his coercing stare seemed to last an eternity. Then he strode over to their table and sat, never taking his eyes off of them.

Before Dan or Selena could say anything, the stranger, in a deep raspy voice with his eyes locked on Dan, spoke. "Aren't you a long way from home?"

"Excuse me?"

He looked to Selena. "At least you didn't have far to travel. Tell me, what did you tell your superior happened to your partner? And the boy—did you happen to mention him?"

Selena spoke up. "I'm sorry, you must have us confused with someone—"

"Cut the crap! I know you two were with Larson and his kid, so tell me what the hell happened to them!"

"So why don't you just tell us who you are?" Dan was intimidated by the man's size, but he knew he couldn't show weakness.

The stranger turned his focus to Dan. "Let's just say I'm here to see the safe return of Larson and his kid. I think we're on the same side … no?"

"But who *are* you?" Dan asked.

The stranger turned to Selena.

"I'll tell you what I know." He leaned back in his chair. "I know there was a large complex right where the big hole is now. I know it's now gone. I know Larson was in that exact spot four days ago. I know it was inhabited by a crazy-ass Nazi with some crazy-ass ideas. I know there's absolutely no debris anywhere on the ground from the blast. And I also know there's absolutely nothing left of the place in the pit … firsthand. Now why don't you tell me what you know?"

"You've been in the pit?" Selena asked. "How did you get by the army?"

"I have my ways. So, I'll ask you again. What can you tell me that I don't know?"

Dan thought about it for a moment. "Even if we knew anything about this, and I'm not saying we do, why would we open up to a complete stranger?"

"We can play this game all day, Mr. Clancy. But shouldn't you do something to try and help your partner and his kid?"

How the hell does he know my name?

The big man slid his chair back from the table and got up. "Give it some thought." He looked at his watch. "I'll check back with you in twelve hours, eight in the morning. I highly recommend you try to help your comrade." Then he turned and walked out.

"But how will we know where to find you?" Selena asked.

"I'll know where you are," he said without looking back.

CHAPTER 5

ORAN, ARGENTINA

IT HAD BEEN A long night for Dan and Selena. They'd been up for hours trying to figure out who the mystery man was who would be seeking them out within the hour. The only thing they could come up with was that he must have worked with Grant sometime in the past and they still had ties. Whoever he was, he obviously had connections and did appear to be on the same side … at least sort of. They had decided to trust him enough to share what little they knew, as it seemed he already knew just about everything they did anyway. The time seemed to drag by, but they drank their coffee and waited.

Just as the stranger had said, he found them at exactly eight. With no wasted motions, he walked into the café and straight to their table, sat down and in his deep voice said one word. "Well?"

"Good morning to you, too." Dan didn't like working this way, but confiding in the big buffoon was a necessary evil, at least for now. So he let the information flow as to what all had happened, starting in Cairo.

The rough stranger listened without the slightest hint of emotion, and when Dan was finished, the man leaned back in his chair for a moment before reaching into his coat pocket and taking out a card. He tossed it in front of Dan and Selena.

"I'm going to stay on this, but it doesn't look like there's much more to see here for now. So why don't you give me your numbers and we'll help each other out if we can." He swung his focus to Dan. "Agreeable?"

Dan looked to Selena. She nodded. "Okay, let's do it."

They both pulled out their cards and handed them over, and the man with the demands stood up and walked out.

After the door closed, Dan picked up the card. *At least now we'll know who this clown is.* He turned it over, and they looked at each other and shook their heads in disgust. It was nothing more than a business card from the same hotel they had been staying in.

United Flight 3591
Buenos Aires, Argentina, to Washington, D.C.

THE BOEING 777 LIFTED off the runway and made its turn to the north for the long flight back to the United States. Butch sat in the window seat and looked out at the Andes in the distance and had to wonder what might have happened on the mountainside and what else was unfolding because of it.

Several days had passed since he had first seen the result of the event that had occurred in the same location as Grant's call for help. In that time, it had become clear that no one really had any idea what had taken place. With a little detective work, he found there had been an old castle-like structure there that had been occupied by a very secretive organization. There were rumors of ties to refugees from Nazi Germany since the early 1950s, but they were never confirmed.

Butch remembered the information they got out of Tom Bruiner about the leftover Nazi group ODESSA and had to make the obvious connection. Mr. Bruiner was the only player whose whereabouts were still known in this crazy affair. Butch's plan now was to track Bruiner down once again to see if he could squeeze any more pertinent information out of the little smartass. He had seen enough to know that no one could have survived the odd explosion. Even though, he still had to do what he could to get to the bottom of the disappearance of his comrade. God help anyone who got in his way.

Just then he recognized the odor of a perfume he'd smelled only a few days ago. He looked up to see the same flight attendant who had given him grief about his seat back on the flight there. She swung her head around, making eye contact with him, and it was obvious she recognized him as well. The smile on her face quickly faded and she turned the other way as she passed him by.

That's what I thought. The hint of a sneer crept over Butch's face.

The young travelers sitting next to him wrenched their necks to get a glimpse of the scenery before it was gone. Butch's sneer didn't fade as he pulled the window shade down, pushed the button to recline his seat and closed his eyes.

TEN DAYS EARLIER
INSIDE THE GREAT PYRAMID
EGYPT

HIS HEAD SEEMED TO be in a deep fog. The only thing he could remember was a bright blue plasma-like flash. *Where am I?* It was hot. In the distance, he could hear something that sounded like ... voices. Something inside him told him to get out of there. The lighting was dim, but he appeared to be in some kind of cave. The walls were smooth, as though they had been polished. He knew—for some reason—that he couldn't confront whoever was speaking in the distance, *but why?*

The only way out was a long narrow square tunnel that led toward the muffled voices. He had to crouch to traverse the long exit. Sweat beaded on his forehead as he went. He knew he had to hurry. Then he came to a small dark offshoot that seemed to almost go straight down, but the entrance was blocked with a locked chain-link gate. He reached into a small crevice, grabbed a key and popped the lock open and hurriedly slipped down into the vertical shaft. The only light now was coming from where he had just been and was fading fast. He went down as quickly as he could until he came to a small room, where he stopped for moment. Then it hit him: *how did I know about that key?* But he didn't have time to figure it out now—he wanted to distance himself from the voices.

As he slipped farther down the shaft, the temperature cooled immensely—it felt good. The light was fading now, and he finally came to another vertical tunnel with a slight uphill grade. The darkness became overwhelming, but the voices seemed to be getting louder.

What is this place?

He shook his head, trying to unleash the haze that engulfed his brain. It was voices he was hearing again—he was sure of it. They were growing even louder. Not loud enough to make out words, but it was as though he recognized them somehow.

His eyes slowly adjusting to the lack of light, he noticed a faint illumination in the distance. Maybe at the end of another tunnel? Then he could see movement in the light. One, two, and then a third blurry figure passed. The last one seemed to pause for a brief moment as though he were looking right at him.

Everything seems so familiar.

A voice with an Egyptian accent said something that seemed to prompt the last figure to move again. The voices started to fade.

After several minutes, he heard someone say, "Helloooooo." Then it dawned on him: not only did he not know where he was, but he didn't know *who* he was.

CHAPTER 6

THE PRESENT
MILLERSVILLE, VIRGINIA

TOM BRUINER HAD BEEN recruited into the secret organization of S.O.J. several years ago by a friend of his father. His fascination with the giants from the Bible was what made him a perfect candidate. Although the task of cleansing the world of anyone with DNA from the Nephilim in their veins seemed pretty far out there at first, it only took one encounter to make him a firm believer that the job needed to be done.

Tom sat in his car up the street from the house he'd been watching for the last few days. He had been waiting for his target to emerge and hopefully lead him to other ODESSA players left in the area—if there were any. Even the CIA couldn't find any trace of the one he was waiting for now. But Tom had not only been keeping tabs on Ty throughout this whole ordeal— he'd also been keeping track of the one and only Ivan Baumann, aka Dr. Eisenberg—his and Ty's archaeology teacher from Alexandria University.

Of course, he'd been in contact with several of his brethren about the meeting he had with Ty's dad and his goon. He'd also heard of their trip to the Middle East and on to South America where the explosion had taken place. It seemed apparent that Ty and his father were killed in the blast. There wasn't much he could do about any of that now, so he'd set his sights on the only other player whose whereabouts he knew: his former Archeology teacher.

The reason the CIA couldn't find hide nor hair of the professor was simply because the cagey Nazi had two residences: the one he held in the name of Eisenberg for his university profile in Alexandria, Virginia, and this one, in the small town of Millersville on the other side of D.C., under the name of Baumann. Tom had discovered this almost right away, since ODESSA had been infiltrated by one of their own. Their spies were able to come away with a handful of names, including Baumann's.

Whatever the reason was that Baumann didn't get out of the country didn't really matter to Tom. Maybe it was just good fortune. Tom and his cohorts in the area weren't going to let him out of their sights now.

Then he saw the front door open and out stepped a slightly different version of the man who had been portraying his teacher for the last couple of months. Instead of a clean-shaven well-kept distinguished gentleman, here was a man with a shaved head, the start of a raggedy beard and somewhat shabby clothes. According to everyone who had been staking out the Nazi operative, this was the first time Baumann had been out of his secret apartment since the final day of his archaeology class.

Okay, you scumbag, let's see what you're up to. His adrenaline flowed as he watched the old man look around the neighborhood and climb into his car.

Tom picked up the small radio off the seat. "The subject is on the move."

He followed their last Nazi connection for close to three hours out to the peninsula across from Chesapeake Bay. He had half expected him to try to get out of the country, but it was evident now that that was not his intention as they drove deeper into the middle of nowhere.

Baumann finally turned off the main road onto a narrow dead end that was overgrown with thick vegetation, making it almost a one-way road. Tom turned his lights off and stayed way behind until he saw a faint light in the distance. After pulling into the brush along the road, he got out and followed on foot.

It didn't take long before he could see Baumann's parked car next to a gate in a tall fence that seemed to enclose private property. As he got a little closer, he could see there was an odd house in the center of the enclosure. It appeared to have three stories, with no windows on the bottom two, and looked to be made of concrete.

I'd better make a call. He slid back into the brush out of sight and got on his phone.

Victor Blackwell's
Delmarva Peninsula, Virginia

Sensing a tone of desperation on the other end of the phone, Victor tried to ease the man's concerns. "I don't know how far they have progressed … It's a slow process when one has to work under the cloak of darkness, but I do know they are getting closer. Hopefully anytime now … What makes you think it will be needed now?" As he listened, he nervously fiddled with the phone cord. "I see … I'll find out and report back then, although it may take me a day or two … Okay, same to you old friend." He hung up with a blank stare.

After standing in thought for a few minutes, he picked up the receiver again and dialed. "It's me," Victor said in a weak voice. "We need to pick up the pace with the Giza project … and try to get me an idea of how much longer … Thanks. I know it's not easy, but it appears as though time may be of the essence."

No sooner had he put down the phone than the direct line to his front gate rang. Picking up his monitor with the surveillance video stream to the outside view of his fortress, he could see a rough-looking man with a shaved head looking directly into the camera.

"Yes, may I help you?" Victor asked.

"I know it's been a long time, Victor, but I need to see you."

At first he didn't recognize the face, but the voice … There was something familiar about the voice.

TOM WAS ALMOST HOME and couldn't help but think about the odd set of circumstances that had just unfolded. Eisenberg was known to have been connected to ODESSA, an extremely important cog in Himmler's plan. Although when Tom had followed him to the strange fortress across the Chesapeake Bay and phoned in what was happening… it just didn't make any sense that his superior told him to leave. Even though he knew that things were never black and white with the workings of the Organization, it was something that was going to gnaw at him until he found out more.

As he pulled into his parking space, his phone rang. *Good. Maybe it's him again with some answers about what's going on.* He grabbed his cell from his pocket and then froze in his tracks as he stared in disbelief at the incoming number. It wasn't the number he was expecting, but it was one he'd received calls from several times in the past—just not one he'd ever expected to see again. The call was coming from Ty Larson's phone.

CHAPTER 7

VICTOR BLACKWELL'S
DELMARVA PENINSULA, VIRGINIA

VICTOR PRESSED THE REMOTE, opening the outside-perimeter gate. He walked to the mantel and stopped to look at an old black-and-white framed photo of two small boys standing next to a uniformed soldier. He picked it up and stared as though he were in another time and place.

The door buzzer sounded, and without turning around he pressed the remote in his hand and heard the clunk of the latching mechanism as it sprang free. His visitor opened the door.

Victor stared at the photo while he spoke to his unexpected guest, "It's been a long time, Ivan."

"Yes ... it has. I see you haven't forgotten."

Victor put the photo back in its place, but it still had a firm grasp on his gaze. "There are times when I think it'd be better if I had."

"We all have our reasons for what we do in life, Victor. It was fate that put me on my path. I had a chance to get even with those Nazi bastards."

Victor spun around and locked eyes with Ivan. "*Get even?* You chose to live with those scumbags!"

"They were not involved with the invasion. Besides, I needed to stay close if I ever wanted a chance. Surely you've heard the expression of keeping your friends close and your enemies closer? If you'd experienced what I had, you'd have done the same. I wish you could understand that."

"Why are you here?" Victor asked. "Have you come to ask for forgiveness for the unfolding calamity you've helped to unleash on the world?"

"Himmler's intentions were kept from most of us. I had no idea of his true intent … brother."

Victor looked back to the photo. "I've gone the last sixty years without any family and you want to call me your brother now?"

"The family that took me in were not the cause of our parents' death and they would have taken you in, too. We didn't have to separate. It was you who shut me out. Or did you forget? That doesn't matter now. We have bigger problems on our hands and something needs to be done to stop it. It sounds as if Himmler's creation is more than anyone thought."

"What makes you think there's any way to stop it?" Victor asked.

"I've spent my whole life following the participants of Project Riese and the billions in Nazi gold that went into more experiments not too far from here. If anyone has a chance to fix this, it's me."

TOM STARED AT HIS phone while it rang. *This can't be … Even if he's not dead, why would he be calling me?* It was just about to go to voice mail when he broke out of his trance and answered the call. "Hello?"

There was a long pause on the other end, but he finally heard a voice, a voice that sounded muddled yet … an awful lot like Ty's.

"Who is this?" the voice asked.

"*Who is this?*" *Who the hell did you call?* "Who were you calling?" Tom politely asked. "And if you don't mind me asking, who are you?"

Again, there was silence on the other end.

"Ty, is that you?"

"I … I don't … I don't know. Your number was in this phone and I … I need help."

Even though he wasn't sure who was on the other end, Tom didn't hesitate. Whoever it was had Ty's phone and it certainly sounded like him. Even if it wasn't, he must be somehow involved in the recent events that had higher-ups across the world scratching their heads over what was taking place.

"You got it, buddy. Just tell me where you are and I'll come get you."

There was a long pause. "That's also something I need help with. I don't know where I am."

Victor Blackwell's
Delmarva Peninsula, Virginia

"What are you talking about? Project Riese? What Nazi gold?" Victor was still appalled by the sight of his long-lost brother, but his interest was piqued.

"Project Riese was born when Allied forces began to bomb the Nazis' 'wonder weapons' factories. This prompted the Germans to move the factories underground. Right in our backyard, Victor, which is why I chose to stay."

Victor nodded. "Yes, I heard they started with their tunnels after I got away. So what?"

"It was in the tunnels where the Nazis built their most coveted weapon, Die Glocke, otherwise known as the Nazi Bell."

"That was a myth, Ivan. There was never any proof of that."

"Trust me, brother." He put his hand on Victor's shoulder. "It was there. I saw it."

"You saw it?" Victor knocked Ivan's hand off. "How?"

"I will get to that later. First we have to focus on the best chance we have to stop this situation from going too far."

Victor was brief. "I'm listening."

"You must remember what was known as the Philadelphia Experiment."

"I remember, and I recall the cover-up that followed the disastrous event. What does that have to do with anything? And what about the Nazi gold you mentioned?"

Ivan turned from his brother and walked to the photo on the wall. "I remember the day this was taken. A lot has changed since then."

"Please!" Victor snapped. "Save the reminiscing for later."

"Of course." Ivan nodded and continued. "The Philadelphia Experiment was just the tip of the iceberg with what they—*your* government was trying to do. The fact that the inhuman experiment morphed into the even more inhuman Montauk Project is more proof that the good ol' U.S. of A. has no regard for the well-being of anyone except for those in charge."

"That project was just a hoax and you know it!"

Ivan spun around. "Was it? Or was it a continuation of the experiments with the Bell, which the U.S. was so envious of? You do remember Operation Paperclip, don't you? All the Nazi scientists that were recruited into the secret operations of your homeland? Against their will, I might add."

Victor was silent as he stared at Ivan.

"You have to trust me on this, brother. Because of my experience, I had connections at Camp Hero. One of those connections went to Kecksberg when Die Glocke reappeared. Please believe me." Ivan stared into Victor's soul as he spoke. "You must make the call. … This is the fastest way to fix things now."

"What do you mean 'when the Bell reappeared'?"

CHAPTER 8

VICTOR BLACKWELL'S
DELMARVA PENINSULA, VIRGINIA

"WHAT DO YOU MEAN 'when the Bell *reappeared*'?" Victor glared at his long-lost brother.

"You see, brother," Ivan said, "when it was apparent Berlin would fall, Hans Kammler had orders to move Die Glocke out of the underground laboratory to a waiting U-boat. The U-boat would then transport it to Argentina, along with Kammler and several lucky SS members who–"

Victor cut him off. "So that's how Himmler acquired the Bell?"

"Actually, no," Ivan said. "What no one knew at the time and, for that matter, still, is that an American spy had infiltrated Kammler's life, and when it became obvious the Germans were not going to come out on top … well, let's just say Kammler was made an offer he couldn't refuse. So, while the bombs were dropping on Berlin, Kammler was smuggling out the Bell, all right, just not to the U-boat that was waiting for it."

"I don't get it. So if that's not how Himmler came up with it, then where *did* he get it?"

"That's a rather odd story. After it was smuggled out of Poland to the nearest Allied airport, which was no easy feat since the Russians also wanted it, the Bell was flown back to the states and was on its way to none other than the infamous Area 51."

"Not surprising," Victor said.

"No, but what was surprising was that it never arrived."

"Never arrived? What happened?" Victor furrowed his brow.

"According to the crew on the flight, the Bell started to hum not long after takeoff. The humming began to grow louder in time. They said it sounded like … like a bee hive. Then it started to vibrate."

"What? Well, what the hell was powering it?"

"Good question. Nobody admitted to tapping into the plane's electrical system. I don't even know how they could have done that, the theory is that as the aircraft carrying it was flying east to west and was cutting the earth's magnetic lines of force. Basically, causing induction, which is—"

"When a conductor cuts across the lines of force in a magnetic field, it generates a current. I know how induction works. But how could that possibly create enough electricity to power the Bell?"

"I don't know, but when the Bell started to vibrate, they were concerned about the plane shaking apart. So, just as they were starting to scramble to try and shut it off somehow … it disappeared."

"What? What do you mean it *disappeared*? Where the hell did it go?"

"All good questions, brother, but it's not *where* it went but *when*."

"When?" Victor cocked his head and focused on his long-lost brother.

Ivan nodded. "Oh, yeah, it was when, all right. Do you remember the Kecksberg, Pennsylvania, incident?"

"Yeah. The Kecksberg incident. I remember. It was in the news and nobody really knew what it was. They thought maybe a satellite. But that was long after the war. The sixties, if I remember right."

"Yes, brother, 1965. The Bell fell exactly twenty years into the future."

DULLES INTERNATIONAL AIRPORT
WASHINGTON, D.C.

TOM STOOD IN WAIT of the passengers who were about to arrive on Egyptair flight MS981 from Cairo. It had only been a day since he had been on the phone with who he thought might be Ty. If it had been Ty, he would know for sure in just a few minutes. After having deduced that Ty—if it really was him—was in Cairo, it didn't take long to find another member of the Organization in the area who was able to track him down. The photo Tom's comrade sent of the subject looked like Ty, but something about his face looked extremely odd. Whoever he was, he had Ty Larson's phone, but no other documents whatsoever. Even then it didn't take long to get him set up with a fake passport and driver's license and on a flight back to Washington, D.C., which had just arrived and was now deplaning.

Several passengers came down the escalator that led to the baggage claim for the flight from Cairo, but no one he had seen before. Then he saw two men coming down side by side, one of which was dressed in all black. It was Ty, there was no doubt about it. Odd, though—something about Tom's buddy was very different. It was more than the confused look on his face—he seemed to have changed somehow. It was apparent that Ty didn't recognize him at all. The look on Ty's face was something Tom had never seen before.

"Good to see you again, buddy," Tom said as he stretched out his hand.

Ty looked like he was lost but still reached out and grabbed his hand. "I apologize, but I really don't remember anything of my past, but there's something about you that … that, well, I just can't put my finger on it … something familiar."

"Don't worry about that now. I think I know someone who can help pry into what's in that head of yours. In the meantime I'll fill you in with what I know about you. Maybe something will jar your memory. I have a feeling that whatever's in the recesses of your brain is going to be truly astounding, my friend."

Ty nodded. It was obvious he was trying hard to remember something, or just anything at all.

Tom let go of Ty's hand. There was something very different about him now, something much deeper than just a failed memory.

CHAPTER 9

TOM HAD DRIVEN FROM the airport into the city to take Ty to see a hypnotherapist who specialized in retrieving memories and was also a member of the Organization. The rendezvous to clear out the cobwebs from Ty's mind had been set up deep in the underground facilities in the 1090 Vermont Avenue building.

The S.O.J. had recruited Erica Hahn—the hypnotherapist—a few years ago because of the amazing results she had with all her patients. The fact that she lived in the D.C. area also made her a prime candidate to help keep tabs on Ty during his time at Alexandria University. Getting a librarian job at the local library had been the perfect cover for just that. And though Tom had been unaware of her being a member then, it made sense now. Celeste Peterson had been the beautiful woman the Nazi used to lure Ty into unknowingly finding a descendant of the Nephilim, but it was Erica's natural beauty that may have played a part in the countless hours Ty spent researching at the library.

While working with the attractive hypnotherapist, the story Ty had revealed to her while under deep hypnosis was a compelling one indeed. Might he just have hallucinated as a result of the traumatic experience, though? He said the first thing he could remember was waking up inside a deep dark tunnel that turned out to be located in the Great Pyramid of Giza. Of course, he had absolutely no recollection of how he got there. He only knew, somehow, that he had to stay away from the voices he was hearing at the time. Once he was able to get out without encountering whoever it was he was trying to avoid, he was able to get into the city, where he had been roaming the streets for the last ten days—several days *before* the explosion in Argentina!

Is it possible Ty's account was true? If so, that could only mean that not only had he somehow been transported across the world, but he also was transported back in *time* by several days! Could time travel actually be possible? If that is what indeed really transpired, it would appear so.

Then there was the brief mention of the serpent. It was vague but seemed to affect Ty in a profound way. He had started to twitch and then muttered, "It's here. The serpent is here. It's … it's trying to tell me something, but I … I can't understand." Those were Ty's last words before he awoke back to the present.

Erica paused and stared at Ty, whose eyes were wide. "Serpent? What serpent?"

Ty looked from her to Tom and back. "What?"

"You mentioned a serpent. What serpent did you see?"

Ty shook his head. "I don't remember any serpent."

"Okay, let's forget that for now and try again, Tyler. Can you remember anything at all before waking up in the Great Pyramid? Maybe an odd feeling or even a strange smell? Anything at all?" Erica had asked this before, but it seemed as though the fog might be lifting a little in Ty's subconscious.

"There was a light … an intense light. An energy. I can remember an energy that was … all-knowing? It … it was like I was a part of it, if that makes sense. Like I knew everything it knew, which …

was *everything*. But now I just can't remember ..." Something was keeping him from reliving the experience. Was he subconsciously blocking it, or was it something else?

"Maybe we should let him rest a bit now." Erica seemed genuinely concerned for Ty, although Ty didn't seem to be in any distress, just in a fog. "As for what you've experienced, Tyler ... have either of you heard of the Philadelphia Experiment?"

Ty looked at Tom, and they both shook their heads.

"Well, gentlemen, let me fill you in." She leaned back in her chair. "I've done quite a bit of research into this event, for reasons I can't divulge, but what I firmly believe now is ... Well, let's say I think Ty's little jaunt through time was *very* real."

"The Philadelphia Experiment is an enigma that's been around since the early 1940s. As with many of the military's top-secret projects, the Philadelphia Experiment was also shrouded in secrecy to the point of denial by all government agencies."

For the next several minutes, Ty and Tom listened intently to what their new confidante had to say.

Apparently, in the fall of 1943 in the Philadelphia Navel Shipyard, the Navy warship USS Eldridge may have had a part in one of the most popular conspiracy theories of the time. According to some reports, the Navy had been working on a project to help keep warships invisible to enemy radar and avoid more casualties from German U-boats. Through the use of two Tesla coils on board, an electromagnetic field was created that not only made the ship and crew invisible to radar but was also undetectable to the human eye. To make the story even more compelling, the ship was somehow teleported to Norfolk, Virginia—several hundred miles away.

"Are you saying the same thing happened to me?" Ty asked.

"Well, it would appear as though your experience is quite similar. The entire process only lasted a few minutes, as with you, but the effects to some of the crew seemed to have lasted a lifetime."

"What do you mean … lasted a lifetime?"

"Well, according to some stories, while the ship was in the invisible state, the crew could move about freely, somehow able to pass through solid parts of the ship. When the ship materialized again, some of the crew members were completely missing, and if that wasn't bad enough, some were found dead. They were physically stuck in various parts of the vessel, such as the decks and the metal walls, literally fused to the ship. Some of the survivors were said to have had lingering effects, including fading in and out of sight, going crazy and ending up in insane asylums and even bursting into flames sometime after."

Tom looked over at Ty and slid his chair a little in the opposite direction. "Nothing personal, buddy." He turned back to Erica. "So what could have happened to cause such a thing? Not to only disappear temporarily but to actually pass through some kind of portal to another place miles away?"

"We don't know for sure, but if these events truly did occur, it would be no wonder the government would want to refute it. Supposedly there were eyewitnesses, though, so obviously someone is lying.

"It was rumored that the one and only Nikola Tesla was even a part of this project, along with Albert Einstein. If Tesla was indeed involved, it would further substantiate another story of his experimentation with time travel in the mid-1890s.

"Tesla had been experimenting with magnetic fields and found that the time-space continuum could be altered if a certain process was used. Of course, after his death, all of his papers were confiscated by government officials, so there's no documentation to back up this claim. There is, however, a witness who claims to have seen Tesla in a coffee shop after he had a brush with some three and a half million volts of electricity while dabbling with time travel. He was reported to have said while stuck in the magnetic field that he could see the past, present and future all at the same time. It was this same process that was used on the USS Eldridge almost fifty years later."

WHEN TY HEARD THIS, it was as if another memory were trying to resurface. Something about electricity was needling him, but he couldn't quite put his finger on it.

"Einstein's theory of relativity," the hypnotherapist said as she leaned forward in her chair, "relates to the fabric of space-time, which could indicate why he might have been involved with the Philadelphia experiment. Personally, I think time travel was just a lucky side effect of trying to make the ships invisible to radar, but I seriously doubt it was a surprise to Tesla or even Einstein as far as that goes.

"If the device you described while in your trance truly was the long-lost Nazi Bell, it would appear the story of its true purpose was indeed to manipulate the fabric of space-time—unless Hitler's scientists just got extremely lucky. Of course, being executed at the order of the Führer would hardly classify as good luck."

Just then the mind specialist's phone beeped, which was odd, since both Ty and Tom had watched her turn it off before the session. She glanced at the message and quickly motioned to the corner of the room.

Ty and Tom turned to look, noticing the small dome in the upper corner of the ceiling, which looked to house a security camera. No sooner did they realize that others must have been watching than two large men wearing suits came through the door and closed it behind them.

"My apologies, my new friends," Miss Hahn said, "but it looks like you'll have to stay here for a while yet. It appears we have a situation on our hands."

CHAPTER 10

"**W**HAT DO YOU MEAN we have to stay here?!" Tom said. "I brought him in to get some answers and this is how you thank me?"

The therapist looked up from her phone. "Actually, Mr. Bruiner, you're free to go, Tyler is the one that's needed here. Having said that, by no means do you have to leave. You're more than welcome to stay. Everything will be explained to you shortly, but for now, let's just say we need to keep close tabs on you, Tyler. I'm sure once you've heard what's going on, you'll be more than willing to help. After all, where would you go?"

Ty looked around the room. There was no way out other than the door, which was blocked by the two men. And their host was right—where would he go? He had absolutely no memory of anything before finding himself inside the Great Pyramid of Giza.

"How did you really end up back in Egypt, Ty?" Tom leaned back and furrowed his brow.

Before Ty could answer, the therapist cut in. "Excuse me, gentlemen, but we thought we had an upper hand in this matter, and it turns out we don't."

Ty was quick to reply. "Just what matter are you talking about?"

"I know you're quite versed in Edgar Cayce's readings, so I'm sure you're aware of the Hall of Records he spoke of that were located under the right front paw of the Sphinx?"

Ty leaned back in his chair and slowly nodded his head. "Yeah, I remember now. I went to his library … in Virginia Beach, I think. I do remember reading about the Hall of Records. I also remember they've never been found."

"Unfortunately, it appears someone's recently found them, as they're missing."

"Missing?" Tom asked. "From where?"

"For years we've been trying to find these records through legal channels with the Egyptian government, only to be denied time and time again. It wasn't until we heard about Himmler's plan that we thought we'd better skirt the legal channels and recover the records at any cost."

"Are you saying you found their hiding place and they weren't there?" Ty said.

"Yes." Erica nodded. "That's exactly what I'm saying."

"How do you know they were ever there?" Ty looked at Tom, then back at Erica. "I mean, you find an empty chamber in the ground and just because it's under the paw of the Sphinx you assume it was used to harbor the records Cayce talked about?"

"Oh, they were there, all right. Mark my words. We found evidence of that. Unfortunately, we were beat to the punch by only a few days."

"What's so damn important about these records anyway?" Tom asked.

"It's the lost knowledge of the ancients they contain. God help us if the wrong person is the only one who acquires it."

"Any idea who found them?"

"Oh, we have a good idea, all right, and if it's who we think it is … well, let's just say we need to intervene."

"So, what can we do?" Ty asked.

"Well, we do have another option here."

"Which is?" Tom fixed his gaze on Erica.

"Find one of the other sets."

"Other sets?" Tom shifted his attention to Ty.

"Yeah, I know what she's talking about," Ty said, "Cayce said there were three sets of records sealed up after the fall of Atlantis. One in Atlantis itself, one in Egypt, and the other—"

"In the Yucatán Peninsula," came a voice over a speaker.

The therapist stared at the two as they turned their heads to face the camera dome.

"What's this got to do with me?" Ty asked.

The voice came over the speaker again. "Because, my boy, you seem to have an uncanny knack for finding things."

MANHATTAN, NEW YORK

ETHAN ALDRIDGE CLICKED OFF his microphone and turned away from his desk to look at the Manhattan skyline. *He sure doesn't come off as anything special. How am I supposed to rely on him to save mankind?*

He stood and walked to the window and stared. He hadn't chosen the role of Organizer—it was his birthright, handed down through the millennia. Probably a role he would not have taken had he a choice.

It was only a few moments of window time before he spun around and picked up his phone and hit speed dial. "I'll need you to set up some travel arrangements … As close to Piedras Negras as you can get … It's in the Yucatán, Guatemala … Three … I'll send you a copy of their passports this afternoon … Yeah, thanks."

After he hung up, he walked to the wall and took a painting down. Hidden from view by the art was a small wall safe, and he plucked away at the keypad and the door sprang open. He reached inside and grabbed a small black notebook and flipped it to the first page, then opened his cell and sent off a short message. In all his years in this position, he'd never had to use this mercenary before, but his reputation was unrivaled. Hopefully, his services would only be precautionary.

WASHINGTON, D.C.

NO SOONER HAD BUTCH gotten off the flight from Buenos Aires than he heard a text come in. Not many people had this number, so he knew that unless it was Grant, it meant work. He glanced at the screen without missing a step and then stopped. *You gotta be kidding me.* He chuckled to himself while shaking his head. *It's a small world.*

He replied to the text. "Yeah, I'll do it."

CHAPTER 11

AEROMEXICO FLIGHT 527
WASHINGTON, D.C., TO PALENQUE, MEXICO

THE THREE OF THEM sat abreast, with Ty next to the window, in the Boeing 777. Erica had the middle seat and wasn't nearly as relaxed as her patients seemed to be when she had them under for a past life regression. Flying wasn't her favorite thing. She was one of the best at what she did, though, which is why she was a lucky recipient of the third seat to the Yucatán. The information she'd extracted from the deep recesses of Ty's mind was the whole reason for their destination and why she was a little nervous. Hopefully, the man who Ethan had hired to watch their backs would be enough insurance for their mission.

It was very rare to do a past life regression that far back in time. Edgar Cayce did it a few times, but he was a master at traveling through the Akashic records.

Most historians across the planet regarded the legendary Atlantis as pure myth. But didn't every myth have a grain of truth buried in it somewhere? Edgar Cayce brought up the doomed continent and its inhabitants more than seven hundred times. If he was right about his medical readings, why would his others be wrong?

She looked at Ty while his attention was outside. *What else is hiding in that subconscious of yours?*

TY LOOKED OUT THE window as the jumbo jet lifted off. It seemed like only yesterday he'd come across Genesis 6:4 and started to wonder what possibilities that one verse might suggest. Now his life was upside down, and why he was such an integral part of this craziness was still a mystery to him. But more prominent than that in his thoughts was what had happened to his dad.

Ty sank back into his chair and closed his eyes. Even though his gradually lifting amnesia and the blunt reality of the situation were weighing heavily on his overtaxed mind, he needed rest. Relaxing as much as he could, he finally drifted to sleep.

Ty pushed aside the vegetation as he made his way through the dense jungle. Then he realized he didn't know where he was going or what he was looking for. But he did know there was something he was supposed to find. What was it? He knew he was getting closer, but to what? Then he heard a hiss. A terrifying hiss from some kind of reptile …

"Ladies and gentlemen, we've started our initial descent into Palenque. Please return to your seats and fasten your seat belts."

Ty's eyes flew open at the announcement over the PA. He looked out the window, then at Erica. "Damn, I must have nodded off."

"You sure did. Looks like you were dreaming. Anything of interest?"

Ty thought for a second. "Not sure, to tell you the truth. But I think we'd better watch our backs when we get down there." He looked out the window. "Looks like we're here."

"Yeah, the adventure begins."

"So, Erica, how long have you been with this organization? I mean, how does someone convince you there are giants and fallen angels running around and you need to help track 'em down and kill 'em?"

She exchanged a look with their companion Clint Bryant—the bodyguard hired to watch over them. "Maybe later, Tyler. There's a lot here to digest for all of us, but let me make one thing clear: you can trust me with anything. Please know that."

Ty smiled and nodded. "A lot to digest is putting it mildly, but thanks."

The jumbo jet's tires screeched as they touched down.

A LARGE MAN IN a parked sedan across from the airport watched as the three exited the terminal with their driver/guide in the Toyota Land Cruiser. The monitor in his hand beeped with a strong signal. He looked at it and leaned back in his seat and watched as they turned the corner and disappeared from sight.

CHAPTER 12

THE YUCATÁN PENINSULA

BLACK STONES IS THE English translation of *piedras negras*, which is the modern name for the ancient once-magnificent Mayan city. Although it's thought to have originated around seven hundred BC, there are some who date the city much older, maybe as far back as almost five thousand BC. As with many ruins throughout Central America, their constructions were built on top of much older sites. Who were the original builders?

Some of the legends refer to the Paddler Gods at the beginning of civilization. In fact, some of their glyphs show them traveling by canoes through floodwaters with active volcanoes in the background. Could this have been a reference to a global flood and Noah in the Ark? Or might it have been the Atlanteans relocating after the fall of Atlantis? If inhabitants from an advanced civilization such as Atlantis were to show up, wouldn't they have the appearance of gods to a primitive race such as the Maya?

Some thought that the ancient gods Viracocha, Quetzalcoatl and Kukulkan might be one and the same. If so, who might it have been? In some of the Inca legends, Viracocha initially created mankind out of stones, which were giants that ended up displeasing him through their evil actions, so he had to destroy them. Just one more story that mirrors that of Genesis 6:4.

The strange thing was that the folklore of not only the Maya but also the Aztecs and Incas included stories of white-skinned bearded gods with blue eyes that came to the land after a great flood. They civilized the inhabitants of the land by bringing order to their world, along with teaching them many things such as farming.

The natives were dark-skinned and had no facial hair. Why would their gods look so much different? They must have modeled their gods after someone they had once seen. Might there be truth buried deep within their legends? If it happened that they were indeed the survivors of Atlantis, Edgar Cayce's story of their records being brought to the area were probably true as well.

Another strange coincidence was that when these "gods" left the area, they all said they would one day return. This helped lead to the demise of the Incas, Aztecs and Maya. When the Spanish arrived in the area in the 1500s, they were thought to be the gods returning because of their lighter skin and bearded faces. They were welcomed as such, and the natives paid the ultimate price for their ill-guided trust.

Ty's group had come to the area of Piedras Negras not only because of what he revealed while under hypnosis but also because of the readings of Edgar Cayce. This had long been thought to be the location of the records of Atlantis in the Yucatán.

The city was rediscovered in the late 1800s by Teobert Maler, who made a crude map of the area. Researchers from the Carnegie Institute came on four trips from 1914 to 1931, but it wasn't until the University of Pennsylvania excavated the ruins from 1931 through 1939 that the most impressive artifacts were found. In fact, in one of his readings, Cayce said an Atlantean artifact had been found there in the 1930s and placed in a museum in Pennsylvania. Ty and Erica were no doubt on the right track.

IT WAS A RELATIVELY short drive from Palenque, Mexico to the point where they would have to continue on foot to Piedras Negras, Guatemala. Though the weather change from the winter season in North America was nice, everyone was focused on the adventure ahead as they left the pavement and proceeded down the primitive road, getting closer to their destination. Unlike some of the other famous Mayan sites in the Yucatán such as Chichen Itza, Piedras Negras was off the beaten path. Only true adventurers would ever see the sight.

Pedro, their local Mexican guide and driver, tried to make conversation, but his broken English and their preoccupation with the task at hand made for a quiet trip. With a pair of expensive binoculars dangling from his neck, he looked like a deep-woods birdwatcher. All of his fifty-five years on the planet had been spent in the Yucatán, so his knowledge of the area was extensive.

"Why you wish to go to Piedras Negras?" Pedro asked. "There are ruins not as far, easier to get to. Palenque has own ruins."

Ty just stared out the window, but Erica spoke up, "We're looking for something in particular at Piedras Negras. We'll know more when we get there."

"You lucky you come now."

"Oh? Why's that?" Erica asked.

"River soon to be blocked off ... to make electricity."

"Blocked off? You mean they're building a dam?"

"Sí, a dam, very soon."

The three of them exchanged a look. "Damn, nothing like cutting it close," Ty said.

Erica shook her head and turned to face Ty. "I'm starting to understand what Tom said about you."

Getting to Piedras Negras wasn't just a typical day trip. Although Palenque was relatively close to the ancient site, there was still about a two-hour drive to Tenosique, at which point the pavement ended and the dirt road began. The road went south to a Mexican military post on the Mexico-Guatemala border. From there they would have to walk on foot into Guatemala for about five hours. The ancient ruins of Piedras Negras were nestled in the thick jungle close to the Usumacinta River.

Several hours passed as they pounded down rough road, but their goal was finally getting closer, although one would never know it—the jungle was thick and had swallowed up anything left unattended too long. Now there was still the arduous walk through the jungle before they reached their destination, but at least the weather was perfect for hiking.

About halfway into their walk they stopped in a small clearing for a water break and to look at the old map they were carrying. Erica turned to their guide. "We're looking for any underground passages that were under water in recent times."

"There is place here like that. It has been submersed until the earthquake only a few weeks ago. Funny you should ask, though."

"Oh yeah? Why's that?" Ty asked.

"There was another that asked same question only few days ago. In fact, I think he will be back with papers to dig."

They all exchanged a glance. "Can you tell us who that might be?" Ty asked.

There were dollars signs in his eyes. "Maybe … for a pri—"

Clint stepped closer to their greedy guide. Without saying a word, the negotiating was over. The massive bodyguard was a quiet man, but his rough looks seemed to intimidate everyone, even Ty and Erica.

"His name I do not know, but his face," he took a piece of paper out of his pocket and unfolded it. "Here." He showed them a newspaper clipping with a photo of a distinguished-looking, well-dressed older man shaking the hand of a local. Ty didn't know Spanish, but it appeared the man was being honored for something. "What happened to the caption explaining the photo?"

"I don't know, but he gave money to the needy for something. I think he is explorer. He is looking for something, but I do not know what."

SEVERAL YARDS BEHIND AND safely out of sight, the large man in the shadows looked at the monitor in his hand then came to a stop. *Come on, people, let's keep moving.*

CHAPTER 13

PIEDRAS NEGRAS

AFTER ANOTHER COUPLE OF hours, they finally reached the outer edge of the overgrown ruins of Piedras Negras. The once-magnificent city was now nothing but a distant memory. Even though it appeared that the jungle had tried to swallow the city whole, there was still enough exposed to recognize an ancient civilization had once thrived here. It was as though the city didn't want to be forgotten.

It took a moment for everyone to take in the sight before their guide spoke up. "The sun will go down soon. We must set up our tents while we can still see."

"Yeah, that's probably a good idea. We'll have plenty of time in the daylight to start our search." Ty looked over the area. "So, with only two tents, what are the sleeping arrangements going to be?"

Erica spoke before anyone else had a chance. "I think I should be as close to you as possible right now, Tyler."

The bodyguard gave the guide a look, then winked at Ty.

"Just in case you start to remember anything else," she added. "So don't get the wrong idea."

Ty nodded and grinned and looked at the others. "Any objections?"

"Lucky, amigo." The guide smiled and walked away.

THERE'S A LOUD CRASH and the ground trembles. Ty's in an ancient city with several pyramids around a courtyard. People stop what they're doing and listen. Another deafening noise, followed by an even bigger quake. A rumbling sound in the distance gets everyone's attention, but instead of stopping this time, it only gets louder.

Someone rushes through the mesmerized crowd and disappears through a side entrance to a shimmering white pyramid. Moments later he reemerges carrying a wooden box emitting a greenish glow.

The eyes of the people grow larger as they stare at what approaches, and then they flee in a panic. In the distance, something can be seen over the tops of the trees—a wall of water. Then he hears it again. The hiss comes from directly behind him this time. He turns to see.

Ty jolted awake. His dreams were getting more real each time.

"Easy, Tyler. Everything's okay." Erica put her hand on his chest.

"Just another dream." His breath was returning to normal. Her touch gave him comfort and felt good.

"Anything important?"

"I'm not sure." He paused. "I think we might be in the wrong place, though."

"What? Why?

"Just a feeling. I think the records *were* here but were moved long ago."

"Any idea where?"

"Yeah, I think so."

THE MORNING CAME, AND so did the rain. This was the rainy season for Central America, but they couldn't afford to wait. The Organizer had been tight-lipped about the bigger picture of their mission. He only stressed that if what he suspected was truly unfolding, they not only needed to find what they were searching for but also be able to decipher the ancient texts in time to somehow stop the unfolding calamity.

"So, you're saying we're in the wrong place?" Clint had a slight accent, but Ty couldn't quite place it.

"I am. I feel we need to move inland more."

"Is this a wild hair, or do you have some intel?" Clint asked as he sopped up the last of his morning eggs with a piece of bread.

Erica jumped to Ty's defense. "You aren't getting paid to ask questions, Mr. Bryant, so ease up a little."

"Easy, you guys." Ty put his fork down and focused on his travel companions. "I know it must be frustrating to be led by a blind man, but you'll have to trust me on this. Although there's no guarantee we'll find anything."

"I was just playing with ya, kid. Someone needs to try and lighten the mood a little." Clint stood and looked out at the rain. "Now if you'll excuse me, I need to hit the head before we get moving."

"Yeah, I'll go freshen up a bit, too," Erica said. "We don't have much to pack up." She scanned the area. "Say, have you seen our guide?"

Ty looked around. "Yeah. I mean, I thought he was just here. Wasn't he?"

"Actually, now that I think about it, I don't think I've seen him since last night."

"Clint probably knows where he is. I saw them arguing about something before we called it a night. I'll ask him when he gets back. Go ahead and get ready." Ty said it nonchalantly, but as Erica walked off, the look on his face changed. *Where the hell is Pedro?*

Just then, he heard something from the thick brush behind their campsite. He strained to hear, but the rain was still muffling the sounds from the jungle. There it was again. It almost sounded like someone was calling to him.

Ty stepped out from under the shelter and slowly walked toward the thick brush. Through the drizzle, he heard it again. It was a voice.

"Ty," the voice said faintly.

He moved closer. "Who's there? Pedro? Is that you?"

A powerful arm grabbed him from behind and pulled him into the shadows of the jungle and he disappeared from sight.

CHAPTER 14

PIEDRAS NEGRAS

TY TRIED TO RESIST, but the man was just too powerful. With one of his abductor's massive hands over his mouth and the other wrapped around his torso, securing his arms, Ty was unable to do anything but listen.

"Ty, I'm not going to hurt you, but I need to talk to you. You're in danger."

Ty tried to free himself, but it was as though he were encased in a living cocoon.

"I'm going to let you go in just a few seconds, but first I need for you to trust me." The man's voice was rough even though he whispered so that only Ty could hear. "First I want you to know I'm friends with your father. We've known each other since we both worked at the border patrol in Montana."

The stranger paused and Ty could sense he was listening for anyone who might happen by.

"Your dad sent me a message for help on the same day you and he disappeared in Argentina. I was working with him back in

Alexandria last month trying to figure out who was following you. I was the one who was with your father when we interrogated your friend Tom."

He paused again and Ty could feel the man's head swivel as though he had heard something.

"I'm going to let you go now, Ty, but please promise me you will stay quiet and hear me out. Your lives depend on it and I'm here to help." He loosened his grip some as he spoke, "And remember, Ty, my main goal is to find your father. And with your help, I intend to do just that. I'm going to let you go now, but you must trust me."

Ty felt his abductor's arms relax and slowly let him go. He took a step back as he turned around to see the stranger. At first, he just saw the silhouette of the man, which was very large. The man stepped closer, allowing the light to fall on his face. There was a scar on his cheek and he looked rough. He was dressed in camo and looked as if he were part of the jungle. Ty could tell this was someone who could take care of himself and probably anybody else if need be.

"You fit the description Tom gave me, all right." Ty looked the large man over. "If you've known my dad that long, how is it I've never seen you before?"

"Your father and I were ... well, we interacted more on a professional level than a personal one. But we did meet once. Long ago when you were about two feet shorter."

Ty narrowed his eyes and looked hard at the man, then slightly cocked his head. "In that park. The park across the river?"

"Yeah. You were a lot smaller then."

"I remember Mom and I were going to meet one of her friends. She'd never been to that park before, and I remember Dad was surprised to see us."

"Yeah, you caught us off guard, all right. Your dad had to do some fast talking to explain what I was doing there. I hadn't seen your mother since our border patrol days."

Ty nodded. "I remember that."

"Listen to me, Ty. We have to get back to the matter at hand. You and the girl are in danger."

"Danger? How … why?"

"Shhh. Keep your voice down."

"What do you know about my dad?" Ty whispered. "Do you know where he is?"

"Sorry, kid, I was hoping *you'd* know where he was." He kept scanning the entire area as though it were a reflex.

"So you used to work with my dad?"

The big stranger glanced around before he answered. "Yeah, I've worked with him now and again over the years, and I'll gladly talk to you more about that later. Right now, you have bigger problems."

"Bigger problems? What are you talking about?"

"That brute you have with you—what do you know about him?"

"Clint? He's been hired to travel with us. Kind of a bodyguard, I guess."

The man scanned the area again. "I can tell you that's *not* who he is. I was hired just for that job. That son of a bitch hit me with a lead pipe and left me for dead. I don't know how, but he hacked into my phone and stole the identity I was going to use on this job, then stepped into my place."

"What the hell?"

"That's exactly what I thought, too. I was able to follow you guys, though, and don't worry—I've been keeping a watchful eye on you two. I was hoping to find out who he's working for, but it's to the point now that I think he's going to act. I'm not sure what he has planned, but I can tell you this much: whatever it is, it ain't good."

Ty looked him over a little closer now. "I admit he seems a little odd, all right."

He looked around again. "The brute, whatever his name is, dispatched your local guide, shall we say. That's why I decided it's time to step in. Whatever he has planned is about to start, so I'm going to put a stop to it."

"Jesus, I never would've guessed. So, what do you plan on doing?"

"I need to get him alone and away from you two so he can't use you as a human shield."

Ty noticed that he had a semiautomatic pistol strapped on his side and a shotgun with a pistol grip slung over his back. There was also a Rambo-style knife stowed nicely in a sheath in his tactical belt. At first glance, all his weapons had seemed to blend into his wardrobe and where barely noticeable, but now they stood out loud and clear and gave Ty the chills. "So, what do you want me to do?"

"Were you planning on staying at this site any longer?"

"Actually, no. We're going to be moving inland some more."

"Okay, after you've packed up your things, leave one of your bags behind. Then once you're out of camp—say, about a hundred yards or so—realize you've left a bag behind and ask him to go back for it. I'll take it from there."

He couldn't believe what was happening. His life had transformed from that of an ordinary college kid into a cloak-and-dagger adventure that just seemed to grow by leaps and bounds every day. "I can do that."

"Good kid. You remind me of your father. He was never afraid to get his hands dirty either. And don't tell your girlfriend anything yet. The last thing I need is for the broad to tip this guy off. Especially after seeing what he did to your guide."

That remark gave Ty a sick feeling. "Okay, I'll get back." He started to leave but stopped and turned around. "Hey, so what's your name?"

"Call me Butch."

CHAPTER 15

THE RAIN HAD STARTED to let up as the three made the final adjustments to their gear.

Erica was tightening up her backpack. "Any sign of Pedro yet?" she asked as she scanned the area.

"I think he abandoned us," Clint said. "Dumb-ass left his binoculars, too, and I'm keeping'em." He zipped up his pack and put the binoculars around his neck.

"What? What makes say you that, and why would he leave us?" Erica continued to look over the area.

Clint stood up, throwing his pack over his shoulders. "Well, to the first part of your question, have you seen any of his things around?"

Erica looked around. "What? That just doesn't make any sense. I mean, why would he just leave us?"

"Just a guess, but did he get paid in advance?"

"I don't know about that, but I'll find out."

Clint looked up into the canopy of the jungle. "Oh yeah? You think you're gonna get cell service out here?"

"Shit!" She looked at her phone. "What about the car? Is it even going to be there? If it is, how are we going to start it without the keys?"

"Don't worry about that. Those older rigs are easy to get into without a key and even easier to start. I'll take care of it." Clint tightened up his pack.

"I guess the only thing we can do is keep moving," Ty said, looking up from his phone. "Maybe he'll show up down the trail."

"Don't hold your breath, kid." Clint stared out into the jungle. "That's the problem with paying these people up front. Live and learn. So where to now?"

"Inland. Wish I could tell you more, but that's all I know now."

"Looks like we won't be needing a guide then anyway. Not if we don't know where the hell we're going." Clint shook his head and gave Ty a glare.

"Let's go back and get the car, then head downstream from the river. That much I know."

"Shit, kid, that's where we just came from."

"Never mind," Erica said. "Let's just get going."

"Okay, you're the boss," Clint said as he rolled his eyes.

A few hundred feet down the trail, Ty stopped and patted his belt. "Damn it!"

"What is it, Tyler?" Erica said as she adjusted her pack.

"I forgot the little bag I brought. The map is in there, too." He looked at Clint. "Would you mind getting it for me while I step into the trees and hit the head real quick? I'm sure I left it right next to that rock altar I was sitting on."

"Jesus, kid, you'd forget your head if it wasn't glued on. Yeah, I'll get it for ya. You need me to wipe your ass for ya too when I get back?"

"Funny. I think I can handle it."

"I ain't so sure about that. All right, hurry the hell up so you're finished when I get back." Clint spun around and disappeared down the trail.

Erica stood and watched as both men left. Then Ty returned and looked in the direction Clint had gone.

"Tyler? What's wrong?"

CLINT WAS MUTTERING TO himself as he walked back into their campsite. "I hope that kid knows what he's doing … for everyone's sake."

He looked the spot over and saw the pack right where Ty had said it would be.

"Dumb-ass."

TY AND ERICA STOOD in silence as they watched the path that led back to where they had just left. Ty had just finished telling her about Butch.

"Are you sure we can trust this guy?" Erica asked.

"There's no cell service out here, so we can't check him out, but I know my dad trusted him with his life on several occasions, so I think we're in good hands."

As they were looking down the trail, they heard something and were shocked to see Butch standing behind them.

"Butch! Where the hell did you come from?" Ty said. "Never mind, I'd like you to meet—"

"Save the introductions for later, kid. We'd better get moving before he comes to. I got the jump on him for now, but I don't want to take any chances. This jungle is dangerous enough without a crazy mercenary trying to hunt you down."

Ty and Erica looked at each other and nodded. Then, without haste, they started up the trail.

MARIA AND JUAN HAD been planning all summer for their trip to Piedras Negras. Visiting all the ancient Mayan sites was something the young couple had wanted to do, and this was their first.

They had just made it to the ancient site. It had only been a little over an hour since they passed the only other people on their trek so far, two men and a woman who were on their way out. They had the place to themselves.

Sweat was running down Maria's temples and she was breathing hard. "Okay, Juan, I am going to take a water break before we check this place out. Not everyone is the Olympian you are."

He laughed. "Hey, I'm not judging. So, you gonna pass me some water or make me dig out my own?"

She laughed and tossed him an extra bottle, but her aim was off just enough that he couldn't reach it. The bottle sailed over his head and down a small drop-off and into the dense jungle.

"Damn, girl, anyone ever tell you that you throw like a girl?"

"Luckily for you, that's not all I do like a girl. Now don't be losing my bottle, since you can't catch."

He shook his head and laughed, then jumped up and slowly climbed down the small bank in search of the water bottle. It was just enough of a drop that he had to use both hands to hang on to an exposed root to not fall the six or seven feet down. Being not very traversable, this wasn't a spot most adventurers would ever see on their trip to Piedras Negras. As his feet touched flat ground, he was able to let go and begin his search.

"You sure you aren't trying to get rid of me?" he yelled back up to Maria. "You know I don't have any life insurance, don't you?"

All he could hear was a slight giggle from above.

All right, if I was a bottle flying over the edge of a bank, where would I land? He began poking around the thick undergrowth.

Then he saw a slight glimmer of light reflect back at him from under the thick brush. *Mayan gold maybe?*

He moved aside the boughs of the brush and reached down for the shiny object. Then he realized what had been glimmering at him, and it wasn't the water bottle or Mayan gold but a nice set of binoculars. *Nice! Some poor sucker's loss is my prize!* He grabbed them, but they snagged on something when he tried to pull them out. He bent lower to see what might be holding up his find, and then he saw what it was.

They were around the neck of a body.

BLACK MOUNTAIN
NORTHEASTERN AUSTRALIA

MEANWHILE, DEEP IN THE Southern Hemisphere, somewhere near the mysterious Black Mountain in Queensland, Australia, reports started to surface of sightings of something very odd. It was in an area where there had long been strange happenings, but this time something was different.

CHAPTER 16

They had been in Butch's car driving back toward Palenque for a little over an hour and the mood seemed rather tense. The car Pedro had driven them in was still parked in the same place where they had left it.

"I just don't see why we can't tell the authorities about Pedro," Erica said. "And even Clint, or whoever the hell he really is. I mean, this is serious!"

"Look, Doc, if you want to end up in a Mexican prison or even worse, maybe a Guatemalan prison, then by all means go to the cops," Butch said. "But I can tell you exactly what'll happen. They'll hold us responsible unless we come up with a bundle of cash to buy our way out. That I guarantee. I've seen it over and over again in these places."

"Maybe we could just wait until we get back and then let them know?" Ty suggested.

"Okay, I'll tell you what I'll do. Next town we come to, if and only if I can find a pay phone, I'll call someone"—Butch looked Erica in the eye—"anonymously and tell them where they can find … what's his name?"

"Pedro. I'm sure he has a family!"

"Yeah, yeah, Pedro. And they can take it from there. Deal?"

"Okay, deal. I just know I'd want to know if it was my family."

"All right then, consider it done. Now where the hell are we going?" Butch asked while navigating the narrow road.

Before Ty could answer, Butch stepped on the brakes and slowed to a crawl. "Oh shit, what now?" Butch grumbled as they all looked ahead.

Traffic had been sparse, but now there was a lineup of cars ahead. It appeared to be a roadblock.

Butch looked in front then behind. "Something stinks here."

"I'm sure it's road construction or something." Erica said.

"If it was, wouldn't they be stopping traffic both ways?"

He was right, the steady oncoming traffic didn't seem to be held up at all.

Butch looked to the rear again. "Okay, this is what we're going to do before someone gets behind us." As he talked, he grabbed his pack and threw a few of his items into it before securing it for travel. "I'm getting out here and will meet up with you at the next ruins you're going to. Where was that again?"

"What a minute, Butch," Erica cut in. "I think you're overreacting here. We've done nothing wrong."

"Look, little girl, we're not taking any chances. I already told you the oaf that was impersonating me did away with your Mexican guide. We passed that couple on the trail, and if they by chance found a dead man there, they probably think we may have had something to do with it. They saw three Americans, so that's what the *federales* will be looking for. Now, I don't care if I'm overreacting or not, but I ain't gonna land in a Mexican prison because I was hoping for the best." He turned his rough stare to Ty. "This is a courtesy car from the general aviation side of the airport at Palenque, so there's no name attached to it. Now I need to know where the hell to find you."

"Teotihuacán, the Pyramid of the Sun," Ty said. "That's where we'll be."

"Okay, now I know there's no cell service out here, but I can hook us all up to the same satellite app that your father and I use. Give me your phones and I'll get them set up so I can get in contact with you if need be. We have to hurry, though."

Ty and Erica fished out their phones and handed them to Butch. Ty slid over to the driver's seat while Butch did his thing. It only took him a few seconds.

"Thanks, kid," he said as he handed their phones back. "If you need to call me, just click on the new app and follow the directions." He opened the door and looked back at Erica. "Now get up front and slide your ass over and look like a couple that can't keep their hands off each other. They'll know you've been to Guatemala, but they won't know what you did there unless you tell them. Now, you're gonna have to come up with what you're doing here, but you're not interested in any ruins. Got it?"

Ty and Erica looked at each other and nodded, then Erica jumped into the front seat. Butch paused for a second before clearing his throat and stared at Erica, prompting her to slide over next to Ty.

"Good. Don't screw it up. I'll see you soon." He shut the door and disappeared into the brush just before a car came around the corner behind them.

BUTCH HAD BEEN GONE for roughly twenty minutes as they approached the front of the line. Four Mexican soldiers toting machine guns were going from car to car, and theirs was next.

"Don't take anything I do the wrong way, Tyler," Erica whispered. "I'm not sure if I like Butch all that much, but he does seem to be a survivor."

"Oh, I agree," Ty said as he put his arm around her and pulled her closer. He liked the way her body felt next to his.

She looked in the mirror and gave him a smile just as the Mexican soldiers walked up to their car.

"*Abre, abre!*" the soldier demanded as he motioned for Ty to roll down his window.

Ty did as requested.

"Americans?" the soldier said.

"Yes, what's the—"

"Passports!" he demanded while his cohort walked around the car, looking closely at everything inside.

They quickly produced their passports, and this time Ty kept quiet.

"What's going on?" Erica said as she tried to make eye contact with their interrogator.

He ignored her as he looked over their papers. "What are you doing in Mexico?"

"We're just taking our first trip together," Ty said. "Just a little getaway so we can be alone."

The soldier studied them closely as his companion came to a stop next to him.

"Anyone else traveling with you?"

Ty looked around, then back at the interrogator. "No, just us."

"You think you are funny, gringo?"

"Sorry sir," Ty said. "It's just that we came down here so we could be alone."

The *federale* looked down and continued to go through their passports. "Looks like you've been to Guatemala. What did you do there?"

"We just wanted to get to know each other in as many countries as we can," Erica said as she smiled at Ty.

The soldier lifted his gaze this time. Erica smiled and moved her hand a little farther up Ty's leg.

With no change in expression, the soldier belted another order. "Open the back!"

Ty did as requested and waited until the two came back around to the front.

"Where are you going now?"

"Mexico City," Ty said as his palms started to sweat.

"What are you going to be doing there?"

"Just seeing the city, sir."

Erica winked and smiled.

He looked them over one last time before handing Ty their passports and motioning for them to leave. "You can go now."

Sighing with relief, Ty put the car in "drive" and started forward.

"Stop!" It was the soldier.

"For God's sake, what now?" he whispered to Erica. "I just want to get the hell out of here."

The soldiers walked back up to his window. "Señor, it is against the law to drive like that."

"Sir?"

"The back of your car," he said as he pointed to the back. "It's still open."

Ty looked in the mirror. *Crap!* "Oh, sorry, sir, but it was you—"

"Yes, gringo?"

"Sorry, sir. I'll shut it right now."

"Good idea," the soldier said and walked back to the next car.

CHAPTER 17

SOUTHERN MEXICO

THEY WERE NOW DEEP in the heart of Olmec country, supposedly the oldest complex society in the Western Hemisphere. Many mysterious artifacts and stone carvings had been unearthed here over the years. The massive stone heads were the most famous, but there were many others that seemed to tell an even stranger tale.

Of course, the carving and transportation of the colossal Olmec heads of stone from nearly a hundred miles away was intriguing, but the much smaller stone reliefs and statues depicted a peculiar dilemma. There were numerous small stone figurines of people with elongated heads. Several other carvings found in and around La Venta, Mexico, in the Tabasco region, depicted men who appeared to have heavy beards and European appearances. Was it possible that another culture from across the vast ocean visited the ancients in the area long before first thought? Or were these depictions of the white gods, the beings in the local folklore?

Maybe the most intriguing stone relief found in the area was what was known as Monument 19. Monument 19 has baffled experts since its discovery just north of what is known as the Great Pyramid at the La Venta pyramid complex in central Mexico. On the stone carving is a man in an odd seated position with a large snake-like serpent in the background. Of course, some have theorized the man to be in a space ship, but what did this stone carving really depict? Could he be in a boat of some kind? And what of the serpent? Was it the famous Feathered Serpent of the native lore? And why does it seem to be part of the vessel? But the strangest things about the carving are what the man has in his hands. In his right hand, he holds one of the most mysterious objects in ancient Sumerian art: the famous purse.

Depictions of this handbag have been recorded not only in Sumer but also, most recently, in what may be some of the oldest ruins on the planet: Göbekli Tepe, in Turkey, a site that predates Stonehenge by some six thousand years, making it about twelve thousand years old.

Göbekli Tepe consists of numerous vertical stone pillars varying in height and weighing several tons. Carved on them are several types of animals and symbols, in addition to the mysterious handbag. But what makes it even more mysterious is that this place was intentionally covered up. Why would anyone go out of their way to cover up these ancient ruins? With some of the pillars over twenty feet tall and weighing around ten tons, transporting the earth necessary to completely hide the structure would have been a more daunting task than building it in the first place.

The locals believed the hill where the site was uncovered to be sacred. Why would it be sacred to them if they didn't know anything about the buried structures? German archaeologist Professor Schmitt discovered it in 1995. Humans, at the time it was built, were said to be in the Stone Age, but if that was true, how did they achieve such a feat?

The true purpose of the Sumerian purse still baffles experts. And now to see the same handbag on the other side of the world just deepened the mystery.

Monument 19 also has other interesting features. As if the handbag weren't fascinating enough, what was in the other arm of the man may have been even more interesting. He was carrying what appeared to be several stone tablets. Could this have depicted the actual moving of the records that were from Atlantis? Edgar Cayce said they had been moved inland because of more flooding, so it was entirely possible. And maybe the eeriest thing about the situation was what Cayce said about who would find the records: two men and one woman.

CHAPTER 18

TEOTIHUACAN, MEXICO

THEY HAD BEEN ON the road for several hours after getting safely through the roadblock. What the Mexican soldiers had really been looking for, they had no clue, but if Butch had been right, their actions were indeed justified. That all seemed almost a distant memory now as they gazed in awe at the magnificent sight before them. Teotihuacan is known as the city of the gods, but it can also be translated as "the place where men become gods."

Located in the heart of Mexico, Teotihuacan is an ancient complex of several pyramids, including the third largest in the world, the Pyramid of the Sun. It's about the same size as the Great Pyramid of Giza at its base but not quite as tall. As one of the largest cities in the new world, Teotihuacan was home to possibly more than two hundred thousand people at its peak. It's estimated that the city was founded around 400 B.C., and when the Aztecs discovered the site in the 1400s, the city had already been abandoned for centuries.

No one knows for sure who built these amazing structures, but there had been stories that the ancestors of the founders were from

Atlantis. Even now, it's still a mystery as to what happened to the people, as they seem to have mysteriously vanished. What could have caused the collapse of such a great city? Was it climate change or maybe something more mysterious?

Could it be that the continuing references to Atlantis were just a coincidence? Again and again, Atlantis, or civilizations that mirrored Atlantis, seemed to be at the root of the local legends. Was this just another coincidence similar to the Greek mythology parallels with the story in the Bible of Gods having giant children with human women?

Unlike Piedras Negras, Teotihuacan was in a currently populated area. This made it a natural tourist destination and also meant they would not have the grounds to themselves.

Ty looked out the window in awe as they pulled into the parking area. "Wow, it's hard to believe what the ancients built without machinery."

"It sure is," Erica said as they stepped out of the car. "They built things to last, too. In the town I'm from, the houses are all fairly new. Everything over fifty years old has been torn down it seems."

"Yeah, yeah, lotta old shit here," they heard from behind. "Either of you two got a plan?"

They both reeled around in shock to see Butch standing behind them.

"What the … How did you get here so fast?" Ty asked.

"Easy there, partner, we're just strangers who happened to meet in the parking lot. They're still looking for three Americans, so I'll meet you inside."

Ty nodded. "Yeah, right. Well, we're going to have to be able to roam around at will, and I'm betting some of the places are off limits to tourists."

"Yeah, I bet you're right," Erica said. "You got any contacts here that can set us up, Butch?"

"I wish, but no." Butch turned to face them. "Looks like we're going to have to improvise. I made a reservation at a motel close by." He handed Ty a piece of paper with an address on it. "Go check in first, then come back here. I'll meet you inside later."

EASTER ISLAND

THE ANCIENT MOAI STAND motionless on the shore with their gaze fixed toward the setting sun while they wait for the return of their maker's god. Their silhouettes grow longer as the sun begins to disappear below the horizon. As the last sliver of the luminous body vanishes from sight, the entire island is lit up as though a bolt of lightning has blown out the bottom of an enormous thunderstorm. Although there are no clouds anywhere in sight.

CHAPTER 19

TEOTIHUACAN, MEXICO

THE SUN WAS JUST about to drop over the horizon, which made the ancient site even more mesmerizing. Ty and Erica had paid their seventy pesos for entry but had no intention of leaving with the last of the crowd at closing time, as they still hadn't seen Butch. They did, however, have plenty of time to scope the place out and prepare for any night operation that might ensue.

Between the few hours they had browsed the place and searching the very limited Internet available back at the small motel room they had rented, they had a pretty good idea of where they needed to go. The real breakthrough, though, came when Erica put Ty in a deep trance and showed why she had been chosen for this particular mission.

Past life regressions have been taking place since before Christ. Even the early Jews who now follow the kabbalah believed in the reincarnation of the soul. Of course, there are plenty of skeptics who claim the "patient" is only experiencing delusions, but nevertheless there have been several examples that do indeed suggest it is very real.

Although Edgar Cayce's work with past lives was better-known, it was Erica's study of Dr. Brian Weiss's work that first made a believer out of her and pushed her into the field of hypnotherapy.

Brian Weiss, M.D., graduated from Columbia University and Yale Medical School. It was his work as a traditional psychotherapist that gave rise to his fame. In 1980, one of his patients who was suffering from several phobias slipped into a past life while undergoing a hypnotherapy session with him. At the time, Weiss was not a believer in reincarnation. It wasn't until after several regression sessions with this patient, during which she produced some information about Weiss that only he would know, that he finally became a believer in reincarnation.

Since that time, Weiss has regressed thousands of other patients into past lives to try to help them with issues they have carried into their current lives. He has since documented most of these and written several books regarding these events.

Although Erica had successfully put Ty under when Tom first brought him in to try to clear him of his amnesia, she hadn't had the same luck at Piedras Negras. This time, though, was a huge success. The strange thing about the experience was that Ty never divulged who he was speaking as. Even his voice was different. Nonetheless, the information flowed freely.

Ty revealed not only that the records from Atlantis had made it to this site but also that the inscription on Monument 19 was in fact a record of the event. Just as Cayce had said, the records were first brought to the Piedras Negras site. Due to some flooding in the area, they were indeed moved to Teotihuacan, where they should still be. And after a thorough investigation of the ruins, they had a pretty good idea where they could be found.

As soon as the crowd thinned out some, they would have their chance. Ty looked at his watch—five minutes to closing. What was keeping Butch?

"Time to go!" one of the workers hollered across the way.

"Guess we don't have a choice," Ty said as he looked around for Butch. "Looks like we'll have to leave"

"I really thought he would have been here by now," Erica said.

"Maybe he has plans for tomorrow."

Just then there was a loud explosion a few blocks away, followed by a thick black plume of smoke that belched into the clear blue sky.

"What the hell was that?" Ty said while watching the plume build.

All the tourists who were leaving stopped to see the sight. The workers yelled to each other in a panic and hurried the tourists out the gate.

"I guess we'd better get out of here, too," Erica said.

As they started to walk across the courtyard, they heard a voice directed at them. "Hey, get over here!"

They both turned to see a man in the shadows behind one of the ancient stone half pyramids motioning them over. It was Butch.

"WOW! THAT SURE TURNED out to be convenient for us," Ty said as he looked around at the deserted complex. "I don't suppose you'd know anything about it?"

"No," Butch said, "but it looks like we should have this place all to ourselves for a while."

"Are you serious?" Erica was fuming. "You caused that just so we wouldn't be bothered here? Are you out of your freaking mind?"

"Easy there, little girl," Butch said as he looked down on her. "I had nothing to do with that. Even if I did, it's an abandoned building in a nonresidential part of town."

"How on God's green earth would you know that? And who's to say it won't spread to somewhere else? You can't just go around starting a local calamity so we won't be disturbed! I'm sure we could have just bribed the right person to have the place to ourselves for a few hours."

"You think an American trying to bribe an authority at an ancient city in Mexico would be a good idea right now? You seem to be forgetting the Mexican authorities are already looking for three Americans that were seen leaving one. It doesn't take a rocket scientist to—"

"Easy, you two." Ty cut him off. "Butch may or may not be right, but we'd better do what we came here to do and get out."

"You're right, kid. Let's get this over with."

Ty turned to Erica. "Maybe we can get Ethan to donate some money anonymously to help anyone who may have lost their home. He seems to have a big bag of cash."

She looked at the nearby flames, then gritted her teeth. "Yeah, I suppose you're right," she said as she stared at Butch. "Let's find what we came for and leave ... before something else bad happens."

CHAPTER 20

TEOTIHUACAN, MEXICO

TO SAY THAT TY'S life had become a surreal event was putting it mildly. All of the reading about Edgar Cayce and the Hall of Records and now to be actively looking for the lost texts was unbelievable. But as amazing as that was, he had mentioned something even stranger while Erica had him in a trance earlier in the day. He mentioned something that he had heard about in passing several weeks ago: the Emerald Tablets of Thoth the Atlantean. Could it be possible the Emerald Tablets and the records hidden away that Cayce had mentioned so many times were actually one and the same?

According to legend, Thoth was an Atlantean priest who lived until around thirty-eight thousand years ago. He is said to have left the doomed continent and fled to Egypt to start a new civilization. He not only brought with him the ancient records of their secrets but was also the architect of the Great Pyramid itself. Within the Great Pyramid, it is said, he incorporated the knowledge of the Atlantean's.

Could this actually be possible? Ty surely didn't believe the pyramid was a tomb, and in his brief visit it was obvious to him it was a machine of some kind. In fact, not once has any pharaoh's body ever been found inside a pyramid. Over and over again, the signs kept pointing him in this direction, but why?

Thoth was said to have eluded death and was able to travel in and out of the spirit world at will. Might he have actually been Enoch? There were several stories Ty had come across that said Enoch was in fact the builder of the Great Pyramid. He was also transmuted from the physical world to the spirit world without dying. Could this all be just a coincidence?

There were even stories that Thoth had brought knowledge to the people of Central and South America. These areas were also linked with the Hall of Records mentioned by Cayce. All of these locations had tales of a long-lost white-bearded god who did in fact bring them knowledge. Thoth was supposed to have incarnated three times, the last time as Hermes, author of the Emerald Tablets. Many think these tablets were what was hidden in Cayce's Hall of Records.

After being safeguarded in the Great Pyramid of Giza for thousands of years, it is said, a group of priests took the tablets and migrated to the Americas, where they found the Maya race. The Maya were said to have remembered much of the wisdom from ancient times. Unfortunately, after the Spanish arrived and decimated their tribes, the knowledge was forgotten, as were the tablets.

Somewhere around 1925, some of the tablets surfaced. Written on a material that was unlike anything else on the planet, the tablets consisted of twelve volumes in the ancient language of the Atlanteans. Shortly after their discovery, they were mysteriously translated by Dr. Doreal. Throughout the peculiar texts were references to vibration and frequency that were at the source of all that is.

As informative as the tablets were, mankind was allowed to view only the first ten. The last two contained knowledge that mankind was not ready for. Whatever secrets they contained were most likely unfathomable.

Could the last two be what he was sent to find?

Butch looked the area over. "Where to, kid? We ain't got all day."

The sweat poured down Ty's brow. "There," he said and pointed at the Pyramid of the Sun. "Under there is where we'll find what we're looking for."

The immense structure loomed ominously on the other side of the courtyard from where they stood. Ty had known that was where they needed to go and had been sizing up the place the entire time they had been waiting for Butch.

EVEN THOUGH ALL THE workers had vanished, they played it safe and stayed to the edge of the courtyard, close to all the half-pyramid platforms that lined the empty ancient square.

Ty couldn't help but imagine what life might have been like here when the citadel was at its peak. To have their world come crashing down when invaders arrived from across the pond—masquerading as friends—must have been a living nightmare for the inhabitants.

They approached the south side of the great structure and proceeded around the back.

"It's back here," Ty said as they got closer. "The only problem is, the entrance is gated and chained shut."

"Not a problem, kid." Butch took off his pack and pulled out a pair of bolt cutters. "I went shopping and bought ya a master key," he said and tossed them to Ty.

Ty plucked them from midair with one hand and looked to the gate with a smile. "All right then, let's do it."

Picking the lock—so to speak—had been the easy part. Once they were inside, it was as though the lights had been turned off.

And, of course, Butch was ready.

"Here you go, children," he grunted as he passed out flashlights to Ty and Erica. "Maybe I'm worth having along after all." He leered at Erica as she snatched hers from his hand.

"The jury's still out on that. If Mexico declares war on the U.S. after we've left, I think we'll know why."

"Enough!" Ty snapped. "We'll worry about defusing the war later. For now, we've got a job to do."

Ty couldn't help but think of Indiana Jones as he cautiously led the way. Unlike the surface, this place had been devoid of tourists for years and probably only visited by a select few.

The air was damp and musty like in an old basement, and the silence was a little eerie, to say the least. But even stranger was that Ty had a feeling he'd been here before.

"So exactly what are we looking for?" Erica whispered.

"I'm just going with my gut on this one." He kept his strange feeling to himself. "Whatever it is, it's not going to be obvious."

"So, tell me, kid," Butch said. "Why is it you were picked for this job? I mean, I know why I was called, and the little woman here seems to have a therapeutic knack, but even your dad seemed in the dark on why you were getting dragged into all this."

His dad. He hadn't even had a chance to process what may have happened to his father. He didn't want to entertain the thought that he wasn't still alive. Whatever happened at the fortress in Argentina had kept Ty safe, so maybe his dad had survived as well. "I wish I knew, Butch. It seems a few people think I'm more important than I really am."

They had been in the underground maze for close to an hour and had made countless turns, but it was as though Ty was gradually getting his bearings as they went. The familiarity was almost like a cross between something that happened yesterday and something that happened lifetimes ago.

Then a strange feeling came over Ty. It was almost like a voice from the past was telling him to stop. He stood still and leaned against the wall, which was comprised of large granite stones that had been hewn to rectangular shapes. The stonework had an uncanny resemblance to some of the stones used on the other side of the planet in Egypt.

Something drew Ty's eyes to a small rock at the top of the wall. It appeared to be wedged between the ceiling and the large stone below it that went almost to the floor. He reached up and started to fiddle with it. He put pressure on one side and then the other. It moved. He worked it some more and it came loose. He jostled it back and forth and pulled at the same time until it came out.

"Nice souvenir, kid," Butch said quietly with his gruff voice. "I hope that's not what we're looking for."

Ty looked at the rock then reached up with his other hand and pushed on the larger one below the now small empty void.

It moved. Ever so slightly, but it did move. There was just enough of a vacuum to cause some air to rush into the crack and make a slight whistle. They all heard it.

"What was that?" Ty slowly ran his hand across the seam.

"Sounded like a faint breeze for a second, but now it's gone," Erica whispered. "You don't think … Could it be what I think it is?"

Ty looked the wall over. "Maybe. There must be an area behind this wall with a slight pressure difference. A cavity with enough volume to draw in air until the pressure equalized. And whatever it is, it must have had an airtight seal … until now.

"If this large stone moved that easily, that can only mean one thing," Ty said as his hand gravitated toward a precise spot. "It must be a door of some kind. I remember reading about Edward Leedskalnin in Florida. He built Coral Castle out of huge chunks of coral rock. One of them was about this size and he had it balanced so perfectly a child could easily move it with one hand."

He pushed some more—nothing this time. He leaned into it harder and it started to move again. Then it started to move much more easily. Ty looked to his right and saw Butch's large hand pushing as well. Just like the door at Coral Castle, the rock pivoted ninety degrees. A small room opened up before their eyes as a stale blast of air hit them in the face.

They stepped in single file behind Ty, with everyone's flashlight illuminating the room. The layer of untouched dust was thick on the floor. What a perfect place to hide the ancient tablets. The only problem was that the room was empty.

"Tough luck, kid," Butch said. "Looks like someone beat us to it a long time ago."

"Sorry, Tyler," Erica said. "Maybe they're not here after all."

Ty ignored his companions and walked to the far corner, reached up, and pulled on a small jagged edge of the cornerstone. To everyone's surprise, it came loose and crashed to the floor.

He aimed his light into the cavity. An eerie glow was faintly visible. Then they all saw it. There, stacked in the small cubbyhole, were two tablets made from a material that emitted a beautiful green sheen.

"Oh my God, is it them?" Erica asked.

They eagerly but gently eased closer to the ageless material.

"This has to be it. The last of the library that has gone untouched since shortly after the fall of Atlantis." Ty carefully reached in to retrieve the glowing slabs. "The one and the same that Mr. Cayce talked about several times, the Hall of Records, the final two Emerald Tablets!"

Could it be? It was in the exact place they had deduced it should be. It had to be true. Forged onto the green plates were texts in immaculate condition. For something to be in existence for that long and still to be legible was extraordinary. The problem was the language they were in—totally unrecognizable.

"This, this writing," Ty said. "I recognize it from somewhere, but where?"

"Can you read it?" Erica asked.

"No, I can't. But where have I seen this before? It almost looks like … like Rongorongo."

Butch and Erica turned to look at Ty. "What the hell is that?" Butch asked.

Ty paused before replying. "It's one of the few languages on the planet that's never been deciphered. The only place it's ever been found is … Easter Island."

"So … it's useless to us then?" Erica asked.

Butch grinned. "Impressive, kid. I don't know how you did it, but very impressive." His grin faded as he turned to Erica. "Our job is only to find these tablets and take them back. Deciphering them is someone else's problem."

A FEW HOURS HAD passed since the trio recovered the ancient texts. The shared bungalow they had rented for the night was silent now that their little celebration had come to a close. It had been a long few days and Butch was the last one to hit the sack, but he had dropped off to sleep pretty quickly once he had laid down fully clothed on top of the made bed.

"Butch … Butch. We need your help."

Butch's eyes popped open and he sprang to his feet with his fist clenched, ready to smash some unlucky soul's face in. In his other hand was a pistol that had seemed to come out of nowhere.

"Who's there?" He panned the room, but nothing moved. He looked at his door only to see the chair still braced under the knob, then at the window, which was also rigged to give him warning of an unwanted guest, and it, too, was just as he had left it.

Could I have been dreaming? It had seemed so real, yet it was obvious he was alone in the room.

He removed the chair from the door and made a sweep of the bungalow only to confirm that no intruders had made their way in past any of his makeshift barriers. Ty and Erica were fast asleep right where he'd left them. He stood there in silence for a few more minutes before quietly going back to his room.

He gently lowered himself into the chair next to the bed, still slowly scanning the room. Finally, he closed his eyes but only for a moment before they shot open again. Something was gnawing at him … something from within.

CHAPTER 21

NORTH AFRICA
AGADIR, MOROCCO

BENEDICT ASHWORTH RAN HIS boney fingers through his thinning hair while he sat at his handcrafted ebony desk. The view of the North Atlantic Ocean out his office window was one to behold.

He had moved to Morocco several years ago because of its central location to numerous ancient mysteries he had been consumed with in his younger days. With the location of Atlantis being just beyond the Pillars of Hercules in Plato's account, this was where he chose to build his empire. He had heard tales of the lost knowledge of the ancients years ago, which is when he made the decision to find their secrets. Now that he had found them, he knew that his destiny of becoming all-knowing was within his reach.

Most everyone at the United Nations had thought the downing of the plane that carried visionary UN Secretary-General Dag Hammarskjöld in 1963 was an accident, but Ashworth had always suspected foul play. Now he knew the real reason Hammarskjöld had to go. With his newly acquired knowledge, it was obvious the UN outpost was put on top of Mount Hermon to hide the ancient secret that only a very few had become aware of.

I wonder if anyone else is left that remembers the secret they were hiding up there. A smile crept over his face. *And the secret in the Meditation Room … in plain sight, too… Genius!*

If the rumor that Hammarskjöld had discovered the Hall of Records was true, it might explain more than just the timing of the tragedy. And if he had found the records, surely he would have destroyed them to stop someone from obtaining the pure power that would come from the knowledge that lay within the ancient texts. Now, thanks to Edgar Cayce's directions, Ashworth finally possessed them. The fantastic story therein was more bizarre than he ever could have imagined. For centuries, most thought the reference to "Enoch walking with God" was only a metaphor, but now he knew better.

Thank God that bumbling Himmler didn't screw this up. Lord knows he tried.

Hammarskjöld may also have found something else that Ashworth was interested in. The last key to making his dream a reality, a dream he was getting closer to every day. The fact that the UN Secretary-General had been infatuated with the occult had always intrigued Ashworth, but when he found there may have been a connection between the encrypted Copper Scroll found in Qumran in 1953 and one of Hammarskjöld's associate's, more pieces of the puzzle came together. When Ashworth deciphered the long elusive tablets from the Hall of Records, his new theory started to make even more sense.

He pressed the intercom. "Send in Hanson."

Alex Hanson had been Ashworth's top aid for several years, and his loyalty had been proved time and time again. Hanson had always been able to get the job done one way or another.

The door swung open and in walked a middle-aged man of average stature, but his eyes seemed to reveal an inner quality of unbridled conviction to see a job through at any cost.

"First things first," Ashworth said just as Hanson closed the door. "The project in New York, the Stone of Light, how are we looking with that?"

"Everything is in place. We should have it by next week. No one will even know it's missing until it's too late."

"Good, very good. Your last message said you think you may have finally found one of the other locations where the records are?" Ashworth put his pen down and looked at his trusted employee.

"Yes, sir. I believe we have."

"How sure are you this is the real site and not just another dead end?"

"Very sure, sir. I'd say 99 percent, but you should really see for yourself."

"Oh, yes," Ashworth said, "this I need to see."

NORTHWESTERN SAHARA DESSERT

THE ROAR OF THE chopper blades reverberated throughout the airframe of the Sikorsky S-92 ten-passenger luxury helicopter as the four passengers looked out at the barren landscape. Sand was the only thing visible as they raced only a few feet above the desert floor.

Ashworth looked at the desert as it passed below. "I thought we had clearance along this entire route. Why are we flying so low?"

"We do, sir, but we just got word of some rebels in Western Algeria that have been shooting anything down they can see," Hanson said.

"You couldn't buy them off?"

"Not these, sir. There's a power struggle in their ranks right now, so the trust factor is too unpredictable. Had we gotten word of this sooner, maybe we could have swung a deal with Western Sahara, but that would have taken too much time." Hanson looked out the window and then back at Ashworth. "It's only a twenty-mile stretch here, sir. We'll be in Mauritania's airspace soon. There'll be no need to avoid their radar."

"And what about that thing." Ashworth motioned to a tripod-mounted fifty-caliber machine gun in the back attended by two military-type personnel.

"I figure it's always better to be safe than sorry, sir. I'm sure we won't need it."

Ashworth nodded approvingly and looked back out the window.

True to his word, as soon as their GPS registered Mauritania airspace, the Sikorsky rose higher into the air. Ashworth gazed at the wasteland. "It's amazing to think how this landscape has changed over the millennia. To think we're close to the greatest city ever to exist is unbelievable."

"I agree, sir. It doesn't look very hospitable down there anymore."

They covered several more miles before they could see a change in the landscape ahead. In the distance, it looked as though there were a gash in the sand on the horizon. It grew as they got closer until they were over the top of a large tear-shaped rift in the sand. Then something came into view that got everyone's attention.

Ashworth finally broke the silence. "What on earth is that? Is that… what I think it is?"

"Atlantis. Yes, sir. We sure think so."

"It … it's amazing!"

"Quite, sir. The locals call it the Eye of the Sahara."

Twenty thousand feet below them, at the southeast edge of the tear-shaped rift, was something that really did look like an eye. An enormous blue eye. Circles surrounding smaller circles, with a colorful tint throughout.

Ashworth couldn't take his eyes off the sight. "You said you were 99 percent sure?"

"Yes, sir. Everything matches to a tee with what Plato said. The same number of concentric circles, the color of the rock, even the diameter of the structure is the same. There's even a freshwater spring in the center. Again, just as Plato described."

"My God, all these years and it's been right here?"

"Yes, sir. The legendary city has been hiding right under our noses this whole time. Even the location. This exact spot on the ancient maps of this area was called Atlantes. There are just too many coincidences to ignore, sir."

"When was it first discovered? Surely it's been noticed for some time."

"It was first discovered in 1965 by astronauts orbiting the earth. They were looking for asteroid craters and thought this might be one at first. Of course, it's obviously not an impact crater."

"So, does this mean Edgar Cayce was wrong about the location?" Ashworth asked.

"We don't think so, sir."

"But Cayce said the location of Atlantis was near Bimini, just off the coast of Florida. He even gave a date of when it would be found, which was the same time the Bimini Road was discovered in 1969. The precise year and the precise location. But Africa? This is nowhere near Bimini. It just doesn't make sense."

"We thought that at first, too, sir, but back in the early 1900s a German scientist by the name of Alfred Wegener came up with the theory of continental drift."

"Yeah, I've heard that, all right. In fact, I don't even think it's really a theory anymore. Didn't they more or less prove the land masses were all connected millions of years ago?"

"I do think so, sir. Wegener spent his life trying to prove it. Of course, the coastlines of South America and Africa sure seem to line up. So do North America and the northern part of Africa. But he came across evidence of fossils of extinct dinosaurs that were found on the coast of each that indicate they were once connected. There are also other things, like similar magnetic variations in the rock on the floor of the ocean that back up the theory."

Ashworth thought for a moment. "So, if that's true, then at one time the northern part of Africa would have been—"

"Right off the coast of Florida, sir. Just as Cayce said."

The rhythmic hum of the rotor went unnoticed as the passengers stared in silence at the ancient wonder below. Ashworth's imagination was running wild at what might have taken place in this very spot long ago before the city was destroyed.

"And, sir." Hanson took an object wrapped in a cloth from his jacket pocket and opened it up so Ashworth could see. "We found this all over the site below."

Ashworth stared in disbelief. "Is that what I think it is?"

"We think so, sir. It must be a fragment of one of the firestones Cayce spoke of that the Atlanteans were using to amplify the natural energies of the earth and sun. It's been tested in a lab, and it's unlike any material known on the planet."

"And its qualities?"

"We're still running tests on it, but so far … quite amazing, sir. We still don't have any concrete ideas about where it came from, though."

"Don't worry about that, Hanson. I've found the secret of its source, and I know how it was formed."

"Really?" Hanson said. "Anything you can talk about, sir?"

"In due time, my friend, in due time."

"Would you like to go down and take a look, sir? It doesn't look like much when you're on the ground, though. If indeed there was a set of records kept there, I'm sure they've all been destroyed."

Ashworth was still marveling at the view out his window. "Indeed, it appears the destruction was immense. No, I've seen enough. Let's go back."

"What about the other location, sir?"

"It's being taken care of now. This was the last one."

"Very good, sir." Hanson signaled the pilot and the luxury machine made a hard right bank toward the direction it had just come from.

CHAPTER 22

IT WAS CLOSE TO noon before anyone began to stir. Butch had set them up with the earliest flight out of Mexico City, which didn't leave until early evening. The late night of celebrating their find was the catalyst for the much-needed sleep for the entire group. Erica's head was resting on Ty's shoulder when he opened his eyes. As soon as he moved, she slowly came to life. Ty rubbed his eyes and looked about the room.

"Hey, Erica. You up?"

"No. Go back to sleep."

"Too late for that now. I think we should get moving."

Erica combed her fingers through her hair. "Who was it that emptied all these bottles?"

"Yeah, I think we all had a part in that." Ty looked around the room. "I see Butch's door is still shut. Hard to believe he's still asleep."

"How is it he got the private room?" Erica asked.

"Good question. I don't remember voting on it." Ty said as he stretched his arms. "Of course, I don't think I want to be on his bad side, so it's all good."

"Yeah, he seems pretty intimidating, all right. How long has your dad known him?"

Ty got up off the futon. "They worked together at the border patrol in Montana years ago. Mom and I ran into him and Dad at a park in Alexandria when I was a kid, but I didn't know they were still in contact anymore."

"Judging from what I've seen, I bet your dad used his help when things were … a little dicey, shall we say?" Erica was standing up now.

"Most likely so. Guess that's why we left the tablets with him for the night. He's like having a portable safe. Well, I'll brave the storm and see if he's up yet. We probably should get to the airport fairly soon in case we have any problems getting through customs."

Ty walked to the bedroom and knocked on the door. "Butch? You up yet?" No answer. He tried again. "Yo, Butch. We should probably get a move on" Still no answer. He looked at Erica, then tried the door. It was unlocked, so Ty eased it open. "Butch? You in there?"

Ty looked in and turned around in disbelief. "He's gone."

"Gone? What do you mean, gone?" Erica's morning smile faded.

"I mean this room is empty … completely!"

Erica was up and moving toward the open door. "Empty? Everything? What about the tablets!?"

They both stood staring into the empty room. No Butch, no suitcase, and no tablets. It looked as though the maid had just left. Even the bed had been untouched.

LONG ISLAND, NEW YORK

A SLIVER OF MOON lit the beach on Long Island's southern tip. This was one of only a few places on this part of the island that was accessible from the water. The majority of this portion of the island that faced the ocean was surrounded by a bluff that would ward off even the most experienced of climbers.

Bubbles came to the surface of the water just a few feet off shore, followed by three men in black dive gear. They arose from the water and wasted no time in getting over the rocky beach and to the base of the bluff.

The divers took off their gear and stashed it in the brush. They quickly donned dark land clothing. All three had packs stuffed full and strapped to their backs. Without saying a word to each other, they started the climb up the steep embankment.

CHAPTER 23

NORTH AFRICA
AGADIR, MOROCCO

BENTON ASHWORTH WAS AT his desk when the phone rang. "Yes? … Ah, yes, please send him in."

He put the phone down just as the door opened and a burly man walked in. He closed the door behind him.

"Mr. Colton. So nice to finally meet you. I thank you for dropping everything for me on such short notice."

Butch looked the swanky office over before settling his eyes on Ashworth. "No problem. Happy to be of service."

"So, it was a success then? You have what I want?" Ashworth's eyes lit up.

"Oh yeah. The kid found them, all right. Just like you said he would."

"And? Where are the tablets now, Mr. Colton?"

"They're safe. Too bulky to be carrying around."

"And the boy?"

"That's not what I hired on for. You didn't mention that until later. Besides, you don't have to worry about him. He doesn't know anything. He's no threat."

Ashworth's smile faded some as he got up and stepped around his desk. "Please, Mr. Colton, take me to the tablets."

"Aren't you forgetting something?" Butch asked.

"Ah, yes. The other half of your fee. I'll have it brought in now, but I'll need to see what I am paying for first. I'm sure you understand, Mr. Colton." He pressed the intercom button. "You can bring it in now."

The door behind Ashworth's desk opened at the same time as the one Butch had just come through, and in walked two men. One had a briefcase and the other had a submachine gun.

Butch gave a cold look to the man packing the heat. "Be careful where you point that thing. I'd hate to see you hurt yourself."

The man didn't move a muscle.

"Easy now, everyone. Remember, we're all on the same side here." Ashworth was as cool as a cucumber.

"About that." Butch turned to Ashworth. "I was wondering about my payment."

"You were hoping for more, Mr. Colton?"

"No."

"No?" Ashworth raised his eyebrows.

"I'd rather you keep your money in exchange for a piece of the action."

"You want a job?"

"That's right." Butch took his eyes off the hired hands and gave all his attention to Ashworth. "I'm not sure what's going on here, but I'd like to be a part of it. That is if you think you can use my services for something more than just contract work."

Ashworth pondered the situation. From what he had seen from Colton, he was someone who had talent, all right, but was he loyal? The few seconds of silence seemed to linger on, and he gave a slight nod. "I think we might have something for you after all. Now, shall we go see what you found for me?"

Butch smiled. "Let's do it."

BUTCH'S RENTAL CAR WAS parked inside the gated area next to the main building. Of course, Butch had seen the ancient tablets already, but the hieroglyphs were all Greek to him. He assumed Ashworth would have a translator close by so he could get them translated.

Butch popped the trunk, exposing a tarp covering his unique cargo. A subtle smile came to Ashworth as he looked under the tarp.

"Are they what you were looking for?" Butch asked, but he had no doubt.

"Yes, they are, Mr. Colton … Yes, they are."

Ashworth motioned to his goons. "All right, boys, you know what to do with them."

"The same as with the others?" the one carrying the Uzi asked.

"Yes. See that they're destroyed."

Butch raised his eyebrows and looked at Ashworth. "What? You don't even want to know what they say?"

"Oh, I know what they say, Mr. Colton." Ashworth squinted and smiled. "I know."

CHAPTER 24

ETHAN STOOD UP AND slammed his fist on his desk. "What do you mean they're gone? Well, where did they go?! … Please tell me you at least have pictures of them!? … Illegible? Are you serious? … Damn it! How could this have happened? … That just doesn't make any sense. His reputation is impeccable. I just don't believe he could have been bought off … Wait a minute, what? Who's Colton? … Damn it, that's not who I hired … No, his name was Bryant, Clint Bryant … Shit! … No, he hasn't contacted me. My guess is he's dead. The only other person on the planet that I'm aware of who might know of those tablets and has the means to acquire them has no problem with killing as many as he needs to get his hands on them … Sorry to take it out on you. It's not your fault. I know it's spotty cell coverage there, but he must have done something to your phones. It doesn't matter now … No, just get back here as soon as you can. We'll have to go to plan B, but we'll need Ty here, so just bring him back."

ERICA'S FACE WAS PALE, but she had one more question for Ethan. "Sir, so what's on those tablets that's so important anyway?" She turned and looked at Ty standing outside the phone booth. "I understand … No, he doesn't seem to know anything about that … Okay, we'll get to the airport then."

Erica stared at Ty again while she hung up the phone. *There must be a connection to his dreams then. But what is it?*

ETHAN'S EYES WERE FIXED on a spot far away as he shut his phone off. *Can this be it? Is this how it will all end?* The Illuminati had been born in Bavaria in May 1776 and were initially focused on keeping the religions of the world from controlling the people. And though their initial goals had been for the good of mankind, one of their members, someone who'd been able to stay hidden in a cloak of secrecy, had ambitions that had become much loftier. His mission had been so secretive that most thought it was an urban legend, but Ethan and everyone in the S.O.J. had long suspected otherwise.

If this mystery man was indeed behind the missing records from ancient Atlantis, what were his plans for them? Could they possibly be for the betterment of humanity? More realistically, his plan would be for world domination. With the latter more likely, it was obvious they would have to try to counterbalance him somehow. As if their original problem of the reappearance of the fallen angels on the planet weren't enough, now they had to somehow stop the almighty power monger from tipping the scales even more.

He could see the potential downward spiral that would most likely ensue if they stood back and did nothing. It was obvious that the last resort was the only option left.

He strode to the window to gaze at the Manhattan skyline. Even just the thought of exercising the last resort had made him cringe in the past, and now it was their only alternative.

Just then his phone rang. "Yes, Victor? ... Yes, it's true. I was hoping to avoid that damn place, but it looks like it's our only hope ... Has he told anyone of this? ... I need you to find out, old friend. The situation is getting worse by the minute and we can't take any chances ... Thanks."

Ethan slid his phone into his pocket and stared off into space while he rubbed his chin. *How many others know of Montauk?*

THE SACRED VALLEY
OLLANTAYTAMBO, PERU

NOT FAR FROM THE famous Nazca lines is one of the strangest places in all of South America. There, at the northern end of the Sacred Valley, is home to some of the most mysterious ancient ruins on the planet. The megalithic ruins at Ollantaytambo rival even those in all of Egypt. Some of the stones in the construction weigh as much as sixty-five tons and are fitted together so tightly that a human hair will not fit in between.

Several tourists roaming about the ancient wonder froze in their tracks and stared in bewilderment. Out of nowhere, a bluish creature appeared as though a bolt of lightning had been frozen in time. With human-like arms, legs, and a head, the very large "energy being" stood and looked over the area as if searching for something. Then, as fast as it had appeared, it vanished.

CHAPTER 25

A PAIR OF MATCHING luxury SUVs bolted through the night heading for the tip of Long Island. Ty and Erica had flown into LaGuardia International Airport and were now speeding down the 495.

"Explain to me again why we are in such a hurry." Ty usually didn't get agitated, but with no time to recoup from the long flight back from Mexico City, he was close to his limit.

"We just got word the pyramids at Giza are closed to the public. They're heavily guarded and numerous construction vehicles are being brought in." Ethan urged the driver to pass a slow-moving truck. "The official word from the Egyptian government is they're doing some 'minor' repairs and restoration, but the magnitude of the activity seems to indicate something much bigger is underway."

"What's this got to do with us, and what's so special about Montauk?"

Ethan turned in his seat to face Ty and Erica. "All right, I'll give you a quick rundown. One of the most secret operations our government may have ever had was the little-known Montauk Project. Ever hear of it?"

"Of course I have," Erica said. "I doubt Tyler's up on it, though."

"Montauk?" Ty said. "She's right. I don't know what you're talking about."

"We got some time now, so I'll tell you what I know. Back during World War II, the U.S. was looking for anything that may tip the scales in our favor. Enter Project Rainbow, better-known as the Philadelphia Experiment and the Phoenix Project. From these operations, the Montauk Project was born.

"You've already been briefed on the Philadelphia Experiment, but the Phoenix project was originally about mind control. Even though twenty years separated the two projects, there was no doubt a connection between the two.

"Several German scientists came over after the war. Too bad none from the Bell experiments were among them, but nonetheless, several did come. Brookhaven National Laboratories were conducting the first experiments prior to the move to Montauk. The goal all along was to be able to manipulate people through mind control. But when the oversight committee found out what was going on, the Senate put a stop to the tests and the scientists were all moved out."

"Where did they go?" Ty was listening intently.

"Well, they ended up at the old Air Force base at none other than Montauk, New York. Now, of course, the armed forces were still involved, but the funding from that point on was all private. This was phase one of the Phoenix project. Hell, they were running up a power bill of around $55,000 a month."

"Sounds a little like the Bell, with that kind of power draw," Ty said.

"Yeah, it sure does. Anyway, long story short, between the concepts of making ships invisible to radar and mind control, along came phase three: time travel."

"Time travel? You've got to be kidding me."

"I'm glad I'm not. Project Pegasus was another experiment with time travel around the same time. Back to Montauk, though. There were even more bizarre experiments going on. Creating objects through thought was one of them, which, of course, reiterates what Edgar Cayce said the first beings were doing here on earth shortly after their arrival. After all, what is matter? Is it really solid or just organized energy?"

"Oh yeah, I remember that from reading Cayce's material," Ty said. "What Cayce referred to as 'thought forms' were the first intelligent creatures to arrive on earth. A spiritual being and a thought form sounds an awful lot like the same thing to me. I remember it took them some time after they were on the earth before they realized they could literally do anything, even manipulate matter. So how were the scientists able to do that at Montauk?"

"Well, a special chair had to be used to make it all happen, which is referred to as the Montauk chair. I'll explain to you how we think it works once we get there."

"So, what happened to the project?" Ty asked.

"It was shut down in the '80s, and all the participants were brainwashed to keep their mouths shut."

Ty pondered everything Ethan had said, and then a light bulb went on. "Huh."

"What, Tyler?" Erica asked.

"Maybe it's just a coincidence, but Nikola Tesla had deep roots out here, too."

"Nikola Tesla? Really?" Erica said as the driver stepped on the gas to pass another truck, briefly drawing all eyes to the road ahead.

"Yeah, he was this eccentric genius that lived in the late 1800s through the early 1900s. By the time he set up out here, he'd already proved it was possible to transmit electricity without wires with his experiments out in Colorado Springs. In one of his experiments, he had lit up light bulbs that were several feet from the power source and weren't connected to anything but the earth."

"Oh yeah," Ethan said. "I know all about Tesla. One thing I remember about that was thunder could be heard several miles away from his lab when he produced artificial lightning. The Tesla coil that was being used was the largest that had ever been built and was probably in preparation for his even bigger plan to come out here to Long Island."

Just then a large U-Haul truck swerved in front of them, barely missing the car in the lead, which Tom and the others were in, and slid to a stop between them. Ty braced himself and instinctively put his arm out to keep Erica from slamming into the front seat while the car skidded to a stop, coming just short of hitting the U-Haul.

"What the hell?" A rush of adrenaline flooded Ty's body. "Is everybody all right?"

Before anyone had a chance to answer, a man jumped from the driver's seat of the U-Haul and bolted out. Ty opened his door without hesitation, but just as he was about to give chase, Ethan grabbed his arm.

"Let him go, Ty. We have more important things to do right now. Besides, no one here's hurt."

"Speak for yourself." The driver finally broke his long silence as he looked at the front tire of the car. "Looks like we had a blowout."

Erica stared in the direction of the hit-and-runner. "Was I seeing things or was that guy carrying a purse?"

Everyone stopped and looked off into the dark.

"Yeah, that's what I thought, too." Ty said. "There was something about him that looked a little familiar somehow. Maybe the way he ran?" He turned to Ethan. "Just what's going on here, Ethan?"

Ethan shook his head. "I don't know, just more damn bad luck."

CHAPTER 26

**THE BASE OF MOUNT HERMON
JUST OUTSIDE AAME, ERNEH, SYRIA**

JORAM SEIF REACHED TO turn on his wipers as the snow started to fall yet again. He had lived in Syria his entire life and worked at the UN outpost for the past ten years, and this was the worst storm he'd ever had to drive in on his way to the pickup station. From there, the UN vehicle would take him and the others to the top of Mount Hermon, where they would put in their two-week stint. The weather forecast wasn't good. It sounded like this might be the last time a wheeled vehicle would be able to make it to the station for quite a while, as a winter weather warning had been issued for the upcoming days.

His days off were always cherished, and his wonderful family was the highlight of his life. Although it was hard to be away from them for two weeks at a time, he still loved his job with the UN. And working at the top of the highest mountain in the area made for spectacular views. Even in the winter months, with the snow blanketing the mountain, the landscape was as breathtaking as it was inhospitable.

Though Sasa, Syria, only had a population of about ten thousand, it was one of the larger towns in the area close to his work site, which is why they chose to make it their home. His two children would get the best education available in the area, and there weren't the toxic situations that came with a big city.

The first hour and fifteen minutes of his drive was the most benign of the two-hour trek to the top of the mountain. As he passed through Aame, Erneh, he doubted he would see anybody else on the road until he arrived at the pickup site at the base of the mountain, especially in this weather. But when he rounded the first bend in the road about a half mile from the last house in the village, he realized he was wrong. There, in the middle of the road, sat a dead SUV with its hood open, lit up like a Christmas tree as the flashers went in sync.

Joram came to a stop. Even if he had wanted to pass by, he didn't have room. He could see someone under the hood, but with the snow, he was indistinguishable. Joram opened his door and got out to see if he could assist.

"Hello. Anything I can do to help?"

He was coming around the front of the vehicle when the man popped his head out from under the hood.

"Oh, yes, thank you. I don't know anything about cars. Would you mind taking a look at this?"

The man looked Middle Eastern, but his accent was American.

"Not sure how much help I can be, but I'll take a look. What seems to be the problem with it?"

"It just died. I have a video here that gives instructions, but I can't understand the language. Maybe you can?" He held his phone in his hand and was keeping it under the hood, out of the falling snow.

"Let me take a look," Joram said as he ducked under the hood and looked at the man's phone.

What he saw almost stopped his heart and seemed to paralyze his entire body.

He turned to look the stranger. "What—what is this?!"

"What does it look like, Mr. Seif?"

On the tiny screen were the family members he had left barely an hour ago. They were all wearing the same clothes they'd had on earlier but now were bound to three chairs and gagged. Standing behind them were two masked men with machetes in hand ready to do the unthinkable.

"Relax, Mr. Seif. They're in no danger … provided you do us a little favor."

"What favor? And how do you know my name?" Joram was still in shock.

"Easy, Mr. Seif. No one wants to hurt your family. Just do as I say and everyone will be fine."

THE REST OF THE drive to where he would park his car for the next two weeks had been a blur. *Am I doing the right thing? If I don't do this, my family will surely be killed … or worse.* He was trying his best to not shake as he drove through the gate.

"Hey, Joram, you're running a little late," the guard said as he closed the gate behind him. "Is the wind trying to blow the road shut again?"

"What?" Joram's mind was far away.

"The snow. Is the wind making drifts out of it again?"

"Oh, no, not yet. Just poor visibility." Joram just wanted him to shut up. "Take care. I'll see you in a couple of weeks."

"All right. Have a good night."

He was having trouble thinking straight. *What else can I do?* He could hear his heart beating, and he felt the sweat on the palms of his hands as he walked to the transport vehicle with his bags in hand.

There were three others taking the same ride up, and he was trying his best not to tip them off that anything was wrong. Everyone else was tired and didn't seem to want to talk anyway.

He stared out the window for the forty-minute ride to the top. With this kind of snow coming down, maybe what he had been instructed to do wouldn't even come into play with whatever their goal was. *What could they possibly have to gain? There's nothing of any importance at this station ... is there?*

MOST UN OUTPOSTS' BUILDINGS were small, and this one was no different, but its location may have been one of the most inhospitable for more reasons than just the winter weather. Being nestled in the religious hot spot near the Israel-Lebanon-Syria border had made for some hairy situations over the years. Maybe one day everyone would be able to get along, but until then there would be a UN presence here.

Joram robotically went through the added security and into his office out of the cold. The attack on the small town of Ain Aata that had occurred only a couple of miles away on the Lebanese side of the mountain a few weeks ago was still fresh in everyone's mind. Security had been beefed up everywhere in the area.

Joram had been at home on his days off during the event, but everyone at the base had been informed. The initial thought was that Syrian President Bashar Assad had ordered the attack, but that was soon dismissed. Some even believed it had been orchestrated from within the Lebanese government in order to blame Israel and justify actions taken against Jewish settlements. The wildest theory he had heard, though, had ties to an old Nazi's elaborate experiment to resurrect one of the long-extinct fallen angels.

He had heard the stories of the two hundred fallen angels descending to the top of Mount Hermon and taking an oath to turn their back on God and give in to their lust for human women. There were those living in the area who believed that that had actually happened. Joram, however, had always thought it was pure myth. The rumors of the old Nazi trying to resurrect one of the fallen ones also seemed too fantastical to be true. Whatever Joram's family's kidnappers wanted just didn't add up.

He nervously looked at his wristwatch once more. His watch had consumed him for the past hour. *It's time.*

Joram had hoped to not make eye contact with anyone as he put on his winter wear next to the entrance. Unfortunately with the added security, that was impossible.

"What the heck are you doing, Joram?" Todd Wright was the only American stationed at the post. "It's nastier than the North Pole out there."

"What?" Joram's thoughts were far away again.

"Where are you going? It's a blizzard out there."

"And it's just going to get worse," Joram said as he slipped on his boots. "If I don't get out of here for a few minutes now, you bastards are bound to drive me crazy from being cooped up with you in these tight quarters for the next couple of weeks."

He finished zipping up his coat and had just started to pull the door open when a hand pushed it shut. It was Todd.

"Not so fast."

"What's your problem?" Joram snapped.

"Easy there, big guy," Todd said as he threw him a handheld. "Don't forget your radio. Not in this weather."

Joram took the radio, only making brief eye contact. "You're right. Thanks."

JORAM STOOD THERE IN the night watching the snow going sideways. There'd never been a question about doing it or not. His family meant too much.

Even though the visibility was poor, he didn't have to go far to get to the three ventilation intakes. They were just at the north corner of the main building, each positioned differently to allow air flow into the building no matter what direction the wind would blow the snow in from. Even the outside gunner's position was abandoned tonight, which would aid in concealing his actions.

He took out three small vials, looking toward the door with hesitation. Then he carefully broke the seals and threw them as far as he could into the tubes. *Allah, forgive me. Please look over my family.*

CHAPTER 27

THE OCCUPANTS OF THE first car saw the U-Haul just miss their vehicle and come to a stop behind them, just in front of the car Ty, Erica and Ethan were in. They stopped and backed up to check on the others.

Tom was the first one out. "What the hell just happened? Are you guys all right?"

"Yeah, we're okay, but we have a blown tire to change," Ethan said as their driver began to jack up the car. "This truck just cut us off and the driver took off on foot."

"What can we do to help?"

"The best thing you can do is get back on the road and get there as fast as possible. We'll be right behind as soon as we get the spare tire on."

"Who else would be interested in Montauk all of a sudden?" Tom asked.

"Himmler was probably acting alone, but he's not the only one with an interest in these spiritual beings. There's one in particular that has an unlimited reach, and he knows what he's doing. And if he's acquired the last two tablets and now knows the secrets they held, it could mean big trouble for everyone. And sooner or later, he'll know Montauk might be a threat to his plan."

"Okay, we'll get there and see that it's secured," Tom said.

"Remember to park where we discussed, and that's the gate you'll have access to. No one will be able to see your car there."

Tom and the other three men scrambled back into the SUV and burned rubber as they hit the road.

What the hell did I get myself into? As if searching for the last of the Nephilim hadn't been crazy enough, Tom had seen a lot of wild stuff since he joined up with the Organization. Whatever had Ethan all worked up must be important enough to risk the identities of the members of the S.O.J. Traveling at such a chaotic pace was not the norm for a group who had gone unnoticed to the public for centuries.

They dodged and weaved in traffic for several miles but were lucky enough not to meet any law enforcement. Maybe their luck had taken a turn for the better.

Finally, after the long day's events, they made it to the end of the island, Camp Hero, Montauk. The abandoned military site where the legendary experiments in mind control and time travel had been covered up for years.

They pulled into the back of the complex and unlocked the gate to the enclosure and slipped inside. Unless something went wrong, the door to the small outbuilding in front of them would grant the access they needed to get down below the complex to the hidden room where they would rendezvous with the others.

The rusty padlock on the door to the shed looked as though it hadn't been touched in years. One man held a light for Tom while the other two watched their backs to make sure no one else was around.

Tom slipped the key into the rusty lock and twisted. It popped open.

"Let's make this quick, you guys. There shouldn't be anyone around, but we don't want to take any chances."

Without a sound except for a slight creak as they closed the door, they were in.

"All right," Tom whispered, "let's get a light on."

Bob switched on his flashlight and illuminated the interior. It was an old gardening shed, cluttered with rakes, grass trimmers and even an old riding lawn mower.

Tom's eyes fell on an old refrigerator. "There … in the back. Move that refrigerator to the side."

Bob and Jack worked their way to the back and grabbed on to the old fridge.

"Jesus. Are you sure this thing isn't bolted down? It weighs a ton!" Bob said as he strained to move it.

"I'm not sure of anything, but it's not supposed to be," Tom said. "Try shaking it some."

That was the key. They jostled it loose and slid it to the side.

"What now? I don't see any kind of door."

"It's there. Look." Tom pointed at the floor. "There's a little seam in the concrete. That's the trap door Ethan said would be there."

Bob knelt down. "Sure enough. But how do we get a hold of it? There's no room to grab anything."

"Allow me," Tom said as walked over.

The others stepped aside while he reached into the duffel he was carrying and brought out a contraption that had three round suction cups attached to a large handle.

"There's a reason this piece of concrete was finished so smooth," Tom said as he put the device on the slab and pumped the air out of the three cups with the small lever on top. "All right, Bob, give me a hand with this. Ethan said it would probably take two to pick it up."

Bob came over, bent down and grabbed the other side of the handle.

"Okay, now we want to be quick in case this thing loses its grip. I played around with it at home, and on a surface like this, it'll only hold for a few seconds. Are you ready?"

"I'm ready."

"All right, on three. One, two, three."

It was about three inches thick and would have been impossible for just one of them to move, but with the two of them, the concrete slab came up rather easily. They slid it to one side, exposing the tunnel and a rusty ladder that disappeared into the dark.

"I got to say," Bob said as he stared into shaft, "Ethan doesn't seem to miss a beat with his intel."

"Yeah," Tom said. "So far, all our information has been good. Now we go down."

Something caught Bob's eye as he started down. "Hey, wouldn't you think this shed would be full of dust? I mean, it looks really clean in here."

Everyone looked the room over.

"Yeah, now that you mention it," Tom said. "You'd think there'd be dust everywhere. Ethan said this place hasn't been used in years."

"Maybe a groundskeeper comes around every once in a while?" Bob suggested.

"Not according to Ethan, but maybe his information was flawed this one time. It sure looks like it's been swept out, but I guess that doesn't really matter now." Tom looked around the interior of the shed. "Let's keep moving and finish what we came here to do."

ONE BY ONE, THEY emerged in a small concrete room with a locked iron door that had "stay out" written all over it.

With flashlights illuminating the antechamber, Tom pulled out another key from his pocket and inserted it into the door. Another perfect fit.

"It sure is nice having friends in high places," he said with a smile as he popped the lock open.

"Damn, when they shut this place down, they sure didn't want just anyone dropping in," Bob said as Tom unlatched the deadbolt.

He slowly swung open the heavy door, exposing the shadows of a disturbing past. The four of them stared into the room as Tom panned his flashlight from side to side. It appeared to be a lab of some kind, with machines that looked like they would have fit in perfectly in a hospital ER. Standing alone in the center of the room was what looked like a dentist chair, only it had probes protruding everywhere that the unlucky participant must have been attached to.

"What ... is that?" Bob asked, frozen in his tracks.

"I'm not sure," Tom said. "Ethan's going to enlighten us all as soon as he gets here."

Tom stepped in, but as soon as he did he heard a click and looked down in time to see a small flashing light attached to the bottom of the doorjamb.

CAMP HERO, MONTAUK
LONG ISLAND, NEW YORK

FIXING THE TIRE HADN'T taken too long, but it put them behind the others by fifteen minutes. Ty stared out the window of the SUV as they raced off the main road and through the now-open gate at the long-deserted Camp Hero, home of the infamous Montauk Project. His mind had been running wild with all that had transpired in the past few days.

"So, when are you going to tell me why I'm so damn important in all this, Ethan? A need-to-know basis is one thing, but get real."

Ethan took a breath and turned to face Ty. "Yeah, you're right. I guess I can tell you a little more. I just didn't want you to freak out and run off. Do you remember in the Bible when—"

"What the … Sir, something's wrong," the driver said.

Ethan turned forward and saw the same thing everyone else in the car saw: a fireball erupting from the earth in front of them. The driver slammed on the brakes and screeched to a stop as all the occupants watched in horror. The entire compound of Camp Hero was being blown apart right before their very eyes. The night lit up as the orange plume of fire shot skyward. An SUV went tumbling by, just missing their car. It was the car Tom and the others had been driving. Ty could feel the ground shake as the explosion continued for several seconds before tapering off.

"Tom!" Ty shouted as he jumped out the door and ran to where the SUV had come to a stop.

He tried to open a door, but they were all jammed. Ethan was right behind him and shone a flashlight into the windows. The car was empty. At the same time, everyone turned back to the fireball, which had now died down to a smaller but steady burn.

Ty started toward the flame, but a hand grabbed him and pulled him back.

"It's no use now, Ty." Ethan stared into the blaze. "There's nothing we can do for them."

Erica gently put her hand on Ty's back. "I'm so sorry, Tyler. I know you two were close."

He just stood there and stared. What was he in the middle of? Whatever it was, there was no way this was an accident.

"I … I just feel so helpless." Ty could barely get the words out.

Ethan stepped up with a blank look froze on his face.

"What is it, Ethan?" Erica asked. "What's wrong?"

"I just realized … Had we not had that blowout—"
"Yeah," Ty said. "We'd all be dead."

CHAPTER 28

**UNITED NATIONS OUTPOST
MOUNT HERMON**

TODD WRIGHT DIDN'T LIKE the look on Joram's face when he returned from the brutal outdoors. He waited until Joram disappeared into the depths of the only hospitable quarters for miles and then quickly threw on his winter wear and stepped out. If Joram had been up to something, maybe he could find a clue before his tracks were completely covered with new snow.

All right, Joram, just what are you up to? He looked down at the tracks that led to the door he'd just emerged from. Had he waited any longer to come out, they would have been completely covered with snow, but he was in luck.

He didn't have to go too far to see where Joram had gone. The footprints stopped at the corner of the building next to the air vents.

What were you doing here? He scanned the area closely. *There must be something here I'm missing.*

His flashlight flickered and then went out. *Damn thing. Must be a loose bulb.*

He tapped it on the closest air vent tube and the light came back to life. Out of the corner of his eye he saw something fall from the tube, and he shone his light at the snowy ground below. Then he noticed something at his feet. He took his glove off and reached down and picked it up. *Looks like a little vial of some kind, but for what?*

He sniffed it. There was no smell whatsoever. Then he noticed the small print on one side. He sheltered himself from the wind as much as he could and pulled out his phone to help light up the wording. *C4H10FO2P. What? What the hell is that?*

He quickly punched the letters into Google on his phone, and his face turned white when he read the definition. *Now, what would you be doing with that?* He stared at the other two vents and then looked at the outpost.

His eyes grew wide.

He frantically whacked the other two tubes several times with his flashlight—nothing. His eyes dropped back to the ground and he dropped to his knees and pawed through the snow—nothing.

"Joram, what did you do!?" he shouted as he got up and raced for the front door.

He threw the outer door open and bolted through the second door, and then he froze in his tracks. Two bodies lay motionless facedown on the concrete floor.

"Joram!" He ran into the back room where his coworker had disappeared.

He was slumped over in his chair. Todd grabbed him by the hair and stared into his lifeless face. There were no wounds anywhere to be seen.

I gotta get outta here!

He took a breath and held it, then turned and ran back toward the front door, but he was losing the use of his legs. Then he staggered and collapsed on the floor. He forced himself to his feet and kept going. He had to get out. With his legs weakening by the second and his vision starting to blur, he stumbled and fell. He picked himself up again only to trip and fall, over and over, until he finally got to the door and fell one last time. He pulled himself into the blizzard and gasped in a lungful of fresh air. *I made it!*

Lying there breathing in the cold air as though they were his first breaths, he saw a faint light, barely visible through the falling snow, coming up the mountain. It was getting closer.

Thank God … help.

With his vision still extremely blurred, he lay there and watched with hope as the light came to a halt. It was some kind of vehicle on tracks. He saw a door open.

"Help us." His voice was week.

Someone got out. It was hard to tell with the snow and wind, but it looked like … an astronaut? No matter, there was someone here to help.

The figure came closer and Todd held up his hand. "Thank God. Please help, there are more inside."

The blurry figure stopped only a couple of feet from Todd. It wasn't an astronaut. Whoever it was had on a hazmat suit. A hand reached toward Todd.

"Thank you," Todd said.

Then he noticed an object in the man's hand. He could almost make it out. Then he saw a bright flash.

CHAPTER 29

MANHATTAN, NEW YORK

I T HAD BEEN A long night for Ethan. He couldn't believe they'd finally had the long-sought records containing the secrets of the universe in their hands only to have them stolen right out from under them. Their only hope after that to stop whatever disaster lay on the horizon was a risky attempt to travel back in time with the use of the infamous Montauk chair. Of course, that was no longer an option.

Ethan finished the whiskey in his glass and refilled it. "All these years and it's going to end like this." He swirled his drink and threw it back. "With our last chance to stop history from repeating itself going up in flames."

"It's not over, Ethan." Ty took a sip from his glass.

"Oh yeah? What makes you so sure?"

"Don't know, but I can feel it."

"I wish I had your faith, Ty, but there's nothing else we can do." Ethan stared hopelessly out the window of his Manhattan high-rise as the sun started peeking over the horizon.

"We still can't overlook the obvious." Erica had been the voice of optimism all night. "Whoever blew that place probably thinks we went up with it, so that might give us an edge."

"An edge to do what?" Ethan said, raising his voice. "That was our last chance! Hell, we don't even know for sure if we could have stopped this had we gone back. To make matters worse, I just got word that that thing Himmler grew has been to Easter Island and now Peru!" He took another drink and slammed his glass down. "Now it's only a matter of time. It's going to find the others."

"Hypothetically speaking." Erica raised her head. "Let's say this... *thing* does find the others and releases them. What makes you so sure they'll do what they did before? I mean, the Creator punished them then, so why tempt fate again?"

Ethan's private line rang. Everyone turned and stared at it except for Ethan.

"Don't you think you should get that?" Ty said. "Maybe it's good news."

Ethan got up and answered the phone.

He listened for a few seconds and said, "Tyler's okay," and went back to listening. His eyes lit up and a slight smile crept over his face. "You say he's willing to help? ... Okay, don't let him leave. I'll have my personal driver pick him up and we'll meet him at JFK ... Don't worry about that—I'll have a new passport for him. And, Victor, thanks, old friend."

Ethan hung up and stood in silence for a moment. Then he turned to Ty and Erica. "Looks like you were right, Ty. We may have a chance after all."

JFK International Airport, New York

IT HADN'T TAKEN ETHAN long to gather up passports and make the travel arrangements. Ty still couldn't believe who was going to meet them at the airport, though. It just didn't make sense, but then nothing about this whole thing made any sense.

Ethan's car pulled up to the curb. With the tinted windows, no one was visible in the backseat. When the door opened, none other than Ty's archaeology professor, Ivan Baumann, aka Dr. Eisenberg, stepped out wearing an Indiana Jones hat over his now-bald head.

Ty didn't know what to say. Tom had told him he'd seen the professor again, but why was he here now?

"I take it you know the man?" Erica asked.

"Yeah, or I thought I did." He couldn't take his eyes off Ivan.

KLM FLIGHT 903
NEW YORK TO POLAND

TY HAD MADE A little small talk with Ivan during the flight but had been reluctant to show much trust in his professor. The lack of sleep over the past several days finally caught up with him, and he couldn't keep his eyes open any longer.

Ty's in an ancient village. It's hot, dusty, but the people are full of laughter and happiness as they move about the streets.

Suddenly a strange sound draws everyone's attention to the top of the mountain in the background. An eerie silence descends. The only sound is the strange noise from above. Then, on the mountaintop ... there's movement. It's a mass of some kind. A volcanic eruption? But where's the fire and smoke? The mass slowly oozes down until individual forms become visible within it. The mysterious forms flood toward the land below.

Ty jolted awake in a sweat. *Damn ... what a dream! It seemed so real.*

He looked around.

"Everything all right?" Ivan asked.

"Oh … yeah. Must have been dreaming, I guess."

"Care to share?"

"It's nothing. Probably just too much TV."

Ty looked at the professor. He didn't know what to say. On one hand, he had always been fond of Eisenberg or Baumann—whoever he was—but on the other, he was a part of a scheme that still had Ty's father missing and his life turned upside down. Still, he'd requested to sit next to the aging European as the group had filled the four center seats on the wide-body aircraft.

Ivan broke the ice on the subject. "Tyler, I can honestly say I had no idea what Himmler was up to. Hardly anyone did."

"So why did you do it? I mean, to go along with a known Nazi?" Ty shook his head and turned away.

"I assure you it wasn't his political views I was interested in."

"No? So what was it then?"

Ivan raised his eyebrows. "So, Ethan hasn't told you anything?"

"No," Ethan was sitting on the other side of Ivan and had been listening in. "I thought I'd wait until you were here. I really don't know much yet anyway."

Ivan took a breath and began to speak. "My interest was and always has been with Die Glocke, the Bell." He turned to Ty. "You are one of the few left alive that have seen the magnificent piece of equipment."

"What's the Bell have to do with what we're trying to do?" Ty turned to Ethan. "And I'm still not even sure what that is!"

"Ah, yes. The Bell's true purpose." Ivan's face lit up. "I can assure you Himmler was a bumbling idiot. All he could think about was his father's legacy. Thank God he didn't know of the Bell's true potential.

"The project started long before the end of the war but only became a working model toward the end. At first the Nazis were just trying to build a better flying machine, but then—accidentally—they found out the Bell could do much more than fly."

"That I saw." Ty said, nodding his head.

"What you saw was nothing. When it was first powered up, it did kill those around it."

"Himmler said that was because it was accelerating the growth of all the cells," Ty said.

"True, but how was it accomplishing that?" Ivan looked at his captive audience. "It was actually changing the frequency of their vibration to mirror that of something in the future."

Ty had been studying the legends of the sacred sites around the world, and most of them were laden with stories of sound as a means to do some pretty amazing things, but this? This sounded more like science fiction than fact.

"Oh yes, my friend. And it gets even stranger. When they finally figured out what was really happening, they thought they could travel through time—forward or back—to do what was needed to win the war on all fronts."

"The Bell I saw didn't look like much of a weapon."

"And it wasn't. The Bell was just the means to transport something through time into the past like an advanced fighter plane and then shoot down enemy aircraft at will."

"I'm all ears now. So what happened?"

"All that was needed was a little more time to work out the last of the bugs." Ivan shook his head. "The irony of it. If only they'd had more time, then they would have had all the time in the world. Nevertheless, the Nazis were very close. The first attempts were with Jewish prisoners, none of which were successful. But then one day a young boy happened to be exploring another abandoned mine shaft in the area. There were mine shafts everywhere, and it just so happened this one was connected to the one the Nazis were using for the Bell project.

"The boy was curious when he saw the commotion and waited for a chance to get closer. He was able to get into the room with the Bell when something else had everyone's attention. There he hid.

"When the workers came back, they made a few adjustments and left the room. That's when the Bell started to hum. The humming grew louder and the boy became scared. He came out from his hiding spot and looked for a way out, but the lead door was latched shut.

"The scientists on the other side of the door could see the boy though the viewing portal and even tried to shut down the Bell, but they were too late. What happened next?" Ivan paused as he looked at everyone. "The boy vanished before their very eyes!"

"So what happened to him?" Erica asked. "Where did he go?"

Ivan grinned. "Exactly one day into the future."

CHAPTER 30

THE PENTAGON
ARLINGTON COUNTY, VIRGINIA

GENERAL MAX BENNET STARED out his office window in the Pentagon. Never in his tenure had he come across anything that even remotely resembled the situation he faced now. When the now-infamous Rudolf Himmler's hideout exploded, leaving nothing but a huge empty crater, it didn't take long for the rumors to start mounting.

Bennet had been brought up as a Christian, but to see Biblical events possibly unraveling before his eyes just didn't seem viable. He'd always thought Genesis 6:4 was about nothing more than a mythical event that humans had manufactured long ago. Of course, that was still what he was hoping for. Unfortunately, there had been too many sightings of an "energy being" that appeared in ancient sacred locations across the planet. The accounts eerily corresponded with the description of the fallen angels written down by Moses all those centuries ago.

He strode back to his desk and pressed the intercom. "I need to speak to the president."

A female's voice came over the speaker. "Yes, sir. How soon, sir?"

"Yesterday, goddamn it! He'll talk to me, just get him on the phone now!"

"Yes, sir. Stand by a moment please."

His phone rang a few minutes later.

"Mr. President … Thank you, sir … Peru was the last place we are aware of, but there's more than that going on now, too … I was just informed the UN outpost on Mount Hermon in Lebanon has been disabled with 100 percent casualty … We have no idea as to the *who*, but we do know the how. Sarin gas, sir. That is, as far as everyone who was inside the base. There was one outside, too. One of ours, sir. He was shot in the head … We still have no idea what they wanted, but I can tell you this: the entire inside floor was torn up, and, sir … it was concrete … three feet thick. Whatever they wanted was under there. Any ideas of what that might have been, sir? … Okay, I'll do what I can to find out. But believe me, someone knows."

Giza Plateau, Egypt

THE GIZA PLATEAU HAD been closed to the public for a few days, although it was anything but deserted. On the plateau, numerous men dressed in combat fatigues had been scurrying about putting up a tall privacy fence around the Great Pyramid. The locals were told an investor had put up enough money to restore the great structure to its original state, complete with the now-missing casing stones and capstone. In the process, the investor would also pay for repairs caused by some minor tremors in the area so it could be reopened to the public soon without posing a danger to anyone.

As Butch walked around the perimeter of the new enclosure, it was obvious there was much more than a little restoration going on. Of course, if that's all that was happening, he wouldn't even be here. Ashworth thought the perfect job for him would be to help make sure no prying eyes tried to see what was really happening behind the curtain.

He stepped back inside the fence. Several trucks had been pouring in loaded with cut white limestone blocks from a nearby quarry. Butch had also noticed numerous weapons hidden from view, and then he noticed something else. Under a camouflage net he saw the barrel of a tank. Then another. In all, he saw four combat-ready tanks completely sheltered from view by camouflage nets. Whatever the big picture was, a lot of precautions were being taken to see that no one interfered with the plan.

Restoration project my ass. Don't need this kind of muscle for that. He looked to the west as the sun was beginning to disappear below the horizon. Something big was going down, that much was certain.

CHAPTER 31

KLM FLIGHT 903
NEW YORK TO POLAND

THE FLIGHT ATTENDANT WALKED by, prompting Ty to keep his voice down to a loud whisper. "Come on. The boy was transported one day into the future? How is that even remotely possible?"

"So, tell me, Ty," Ethan said, "have you ever heard what Edgar Cayce said about the nature of time?"

"Probably, but I don't recall it right now."

"To put it in a nutshell, he said that time is not a linear thing like it appears to us but that everything is all happening in one glorious instant. Of course, he was a seer, but there are many religions around the world that believe the same thing … Everything is happening at the same time."

"I've heard that, too, but how is that physically possible?" Ty asked.

"Let me back up a little first. Nikola Tesla had maybe the most developed mind in the history of modern man. There've been a few brilliant minds in recent times, such as Einstein, Stephen Hawking and others. What separates Tesla from the pack is that not only did he have many theoretical ideas, but he actually put together several successful experiments to back them up."

"What's this got to do with time?" Ty asked.

"I'm getting there. Remember you were briefed about the experience he had with high voltage?"

"Yeah, he told some guy in a coffee shop that he could see the past, present and future all at the same time. I also remember it damn near killed him."

"Yes, but it didn't. And he also said, 'If you want to find the secrets of the universe, think in terms of energy, frequency and vibration.' Couple that with what Cayce said about everything happening at once—"

"Are you saying a change in time is just a change in the frequency of a vibration?"

"Well, simply put, yes. At least that's one theory. And it does seem to make sense. If everything really is all happening at once, each reality would have to be distinguishable by some means, or else life might be rather confusing. So if time is just a change in vibration, then if the vibration of something is changed, you could possibly change the time you're in."

"Jesus, Ethan, do you realize how whacked out this sounds?" Ty said rolling his eyes.

Ethan looked at him. "Well, if you don't believe it coming from me, how about one of Erica's most astute colleagues?"

"Who are you talking about?" Erica asked. "What colleague?"

"There was another interesting person that just passed away a couple of years ago. Delores Cannon. I'm sure you've heard of her. She was probably one of the best hypnotherapists of our time."

"Yes, she was pretty amazing."

"Well, just like Brian Weiss, she did past life regressions to help people with their problems. Back in the 1980s, she had a patient who wanted to see if she had any past lives. Well, wouldn't you know it, Cannon took her back to a past life in France in the 1500s where she was a student of none other than Nostradamus!"

Ty was shaking his head. "That's pretty cool, Ethan, but I still don't see the connection."

"Just hold on, I'm getting there. As with Weiss, Cannon was able to retrieve info from the patient's past life, but then the most amazing thing happened. Nostradamus told the student he wanted to talk to Cannon!"

"What?" Erica's eyes lit up. "No way! How is it I never heard this before? We studied her work quite a bit."

"Well, you missed out on the best part then. Cannon had several conversations through her patient with Nostradamus this way. And she wasn't talking to a dead guy from the spirit world—she was talking to him in real time while he was alive some five hundred years ago! And he told Cannon the nature of time was just like Cayce said—everything is all happening at once. That's how these conversations were possible."

Ty was still shaking his head. "I don't know, Ethan. I mean, this all just sounds so … fantastic."

"How else would you explain what Ivan just said? And how do you think you went from Argentina to Egypt in the blink of an eye … and back in time, no less?"

Ty leaned back and thought about it. "So, the Bell is basically a frequency generator, and if you're near it—"

"You'll mirror its frequency … or that's the theory anyway."

"That doesn't explain how I ended up in the Great Pyramid, though."

"No," Ethan said, rubbing his chin, "we think that has something to do with the pyramid itself. Maybe it corralled your energy somehow after the explosion. We just don't know for sure yet."

"So, let me get this straight," Erica said. "Are you saying that's all the Bell did? Alter the frequency of the surrounding vibration?"

"Exactly. And if you couple that with how Edgar Cayce described time, then anything is possible! Including—"

Ty was nodding his head. "Time travel."

GIZA PLATEAU, EGYPT

BUTCH WATCHED AS THE two-ton truck was let in through the heavily guarded rear gate. Whatever payload the truck was carrying, it must have been pretty important to garner this kind of attention. A strange sensation came over Butch as the truck passed by, an indescribable feeling he'd never felt before. He could feel the hair stand up on his neck.

In the short time he'd been here, it was obvious that more than just restoration was going on. Aside from having to detour a handful of curious onlookers, this had been the easiest job he'd had in a while.

It was obvious Ashworth's right-hand man thought he'd approached Butch without being noticed, but nothing was further from the truth.

"So, tell me, Hanson. What's in the truck?"

Butch could sense Hanson was caught off guard, but he hid it well.

"Just more equipment. What are you doing up so late?"

"You kiddin' me?" Butch turned to face him. "How the hell's anyone supposed to get any sleep around here with all this equipment working all night?"

There had been a steady flow of flatbed trucks hauling in slabs of rock and excavators digging all over the place. Numerous workers were constantly scrambling about. All he had been able to see was the smooth white blocks of limestone being shaped and put into place on the outer surface of the Great Pyramid. With a dragline machine on each side, they had run enough cable to go up over the top of the pyramid, through a pulley and down the other side. Slings were then attached to a partially finished casing stone and hooked to the cable, and the stone was hauled up to its destination in line with the rest. If only the ancient Egyptians had had these draglines.

"It would have been a lot easier if you had taken care of the Larson kid in Mexico," Hanson said as he watched the casing stones being put in place.

Butch swiveled his head to Hanson. "What are you talking about? The kid's no threat."

"How the hell would you know, Colton?" Hanson lit the cigarette hanging from his mouth and took a drag. "Several people way above your pay grade seem to think so." He turned to look at Butch. "But you're right, Colton. The problem has been taken care of. No more threat."

Returning Hanson's stare, he reached into his coat pocket and pulled out a can of chewing tobacco. Without taking his eyes off Hanson, he popped it open, dug out a pinch and firmly stuffed it in his lower lip. He worked the wad in his mouth, then looked to the ground and spit, just missing Hanson's feet. He raised his head back up to Hanson. "So what's the problem then?"

Hanson stood silent for few moments. "Just do what you're told. Our window of opportunity to complete the restoration project is not a limitless one. And I can assure you, Mr. Colton, if we ever need your advice on how to proceed, we'll ask you for it."

Hanson flicked the burned match into the desert as Butch watched him walk into the shadows.

CHAPTER 32

KLM FLIGHT 903
NEW YORK TO POLAND

THE JETLINER HIT SOME turbulence and caused everyone to stop what they were doing for a moment.

Ty tightened his seat belt and looked at Ivan. "So back to your original story. Was the boy okay?"

"Totally unharmed. That was the first successful travel through time. And it was all by accident."

"What was special about the boy?"

"Nothing. He was just worried about getting caught and being in trouble. All he thought about was the day being over. And that's what happened … for him anyway."

"So you're saying it took him to where he was thinking?"

"In a nutshell, yes. Unlike the Jewish prisoners, he didn't think about dying—he just wanted the day to be over.

"Once the Nazis figured that out, advancements in their tests started to happen. They eventually tried to send a fighter plane back to air battles to try to get the upper hand, but they never could quite fully make the transition into that timeline. They tried over and over again but to no avail. The Nazis knew they were close when the Allied fighters reported seeing balls of light in the air, but they just couldn't quite cross over."

"You gotta be kidding me," Ty said as it hit him. "The Foo Fighters? That's what the Foo Fighters were?"

"Ah, you've heard of them." Ivan nodded. "If they only had more time to work the last of the bugs out, but unfortunately it became apparent the Allies were going to win. That's when Kammler made his deal to turn over the Bell to save his own ass. At the expense of everyone else that was involved with the project."

"Excuse me for a minute, but what were the Foo Fighters?" Erica asked.

"That was some bizarre stuff," Ty said. "I came across this, or them, or whatever the hell they were a while back. It seems the sightings were right at the end of World War II in the European theater.

"I think it was late in 1944, just a few months before Germany surrendered. A fighter squadron was flying somewhere over the French-German border and the pilots saw these strange balls of light following them around. Then more and more pilots started to report seeing them, even German pilots.

"Their critics tried to say they were just tired and seeing things. Then, when more and more started to report seeing the same things, they tried to pawn it off as Saint Elmo's Fire, flares and, of course, weather balloons. The fact that the balls of light seemed to be able to turn on a dime and travel at speeds in excess of two hundred miles an hour kind of debunked all those theories, though.

"Then the craziest thing happened. When Berlin fell, the sightings stopped." Ty turned to Ivan. "I guess that makes sense now."

Ivan nodded. "They were so close, but luckily for the rest of the civilized world, not close enough."

"Wow!" Erica's jaw dropped. "I can't believe I've never heard of them before."

Ethan looked at her, then out the window. "Yeah, it's amazing what they don't teach in the school systems."

Ty nodded and turned back to Ivan. "So back to what we're doing now. If everyone involved with the Bell project is dead, why are we on our way to Poland? What's there that's going to give us a chance to clean this mess up?"

Ivan took a deep breath and looked out the window. "It's true, all right. Everyone involved with the project was killed. But the Jewish prisoners the Nazis had working on it saw this coming. They saw it and tried to save themselves."

"How?"

Ivan turned back to Ty. "By building a second Bell. One that Kammler and his superiors knew nothing about. That was going to be their escape."

"Why not just use the first Bell?"

"The security was too high. It was always being watched by the SS, but a Bell in another part of the mine shafts that the SS didn't know about was perfect. Luckily for them, there was a sympathetic German scientist who aided them with the project."

"Huh." Erica bit her lip. "My guess is they were a day late?"

"Exactly," Ivan said. "It was just one day."

Ty thought about it, then turned back to Ivan. "How is it you know so much about this project anyway?"

Ivan stared blankly at the seatback in front of him for a moment, then turned back to Ty. "Because, that young boy … was me."

POLAND

THE FLIGHT HAD BEEN a long one and everyone was tired, but

time was of the essence and the trek had to continue. There were other airports closer to their destination than Warsaw, but it was the only nonstop. They would still get to the Owl Mountain area faster without a layover even after the four hundred-kilometers of roads ahead of them. Ethan had the most energy, so he had volunteered to drive.

Ty stared out the window at the seemingly lifeless trees as they passed by. Visions of the Nazi invasion nearly seventy years ago sprang to his racing mind. He could almost see the German tanks pushing through the forest and shooting anyone brave enough to resist them.

He turned to Ivan. "Do you remember? I mean the invasion?"

Ivan continued to watch the landscape roll by. "Like it was yesterday. They staged a Polish attack on the Germans at the border. The Nazis dressed up like Polish soldiers and then shot several of their prisoners, which were then dressed up like German soldiers. All so they could justify the invasion and give the Germans more space to live and breed. My parents resisted. They were both shot."

"I'm sorry, professor." Ty tried to make eye contact, but Ivan just stared out the window. "There have been so many atrocities people have done to each other over the years. I just don't understand why."

"Money, greed, lust." Ethan shook his head. "We may have a chance to change all that."

Ivan smiled and turned to look out the window again. "I sure hope so."

THEY HAD BEEN ON the road for just over an hour. Ty and Erica had fallen asleep, and Ethan looked back at them in the mirror as they sped down the road. It was still hard for him to believe Ty was the one foretold of who could stop the impending calamity. Although he was starting to see Ty's grit.

He had other sources besides the old woman who called him out of the blue only a few months ago. Himmler wasn't the only one looking for one of the originals. Ethan had spent his entire adult life knowing what he was to prevent, and all the seers he had sought out knew of the original one's existence in this time. All the seers had said the original would be found not far from the great Edgar Cayce's harmonic spot on the earth, Virginia Beach. The old woman even gave him a last name: Larson.

Cayce didn't just happen to build his psychic hospital in Virginia Beach. The greater power that served him told him that that was where it needed to be. Just as the eccentric Edward Leedskalnin knew when he'd found the "right spot" for his famous Coral Castle in Florida. The perfect vibration for anything or anyone was always somewhere.

Ethan hadn't been recruited by the S.O.J.; he was born into it. And keeping the Nephilim from returning to ravage the earth was a role he would gladly take again.

The clock was ticking, as they were only about an hour from the abandoned mine that once housed Hitler's most secretive project. It had become obvious the creature Himmler had created was now in search of its own kind. All of the intel reports he had been getting from his sources around the world confirmed that the mysterious creature had appeared at most of the ancient sacred sites across the planet. Now there was at least one more spot where it would look. It was just a matter of time before the creature found the others, and there was nothing he could do about it—unless Ivan's story was true. Then they would have an opportunity to fix it once and for all. It was just an outside chance, but it was a chance.

CHAPTER 33

HIGH ABOVE ANTARCTICA

TWENTY THOUSAND FEET ABOVE Antarctica, a B-2 bomber escorted by two F-35C Lightning IIs were approaching the Wilkes Land region. The white snow field below looked barren and lifeless. It had only been a few years ago when a satellite sent up to measure the earth's gravity discovered a gravitational anomaly on the edge of the continent just south of Australia. The gravitational pull was much greater here for some reason, and they had been sent to observe.

Several conspiracy theorists had been beating on the Pentagon's door with wild stories of biblical fallen angels buried under the ice somewhere on the frozen land mass. Normally, people with crackpot ideas like this had just been placated enough to get them off of whatever crazy bandwagon they were on and send them home. Of course, they'd be on a special watch list afterward, but this time was different. This time there had been sightings all over the world of some kind of strange energy creature showing up only to disappear shortly thereafter.

"Doesn't look like anything out of the ordinary to me," the mission commander of the B-2 said as he looked the area over. "Anybody else see anything?"

"Negative, all clear," was the response from both F-35s.

"All right then, let's return to base."

"Roger that."

The formation of three turned course back to Anderson Air Force Base, Guam, and picked back up to cruise speed for their long ride home. If they'd only waited one more minute, they'd have seen the ominous blue glow appear on the surface behind them.

JUGOW, POLAND

TY, ERICA, ETHAN AND Ivan sat at a back table in a bar in Ivan's small hometown of Jugow, Poland. It had been a long time since Ivan had been here, and unfortunately, many of the memories of this place that filled his head were not pleasant ones. Of course, there had been good times before the Nazi invasion, but that all seemed like a blur now.

Ivan stared into the bottom of his glass as the others discussed their next course of action. So many years had passed since the German tanks rolled through this area, obliterating anyone who got in their way. How might things have been different had he not stumbled upon the Nazis' most secret project in his own backyard?

His obsession with the Bell and the possibility of getting even with those who'd taken the lives of his parents were all he lived for. And now it looked like he might just have his chance for revenge. The financial backing of the S.O.J. was just what he needed to make it all happen.

Ethan interrupted his thoughts. "So, what do you think, Ivan?"

"What? Oh, sorry. I was just thinking of my mother and father. What was it you asked?"

"You said there's a possibility we might need some equipment to dig with. We should find a place for base and get started. Don't you agree?"

"Yes. The Nazis blew several of the shafts after they shot everyone, and I'm sure there has been other destabilization in the tunnels over the years." He downed the last of his beer. "Have you made arrangements for the other thing?"

Ethan nodded. "It's coming. Wasn't the easiest thing to buy on the black market, but it's on the way."

"Good." He slammed his empty glass down. "Let's get moving, shall we?"

THE NAZI FLY TRAP
LUDWIKOWICE-MILKOW, POLAND

ALTHOUGH IVAN HADN'T BEEN in Poland for years, he was still fluent in the language and had no problem rounding up all the gear they needed to do a little late-night spelunking. It wasn't the supplies that would be a problem but rather getting to the cave entrance they needed to without getting caught. A wealthy foreigner with strong political ties now owned the property, and being invisible was imperative.

The Nazis had dug numerous tunnels in the Owl Mountain area when they launched Project Riese and some were now open to the public for tours. Luckily, the location of the Bell project had never been found after the war. The Nazis probably chose this particular spot to house their most prized weapon of the future because there were already numerous vacant coal mines throughout. There was no need to tunnel into the earth to hide their top secret experiment when the Polish coal miners had already done so in years prior.

Rubble of a once-magnificent power plant partially stood in the background, most of it having been reclaimed by the earth. "The Henge," also known as the Nazi Fly Trap, had been left to stand and was a common stop for the occasional conspiracy theorist. The nickname "the Henge," came from the structure's resemblance to the famous Stonehenge in England. It was a cylindrical construction made from concrete pillars that stood about twenty feet tall with a diameter of about sixty feet. As with Stonehenge, there were concrete uprights supporting a concrete beam that went around the circumference of the top.

There were numerous stories linking the Fly Trap to the Bell project. In fact, there were some who said they witnessed a flying object contained within the Fly Trap during supposed experiments. If these stories were true and it really was connected to the Bell project, then somewhere deep in the ground below they should find the second Bell.

Ty and Ivan would be the first ones in to see what would need to be done to regain an entrance to the Walter Mine Shaft, which, according to Ivan, was where they first needed to go on their way to find the second Bell.

Ivan glassed the area from their perch on the highest peak just south of the complex.

"Not a lot going on. As long as we sneak in at night, there shouldn't be a problem." He handed the binoculars to Ty. "You see the dilapidated power plant just past the Fly Trap?"

"Yeah, I see it."

"Look to the right of that and you can just make out what looks like a concrete bunker."

"Ah … Okay, I see it."

"That's where we need to get to. There's an entrance to one of the first mine shafts dug shortly after the power plant was built. It connects up with the Walter Shaft. That's how I got in unnoticed and was able to leave unnoticed."

Ty handed the binoculars to Ethan. "So what makes you think it's not sealed off? I mean, it's been a long time."

"Oh, it's sealed off, all right. I made sure I was the only one who'd ever go back in that way."

"Oh yeah?" Ethan said as he glassed the area. "How's that?"

"You'll see."

CHAPTER 34

ETHAN HAD ARRANGED FOR all of their supplies to be shipped to the little cottage they had rented in Jugow, which was only a few kilometers from the Fly Trap. The only thing he didn't have yet was the last piece of the puzzle, which Ivan had requested and would be coming soon.

Now they were ready to make their first trek into the old mine shaft. With the cover of darkness and a local festival in the nearby village of Ludwikowice Kłodzkie, they knew this was the perfect time to make their first descent.

They had dropped off their gear and stashed it in the brush while posing as tourists at the Fly Trap earlier in the day. Now they were ready to go back and begin.

"So, tell me, Ivan," Ty said as they packed the supplies. "How is it you found this entrance anyway?"

"Dumb luck, if you want to call it that. Just boys being boys. Before the Nazis invaded, Victor and I would sneak out of the house and come here to play." He paused for a moment. "I think it was just put there as an air shaft, but it was big enough for us to explore. After the invasion, we saw the Nazis in the area a lot, so we knew something important was going on."

"To say the least," Ethan said. "Had you not stumbled onto what you did, let's just say the entire planet would be in jeopardy with no way out."

"Yeah." Ivan seemed to be far away.

"All right, you guys, make sure you check in with your radios every fifteen minutes like we discussed," Erica said. "You've got two repeaters that will extend the range of the radios and enable the signal to make two corners. Ethan will get more once we get going. Of course, we won't know for sure how good they'll work until we actually try them."

"Oh, we will." Ty said. "The last thing I want to do is end up being buried alive over here."

"You and me both," Ivan said as he stood up in preparation to leave.

"So how did the Nazis figure out this ... Bell technology?" Ty asked him.

"Well, what I heard was the Nazis had great interest in most all ancient myths and legends. It was their driving curiosity that led them to the mysterious Vimana."

"Oh yeah, I've heard of them. Weren't those the flying machines in some ancient texts found in India?"

"One and the same. After the Nazis translated these texts into German, they found there was enough technical description to be able to design their own new version."

"You're kidding, right?" Erica asked.

"Nope, just like the moon land rover's wheels were designed from a description out of the book of Ezekiel."

Ty stopped what he was doing and looked up at Ivan. "So you think a mythological machine may have been the inspiration for Die Glocke?"

"Both were said to have rotating containers of mercury at high RPMs to achieve their goal of anti-gravity. Even the ancient drawings of the Vimana were indeed bell-shaped." Ivan raised his head and smiled. "Of course, there's always the chance that the similarities were just a mere coincidence."

THE NAZI FLY TRAP
LUDWIKOWICE-MILKOW, POLAND

ETHAN HAD DRIVEN UP to the turnaround area next to the Fly Trap, where Ty and Ivan had slipped out into the night toward the dilapidated power plant. Ethan had bought the best of everything, including their night vision goggles, which made it easy for them to make their way through the rubble and to the concrete bunker.

"Amazing," Ivan whispered as they crept around the back side and made their way to an opening in the back. "It's been so long ago, yet it seems like only yesterday." He tossed a small rock inside the broken-out corner where they thought they could gain access. "Just in case there are any wild animals making this their home."

The rock rattled around for a moment, and then the silence returned.

"Okay, the coast is clear."

Ty followed Ivan as he crept through the small opening in the corner. The inside was much smaller than it appeared from the outside due to the three-foot-thick concrete walls. About the size of a small bedroom with chunks of concrete littering the floor, there was not much room to spare.

"Keep your light off until we get below ground level," Ivan whispered as Ty was again able to stand upright.

"No problem." Ty looked around the small enclosure. "Are you sure this is where you got in? I don't see anything resembling an underground entrance."

"Trust me, it's here." Ivan pointed to the far corner. "We need to move that slab out of the way first."

Ty stepped around him and bent over. Even though it wasn't a big chunk, concrete was heavy and it was all he could do to slide it aside without making any noise.

"There. Now what? I don't see a trap door."

"Oh, you will. Here, take this crowbar and chip at the surface about two feet from the wall."

Ty took the bar and did as instructed, trying to be as quiet as it was possible to be while hitting concrete with a crowbar. Hopefully, the locals were all still at the festival. At first the bar just bounced off, but then a small chip came off. Then another and another. The pieces were getting bigger and coming off more easily with each blow.

Then he could see a metal lid. He chipped along the seam and followed it. There it was— about a two-foot in diameter manhole cover.

"That was the last thing I did when the Nazis were kicked out. I borrowed a little of the cement mix that the Nazis had lying around and was able to conceal the entrance. Now, pry it up. It's not that heavy and it's sitting on a lip, so it can't fall in."

Again, Ty did as instructed. With only a couple of attempts with the bar, he was able to get into the seam enough to pry the lid up and set it aside, exposing a dark black hole.

He took one of the two battery-powered repeaters he'd brought and attached it to a piece of exposed rebar directly above the shaft. Ty turned to Ivan and smiled as he took out his radio. "Phase one complete. On to phase two."

CHAPTER 35

ABANDONED MINE SHAFT
LUDWIKOWICE-MILKOW, POLAND

TY COULDN'T BELIEVE THEIR luck. Although they had secured their safety rope to a piece of exposed rebar at the top, as of yet they still hadn't needed it. The iron ladder embedded in the concrete wall still seemed extremely stable after all these years. The silence deepened as they descended the vertical shaft.

"So, who put this shaft in?" Ty asked, trying to keep his voice down.

"No need to whisper anymore. The only ones that might be able to hear us now have been dead for over seventy years."

The thought should have given Ty the creeps a little, but he was gradually becoming accustomed to the bizarre. "Yeah, I suppose you're right. If only these walls could talk."

"You'd hear an eerie tale if they could, my friend. One that needs to stay in the past."

"I couldn't agree more. So how much deeper do we need to go?"

"Not much farther now. This only takes us to the Walter Shaft. It's just above the one we are going to. And it was the Polish coal miners."

"Excuse me?"

"The answer to your first question. The local coal miners put this shaft in long before the arrival of the Germans."

Ty could hear the anguish in Ivan's voice. He could also tell he wasn't a young boy anymore from his labored breathing.

"Should we take a break, Ivan? I'd hate for you to have to carry me out of here."

"Thanks, but no thanks, my young friend." His voice was filled with excitement. "I've waited over seventy years to come back to this place. Besides, we're here."

Ty waited for Ivan to move out of the way then planted his feet on solid ground once again.

"Take off your goggles, Ty."

Ty set the other repeater down directly under the vertical shaft and did as Ivan asked. The cavern lit up when Ivan flipped on his high-power flashlight. The shaft had only partially caved in. There was enough room to stand, but not much more. Rubble lined the floor as far as he could see.

"Where to now?"

"About a hundred feet that way." Ivan pointed to their right. "If we can pick our way through that mess, there should be an air shaft that connects to the lower level. That's where we need to go."

Ty took his radio out once again to report. "Are you guys still there?"

The response was scratchy but audible. "Yeah, we're here. How's it going down there?" It was Ethan.

"So far so good. We should know more soon."

"Okay, keep us posted."

ETHAN PUT THE RADIO back on his belt. "I hope Ivan knows what he's doing. We don't have a lot of time for mishaps."

"So, tell me, Ethan," Erica asked, "exactly what do you plan to do when—and if—we find this other Bell? I mean, if this creation of Himmler's really finds and turns loose the original two hundred fallen angels, how can it possibly help?"

Ethan stared off into space for a moment before he answered. "I can't really say yet, Erica. You'll just have to trust me on this for now." He turned to look her in the eye. "I hope you still do."

She nodded. "Yeah, but somewhere along the line, I'd like to know the big picture."

"I know, Erica. And you will. But this is the last chance we have to find a way out of this mess. We have to find the second Bell before we can go any further." He turned his gaze back to the heavens. "Let's just hope Ivan's memory doesn't fail him now."

THEY HAD MADE THEIR way through several feet of debris and were getting closer to the air shaft. The damp air filled Ty's lungs. He was glad he dressed warmly and was concerned about Ivan in the frigid temps.

"How are you holding up, Ivan?"

"Not bad. It was easier traversing this path before the roof caved in." He turned back to face Ty and smiled. "Maybe being a little younger helped some, too."

"Maybe." Ty laughed, then noticed something up ahead. "What's that? Looks like it could be what we're looking for."

Behind a large piece of fallen earth, the edge of a small opening could be seen. It wasn't obvious, but it was there.

"Ah, yes," Ivan's voice was filled with excitement. "I do believe that is it. All these years." He looked back at the shaft, then at the small opening again. "This was the access that allowed me to discover the Bell and the same one that saved my life. I wonder if I was the only one that knew of it. If anyone else did … well, it doesn't matter now. Think you can move that rock?"

Ty nodded and Ivan moved aside. Of course, the rock blocking the passage was one of the biggest around, so Ty had to spend several minutes removing some of the smaller ones from near the base so he could roll it down. When it was clear, he gave it a try.

Nothing.

Ivan couldn't help much, but another set of hands on the boulder wouldn't hurt, so Ty motioned him over. On the third attempt, it moved, and Ty continued to push until it picked up speed and rolled completely out of the way.

"I wonder how long it was after you passed through here that this thing fell. You might be luckier than you think."

Ivan nodded. "Maybe … maybe something went right after all."

"Do you want me to go first?"

"No, I'll go. You wait for me to call."

"Okay, I'll be here," Ty said as Ivan slowly clambered up to the opening and disappeared into the dark.

Several minutes passed silently, and then he heard something. It was Ivan inching his way back. He struggled out and sat on the pile of rubble, shaking his head.

"What's wrong? Has it caved in?"

"Worse than that," Ivan said with a blank stare. "It's flooded."

CHAPTER 36

GIZA PLATEAU, EGYPT

BUTCH STOOD AROUND THE corner in the shadows of the ancient wonder watching the workers as they got closer to finishing the restoration process. The white limestone casing stones going up on the Great Pyramid was a sight to behold. The casing stones seemed to transform the great wonder from a partially dilapidated pile of rocks to the original work of art it once was. The construction had been going on round-the-clock for several days, and more and more sightseers were showing up, which meant Butch had to start earning his keep.

There was always someone willing to stick their neck out to get a closer look, and putting the fear of Jesus into them was Butch's responsibility. One he was more than capable of.

That was the easy part. The hard part was putting up with Hanson and his line of bull. Butch didn't like Hanson, and it appeared the feeling was mutual. Hanson had been with Ashworth for several years, so Butch knew where his boss's loyalty would lie if he and Hanson had an altercation of any kind. So for now at least, Butch would have to placate the little prick.

After watching the immense project with the Great Pyramid, it was apparent that Ashworth was pretty high up on the food chain in the area. To be able to basically take over the last of the seven wonders of the ancient world said it all.

Hanson had made the rounds and briefed everyone that an extraordinary event was likely to occur at the Giza Plateau soon. It wasn't clear what the event was, but the description Butch got made it sound like something paranormal.

Maybe the ghostly event will cause the demise of Ashworth's top dog. He smiled at the thought.

"Just stay calm and let it pass" was the order that came down from the top.

What was it?

Just then, Butch noticed that something had changed. He couldn't put his finger on it, but the air was somehow different now. It was silent. Even the late-night crickets had gone mute.

The lights went dim and then out for a moment before the entire plateau was illuminated with a brilliant neon-bluish light. Whatever it was coming from, it must have been on the plateau toward the Nile.

He heard some murmurs among the workers in front of the Great Pyramid, and he eased out of the shadows to see what the new light source was. He froze in his tracks. Then he took half a step back into the shadows and stared.

Whatever it was, it must have been close to fifteen feet tall. Although it had basic human features—two arms, two legs and a head—it most assuredly was anything but. The light coming from the creature's yellowish eyes lit up even brighter than its transcendental body, which looked like it was composed of trapped lightning.

Butch just stared in awe. Never in his wildest dreams had he thought the Bruiner kid was telling the truth. Now he was probably staring at the same thing his colleague had seen right before the explosion in Argentina.

What in the hell is that thing? Butch couldn't take his eyes off it.

The creature just stood there and moved its head slowly around as though it were lost.

It seems like ... like it's looking for something, but what?

It slowly turned its head and stopped when it was directly facing Butch. He wanted to step back into the shadows even farther, but that seemed pointless now. This was one of the few times in his life he had faced something he didn't think he could somehow get the best of—and it was a feeling he didn't like.

Then just as fast as it had come, it vanished. Slowly, the lights flickered back to life, and it was as though nothing had happened.

JUGOW, POLAND

TY AND HIS THREE companions were looking a little more like they belonged now as they sat in the back booth of the local diner. Ivan's face was blank and emotionless, but Ethan's was just the opposite.

"Believe me, you guys, this is just a little bump in the road," Ethan said.

"But the damn place is flooded!" Ivan said as he threw his arms in the air. "Do you plan on getting dive gear to get to the damn thing?"

"Not if we don't have to. All we have to do is lower some pipe into the tunnels and pump the water out enough so we can access the Bell. Trust me, this isn't a problem."

"He's right, Ivan." Ty assured him. "This isn't over. I can feel it."

"Looks like we need to line up some water removal equipment then, Ethan." Erica said. "So, does Amazon ship out here?"

"I wish. Since it's so far down, we'll actually need two pumps to be able to get the water to the surface. I got them coming, though. Should be here tomorrow. The size of the pumps we need weren't something we could just pick up at the local hardware store. Neither was that amount of pipe."

Ivan looked up from his coffee. "What about the other? Has it arrived yet?"

"No, but trust me when I say it'll be here in time." Ethan turned to Ty. "As for you, my friend, you're going to need some preparation, too. How are you with a bow and arrow?"

"I'm a little rusty, but I can usually hit what I'm aiming at."

"Good. We'll still knock the rust off with some practice, though."

"Why? We going hunting?"

Ethan laughed. "You might say that."

CHAPTER 37

ETHAN AND CREW HAD worked through the night getting the pumps and all the pipe into place. One pump was a submersible type and had to be attached to the end of the pipe in the water. The other pump was at the surface to aid with the extra lift needed because of how far below the surface the Bell was. Nothing about the process had been easy.

Finding the pumps capable of moving more water than what was flowing into the caves was the first battle. Wroclaw was the nearest town of any size, but to find two pumps that big there turned out to be impossible. Ethan had to get them delivered from Warsaw. Even though Warsaw was only four and a half hours away, finding a delivery truck was harder than expected because of the coming holiday of Epiphany.

The amount of pipe they needed also presented a challenge, but Ethan was a very resourceful man and found enough at several old mining camps in the nearby village of Krapkowice. The only snag was that they had to pick it up themselves if they were to have it anytime soon.

Then they were going to need power to run their pumps along with the Bell. With help from an employee of the local power company—and a large cash payout to look the other way—Ethan was able to discreetly have a power line hooked up and snaked through the brush into the ruins of the old power plant from the days before the Nazi invasion. Since the ruins were off limits to the public, there would be no prying eyes into their secret operation.

Inside the dilapidated power plant was a room that was still almost intact. One of the few places that still had a roof left, it was the perfect place for their control room.

The closest place to get rid of the water from the complex of mine shafts below was the old sewer system for the dilapidated power plant. Amazingly, it was still connected to the city sewer. Hopefully, they would have their mission accomplished long before anyone noticed the power draw or extra wastewater.

And as for accomplishing that mission, even with all the little holdups, it looked as though they still might have time to pull it off. Ethan had heard about the odd event at the Giza Plateau two days earlier, which—according to his Cairo sources—seemed to light a fire under the Great Pyramid restoration job.

The appearance of the creature in Egypt was no surprise—it had been only a matter of time. It just meant the man-made Watcher—if that's what it really was—was one step closer to what Ethan was so desperately trying to avoid: the possible release of the imprisoned fallen ones from centuries ago. The very ones whose actions brought on the wrath of God and the destruction of the ancient world.

It would be anyone's guess as to how this man-made creature would interact with the original fallen angels if turned loose. No matter what, their return would probably not be a welcome sight on the planet. If they chose to seek vengeance against their punisher, who knew what would lie in store for the rest of the world?

WITH THE WATER SUCTION pipe now extending from the surface to the tunnels below, the air shaft was barely big enough for one person and his supplies to squeeze through. The pumps had been on continuously for forty-eight hours; now it was time to take a look.

Ty had volunteered to be the first in, and it had been a struggle going down the first thirty feet or so, but luckily the shaft widened out some for the remaining fifty feet. Carrying two more battery-powered repeaters didn't make the trip down any easier either.

"Well, I can say this," he said into his radio as he looked back and forth in the long dark tunnel. "The only water that's left is just enough to cover the intake for the first pump. We'll need to find a low spot to move it to and spool the pumps down some so it doesn't start sucking air."

Ethan's voice crackled over the receiver. "Okay, we'll get ready to push more sections down. In the meantime, I'm coming to take a look myself."

Ty took out the battery-powered lantern from his pack and set in on a protruding rock in the cave wall. It illuminated the cave for several feet. The shaft had been well-reinforced with concrete supports, which had prevented any further collapse from the ceiling.

The walls wept with water like a leaky dam waiting to break loose. Ty wondered if the Nazis also had to run pumps to keep Mother Nature at bay or if the groundwater level had risen over the years.

He heard some grunts in the air shaft and then saw Ivan emerge into the light.

"Ethan, the lighting must be bad. I almost didn't recognize you."

Ivan grunted. "Funny. It wasn't too hard to talk Ethan into letting me be next in line to join you."

"Well? Look familiar?"

"Oh yes." Ivan's face was lit up. "All these years. And so peaceful." Then his eyes narrowed and his smile faded. "The last time I was here, I was running for my life. And the ground … The earth was shaking violently as the bombs fell."

Ty could almost see the memories flooding through Ivan's mind. "Well, which way from here?"

Ivan pointed.

Ty heard the sound of pebbles splashing into the water. "Is that you, Ethan?"

"I hope you weren't expecting someone else," Ethan said as he lowered himself out of the air shaft and into the water.

"See what I mean about the water?"

"Yeah, I had Erica spool the pumps down a little, so we'll have to pay attention to the water level and see what it does."

Ivan had already started down the tunnel and was almost out of sight.

"You'd better stay with him," Ethan said. "I'll find a low spot so we can get rid of the rest of this water."

"Sure thing." Ty nodded and went after Ivan.

For an old man, Ivan wasn't showing any wear in his trek through the mine shaft. It took Ty a few minutes to catch up, and he was in excellent shape.

"So, Ivan," Ty said as he came up behind him, "with all the water that was in here, what kind of shape do you think the Bell will be in?"

"It'll be fine. The room it was hidden in—as was the original— was built with thick concrete walls and an airtight door. I doubt even the bombing on the surface would have compromised its integrity."

"I'll guess we'll soon find out."

They came to a fork in the tunnel, and Ivan stopped and stared down the offshoot.

"It was down there where the executions took place." He paused for a moment as he started to tear up. "I thought I was going to be one of them, but I was young and spry … and quite lucky."

Ty could feel Ivan's emotion. "I don't think it was luck, my friend. I think you were chosen … as apparently I was."

CHAPTER 38

**ABANDONED MINE SHAFTS
LUDWIKOWICE-MILKOW, POLAND**

IVAN WAS STILL RELIVING the tragic events of the past when Ethan finally caught up to them.

"What'd I miss?" He looked down the offshoot, then at Ivan.

Ty answered for him. "The execution of all the workers took place down there."

"What a shame. All those great minds involved in such an incredible project." Ethan patted Ivan on the shoulder. "Thank God they chose to build a second one. It may not have done them any good, but it could save humanity as we know it."

Ivan turned around and pointed. "We need to go down this offshoot. That's where they built the secret room."

Ty set up a repeater at the juncture. The roof of the cave had partially collapsed and a pile of rubble lay scattered on the floor. Luckily, the rocks didn't completely block the way, so the shaft was still traversable. With Ivan leading the way, they maneuvered around the rocks and started down the dilapidated shaft toward their final goal.

Ty tried to imagine what it must have looked like here in the depths of the Owl Mountains all those years ago. That this is where Hitler's most secretive project had been developed was still hard for him to grasp.

Ivan came to a stop. "It's behind these rocks."

"Here?" Ethan commented. "Just looks like part of the wall to me."

"This was the only way they could hide it from the Nazis. The prisoners made it look like a cave-in had closed this off from the rest of the tunnel." Ivan looked at Ty and motioned to the top of the blockage. "Those two rocks at the top—one will slide to the left and the other to the right."

Ty positioned himself to reach the rocks with leverage and pushed. They both moved rather easily and exposed a hole big enough for a man to get through.

"On the ledge … Reach back," Ivan instructed. "There'll be a rope coiled up."

Ty reached back into the darkness and felt around.

"There's nothing here."

"It has to be there. Check again."

Again, Ty did as directed and again he felt nothing. But just as he was about to pull his hand back, he felt something foreign. Could it be?

He snagged it between his forefinger and thumb and pulled, and out came the end of a rotten piece of rope. It had gone back to the earth over the years spent submerged in the watery grave.

"I was afraid of that, but no matter." Ivan took his pack off and unfolded a small shovel that had been tightly stowed inside. "We only need to dig down a little so we can crawl in easier. Might as well make the opening a little bigger anyway. The only reason it was so small was to keep it hidden from the SS."

Ty took the tool and started to pull down debris. It was only a matter of time now. Of course, time was running out.

IT HAD TAKEN SLIGHTLY less than an hour to open the hole enough to be able to crawl in without the use of a rope. They had progressed so deep into the earth that they could just barely talk to Erica on the surface even with the repeaters. The good news was they were now standing in front of the lead door that separated them from the second Bell.

The three stood in the nostalgic moment staring at the only barrier left in the way of their goal.

"Thank God those Nazi bastards never found this place," Ivan said. "It was only by the grace of God the scientists and the Jewish workers were able to keep it hidden."

Ty looked at the seeping walls of the shaft. "What are the chances all the equipment inside has been kept dry when everything else has been submerged?"

"It'll be dry. Both rooms containing the Bells had to be airtight in order to keep everything on the outside safe from withering due to its powerful force."

"Let's hope so." Ethan looked the lead door over. "This is our last chance."

Ivan reached for the latch, but it didn't budge.

This time Ty didn't wait for an invitation. Ivan moved aside and Ty stepped in and grabbed the handle with his powerful grip. At first it didn't move, and then they heard a creak. He pulled even harder—movement. Seventy-five years of corrosion began to give way as Ty forced the handle up, causing the door to pivot open in the process. He stopped and stepped back, allowing Ivan to be the first.

Ivan didn't hesitate. He took the handle and pulled the door open the rest of the way, exposing the darkness from within. Ty handed him his light and he cautiously proceeded in.

Then he stopped.

Ty took the light from Ethan and peered over Ivan's shoulder into the hidden chamber. In the middle of the room stood something he'd only seen once before in his life but would never forget: Die Glocke, the infamous Nazi Bell.

The three were silent. Ty stood there and stared. His head was flooded with memories of the events of only a few short weeks ago. *So, it's true. There really had been two Bells.* Ty's facial expression went flat. *Maybe Dad was somehow transported to another location like I was.*

Ethan broke the silence. "Look familiar, Ty?"

Ty nodded. "It … it's an exact duplicate."

"Yes, my young friend," Ivan said without moving his gaze, "and we're the only humans alive to know of this one."

Ethan pressed forward to get a better look. "History literally staring us in the face."

Ivan stepped in farther and turned his light to a higher setting, illuminating the room as though it were broad daylight. The pristine condition of the entire contents of the chamber confirmed that the replica of Hitler's most prized possession had gone undisturbed for decades.

Ty couldn't help but think of the Nazi scientists and Jewish slaves who worked on the Bell project who were all shot as Berlin was falling to the Allied forces. The Nazi Bell he had seen only a few weeks ago seemed to be alive as he remembered how it hummed with power from Himmler's generators. As ominous as it was, this one looked like it should be in a museum, dead … lifeless.

The three were quiet as they slowly walked around the thing. The undisturbed relic from the Third Reich had rendered them speechless. *All these years and here it still is!* Ty's jaw was frozen.

He put his hand on the machine to feel the smooth flawless

surface. "All the lives sacrificed for this to survive. Unbelievable it's lasted all these years."

"Since the fall of Berlin." Ivan's eyes were glassy. "The Allied forces saved the world. It could have easily gone the other way. The only reason the Jewish prisoners built this was to desperately try to escape their imminent doom."

Ty continued to touch the relic as he walked around it. "Hitler was so close. Just days away from conquering the world."

"Yeah, this turned out to be a lucky break for us, all right. Thanks to you, Ivan, we still have a fighting chance."

"Yeah," Ty nodded then asked. "So how did Himmler get the other one?"

"We're not sure, but we think whoever found it when it fell out of the sky over Kecksberg—someone at Wright-Patterson Air Force Base in Dayton, Ohio—must have sold it to the highest bidder. Whatever the case, it's a good thing he didn't know of this one or it'd be gone, too."

Ty bent over and traced his finger over the hieroglyphic-like markings near the bottom. "So what does this mean?"

Ivan shook his head. "Not sure. Almost looks Egyptian, though."

Ivan moved closer to the Bell and pressed a hidden panel, which swung wide and reveled a mechanical latch. He grabbed the handle and twisted, and a larger panel sprang open, exposing the inside of the old machine.

It was surprisingly simple-looking. There was a vertical shaft with two cylinders attached to it in the center. There were gears directly above the cylinders, and on top of those was what looked like an electrical motor. Ivan reached in and grabbed an odd-looking handbag that was in the void on the bottom of the unit and opened it.

"Thank God, it's still here," he said as a smile crept over his face.

"What is?" Ty's gaze went from inside the machine to the bag in Ivan's hands.

"There were only a few days the Nazis held me captive after they found me. When the Allied forces attacked, the Nazis had to abandon the caves and move the Bell. In that brief time—and since I was only a boy—the scientists talked freely in front of me about the nature of the machine. I know there are two crucial elements that are needed to make Die Glocke work. One of those was stockpiled in the caved-in shaft where the first Bell was. Only problem is, that was in 1945, and I'm sure the Nazis took it when they moved the Bell out. Now there are only a very few places on the planet where it might be found." He looked at Ethan.

Ethan nodded. "The red mercury. Yes, two of the vials just arrived this morning."

"Only two?" Ivan asked.

"The other two will be here in a couple of days. We can still use the first two for practice like you recommended and have some time to prepare."

"Two more?" Ivan looked from the machine to Ethan. "I thought we only needed three."

Ethan nodded and smiled. "Insurance, just in case."

"Red mercury?" Ty raised his eyebrows.

"Yes. It has the perfect qualities. When it's energized with electricity and spun at just the right speed against another equal amount, which spins in the exact opposite direction but at the same speed, a torsion field will be created. The torsion field creates a vibration, and then the frequency can be changed to mirror that of any other time in history, past or future."

"Wait a minute." Ty cocked his head. "That doesn't make any sense. How do you know where you'll end up? I mean, surely there has to be a way to control the frequency of the time frame you're trying to go to."

"Ah, yes. The other element that makes time travel possible." Ivan reached into the bag. "This one isn't so easy to come by."

Ethan cleared his throat. "Excuse me? Easy? Trust me, finding red mercury and someone who's willing to part with it is no picnic."

"Maybe not." Ivan brought out the contents of the bag. "But this … No one I know of knows the source of this material."

In his hand was a cone-shaped semi-translucent object that looked like a giant emerald. Then he noticed something strange—the mysterious object started to pulse. It was as though it were coming alive.

There it was again. *Déjà vu.* It was as though Ty were reliving something from a time long ago.

He turned from the emerald-like object to face Ethan. "I've been patient so far, Ethan, and I know you have your reasons, but it's time you tell me. Just why am I here?"

CHAPTER 39

ASHWORTH LOOKED OUT THE window of his luxury Sikorsky helicopter. He felt giddy as he watched the restoration process of the Great Pyramid of Giza unfold. Soon the last piece of the puzzle would be set in place on top of the ancient structure and the process would be complete. The Emerald Tablets had given up the long-kept secret of its true purpose, and as far as he knew, he was the only one on the planet who knew what that was.

It all started when the spiritual beings Edgar Cayce spoke of—known as "thought forms"—first came to the earth. They eventually realized they could literally do anything they wanted. Even manipulate matter at its very core. It wasn't until they began to create abominations across the planet that, literally, all hell broke loose.

Enoch, the original son of Jared. According to the tablets, he was the first to try to reverse the mutations that were created by the first thought forms that came to the planet. Better-known as the fallen angels, these spiritual beings not only mixed with mortal women but all forms of animals as well, just as mentioned in the

Book of Giants found in the Dead Sea Scrolls. These mutations were the stuff of legend and folklore. Mermaids, centaurs, the Minotaur. These were all actual creatures that existed—as a result of the experiments of the Watchers.

Ashworth learned that Enoch wanted to correct this travesty, which is why Enoch constructed the Great Pyramid of Giza. It was never a tomb of any kind but rather a machine—a machine that operated through all the vibrations in all spectrums, from color to sound. The abomination the fallen angels created would stand in what is now called the Queen's Chamber. When the ancient wonder was turned on, the subject to be transformed would, in essence, absorb the combination of frequencies and be transformed into a spiritual being and set free from its torturous state.

It was the exact opposite of what happened when these spiritual beings—the fallen angels—came to the planet on top of Mount Hermon ages ago. When the fallen angels made the transformation from spirit to human, the very granite they were standing on absorbed the vibrations and underwent a physical change. A new element was born. An element that existed nowhere else in the universe was literally formed under the feet of the Watchers as they made the change from a spiritual being to one of, more or less, flesh and blood.

That's how they were able to mate with the human women. But it was the new material that had literally formed under their feet that made the reverse transformation possible. That was the key ingredient that made the Great Pyramid work. The mutated granite that had been unknowingly hidden under the UN outpost all these years on the top of Mount Hermon. Enoch knew this was the final piece of the puzzle that was needed to make the pyramid work.

The Bible—along with the Dead Sea Scrolls—made it clear that *he walked with God.* That was how he did not die. Enoch was the first to try the machine when it was finished. This was how he passed straight from the physical world to the spirit world. The machine worked!

Now Ashworth was in control of the ancient wonder and he, too, would soon *walk with God*. All the years he had spent searching for immortality would soon come to reality and he would be a god among men.

"It's amazing, sir," Hanson said, admiring the view.

"When will the capstone be ready?" Ashworth asked.

"Only a day or two more, sir. The final touches are being made to it now. That material is really quite challenging to work with, but it'll be ready soon."

"Good. And the waterways?"

"All done, sir. Ready to turn on at your command."

"Excellent." Ashworth's eyes lit up as he looked at the view.

Soon all will bow down to me!

BUTCH WATCHED THE CHOPPER overhead. *So you did away with the kid after all. Sure wish you hadn't done that.* An approaching semi caught his eye as it crept through the well-guarded gate at the west entrance of the newly constructed fence around the pyramid. Whatever it was carrying was heavy enough to require the use of two extra axles on the big rig. Even then, the tires still sank into the desert, leaving ruts all the way to the back side of the pyramid, where it finally came to a rest.

What are you up to, Ashworth?

Butch walked away as security surrounded the truck.

Soon. Whatever's going down, it'll be soon now.

CHAPTER 40

JUGOW, POLAND

ETHAN HAD THOUGHT HARD before he answered Ty's question about why he was here, and Ty took it even better than he had hoped. To find out who one was in a previous life can be traumatizing to some, but to find out you were a notable figure whose actions changed the course of history can be immobilizing.

When Ethan continued on with what the mission at hand was to be, Ty didn't say a word. He just got up and disappeared into the back room.

"No wonder Himmler wanted him. He obviously knew that as well." Ivan got up and walked to the window. "I could tell there was something special about the boy, but I never would have thought that."

"And you're sure about that, Ethan?" Erica asked. "I mean, I have no doubt we've all had past lives, but that's just so fantastic."

"Oh, I'm sure all, right," Ethan answered. "And believe me, at first I had a hard time with it too, but when the old gypsy woman called, that confirmed what we had already known. The first of the original giant hunters, son of Jared. And if I had to guess, it wouldn't surprise me if it was him in another incarnation who moved the last two tablets to Teotihuacán where you guys found them."

"That would explain how he went right to them." Erica bit her lip while she stared out the window. "To notice that small stone at the top of the hidden door and then know to take it out … and all his weird dreams … Yeah, it's all coming together now."

"Indeed, that is a lot to impose on someone. I guess he had to know sooner or later." Ivan turned to Ethan. "So about the fallen angels. Is your intel on their location reliable as well?"

"It is. I've known where the Creator imprisoned them since I found out my true mission in this life long ago."

Erica turned from the window to face Ethan. "So how is it possible to hold a spiritual being captive here on earth? I mean, if they can pretty much do whatever they want, how could they be held against their will?"

"Yeah, it's hard to imagine how it would be possible to physically immobilize a spiritual being in a physical world." Ethan stood up and began pacing. "I'm not entirely sure how the Creator has accomplished it, but I can assure you it's not through magic.

"We've recently discovered a force called quantum locking, which is when a superconductor that is cooled to absolute zero can be locked in place through a magnetic field. The only way it can be moved is if an outside force disturbs it. This quite possibly could be the same process the Creator used centuries ago to contain the fallen angels."

"Come on, Ethan, if the Creator is the Supreme Being, wouldn't it just be a snap of his fingers to control these lesser beings?" Erica said. "I mean if God created the entire universe, controlling the Watchers should be a piece of cake."

"True, but even the Creator still has to play within the confines of the physical realm. Here's how we think this was accomplished."

Ethan continued to pace. "With spiritual entities being made of pure energy, in essence, they have the same qualities as a superconductor. Basically no electrical resistance whatsoever. And unlike any superconductor on the planet, we don't think they need to be cooled to absolute zero to obtain the same properties."

"So you're saying they're being held in place somewhere by a magnetic field?"

"In nutshell, yes."

Ivan took a slow deep breath before he spoke. "So where are they?"

"Actually, in two different spots." Ethan unfolded a small map of earth and pointed to Australia. "Here, in the wilderness of Queensland, only a few miles south of Cooktown, surrounded by brush and eucalyptus trees, stands an out-of-place mountain comprised of thousands of giant black granite boulders."

Ivan perked up. "Ah yes, Black Mountain. A very intriguing place indeed. It has long been a place of inexplicable happenings. I believe the indigenous people have claimed to have witnessed strange creatures, eerie lights, and numerous disappearances there over the years. Are you saying that's where the Watchers are imprisoned?"

"Well, we believe the most evil one is there. It seems with the small amount of magnetic force found in black granite boulders, when piled high on top of a superconductor—or a spiritual being—the quantum locking phenomenon will take hold. So as long as the boulders stay where they are, all of the imprisoned fallen angels would be immobilized. Forced to stay put in the dark dungeon for all eternity."

Ivan and Erica listened intently as Ethan went on to explain the mysteries of the mountain.

From a distance, the mound looks like a normal black mountain. It isn't until one gets close that the true nature of the terrain is exposed. Thousands upon thousands of enormous black granite boulders are piled to around nine hundred feet above the surrounding area with absolutely no soil cover at all. What could have caused such an odd occurrence in this great country down under?

With estimates of 250 million years of age, the black surface of the ancient stones gets so hot from the sun that the place feels like the gates of hell, and sinister noises from within can be heard to further solidify the sense. Screaming and crying noises are not the only eerie claims. Sometimes an unbearable stench is also present in the hellish rubble.

One of the translations of the local people's name for the mountain is "The Mountain of Death." In Aboriginal tales, there are numerous stories of evil lurking from within, and ghosts have often been seen. Some of the stories go as far as to say that if anyone got too close to the mountain, they would be grabbed by unearthly beings and dragged into the granite maze to their death. To this day, many Aborigines will not go near the mountain.

Even more strange stories of the mountain include navigation problems that aircraft experience when they get too close and even tales of animals becoming frightened. Unsurprisingly, the area is a hot spot for UFO sightings. What could possibly be causing all this weirdness? Could there really be something evil buried in the depths of granite rubble?

Australia has no shortage of dangerous animals, so maybe they are behind many of the legends, but that surely wouldn't explain all of the disappearances that have occurred over the years. What could cause an entire herd of cattle to disappear without a trace?

Of course, the Aborigines have ancient tales of people vanishing near the mountain, but it wasn't until 1877 that a modern instance was recorded when a courier disappeared. On horseback while looking for a stray calf, the courier vanished with the horse and the calf and was never seen again. Some thought they may have fallen into one of the many caverns in the pile of boulders, but this story just marks the beginning for many more such instances to come.

One who was lucky enough to find his way out after unsuccessfully looking for a fugitive was so terrified he could never say a word about what he saw.

Of all who've gone missing inside the hellhole, only the body of a lost backpacker was ever found. Cause of death unknown. Could the mountain really have devoured most of those who dared to enter?

"But you think only one of the Watchers is buried there?" Erica had been listening intently.

"Yes. The worst one," Ethan said as he folded up the map.

"How can you be so sure of this, Ethan?" Ivan asked.

"I don't have time to get into that now, so you just have to trust me for the time being."

Erica spoke while she paced. "So, if any of these… Watchers have really been under that pile of rocks in Australia for all these years, shouldn't they remain there forever?"

"Theoretically, yes. As long as those rocks stay where they are, we don't have anything to worry about. What concerns me the most right now is this creature that Himmler has unleashed on the world. How can we possibly trust it to not roust them out?"

"Well?" Erica stopped and looked at Ethan. "How can we?"

"Simple. We have to—" Ethan shifted his gaze to Ty who was now standing in the doorway of the next room. "I should say *you* have to go back and stop them before they have a chance to screw shit up."

"Yeah, I get that I'm the lucky one." Everyone turned to look at Ty. "What I don't get is, how do I do that?"

Ethan smiled. "Glad I didn't scare you off." He opened the duffel bag he had with him. "With this."

The contents looked like a demolitions expert's wet dream.

"You want me to blow 'em up? A spiritual being? I think you'd better rethink your plan, Ethan."

Ethan nodded with a slight laugh, and then the smile left his face. "You're right. There's no way that would work. But you've got to think about this for a minute. All two hundred fallen angels originally were in fact spiritual beings, and most assuredly are now as well. There's no denying that. But in order for them to take human women as wives and conceive children, they had to become human."

"Surely you can't expect Tyler to travel back to when they were living here, hunt them all down one by one and blow them up?" Erica narrowed her eyes and pulled back.

"No, I don't think he'd have a chance in hell of getting them all one at a time."

"So what then? Have Ty hang around until they're all together? When would that be? Hit them up at a reunion? Will they ever all be at the same place at the same time?"

"Oh, they'll all be together, all right." He looked at Ty. "And I believe you know where that is. Am I right?"

Ty only had to think for a second. A grin began to form. "Mount Hermon!"

"Bingo! And that's where—"

"Yeah, I get it. That's where I blow them back to the spirit world."

Ethan nodded. "Yeah. That's where you blow them back to the spirit world."

CHAPTER 41

Erica had come with Ty to the small open field behind their rental cottage to watch him practice with the bow Ethan had got for him. Ty's father had encouraged Ty to get into archery at an early age. And though he eventually worked his way up to a state-of-the-art compound bow, he'd gone back to shooting the simple long bow, which is what he had now. Ethan had also given him an ornate razor-sharp sword that looked to be from Sumerian times but very lethal in any era.

He had started out shooting at a target twenty-five yards away and was now hitting the bull's-eye at fifty yards.

"You make that look easy, Tyler," Erica said. "I probably couldn't hit the target if I was standing on it."

"Trust me, I didn't shoot like this when I first started. It's amazing what years of practice can do." He gave Erica a smile. "Would you like to give it a try?"

Erica looked at the target off in the distance. "Can I get a little closer?"

"I insist." Ty grinned as he picked up the quiver of arrows. "After all, we can't afford to lose all these arrows."

"Funny guy." She elbowed him in the side. "Now show me how to do it."

They walked up and stopped about five yards in front of the target. Ty took an arrow out, set the quiver down and handed the bow to Erica.

"I guess I haven't noticed," he said. "Righty or lefty?"

"Righty."

"Okay, now grab the grip with your left hand like I did. Then take this arrow and put the groove over the string. Now rest the arrow in the notch on the bow right above your hand. Then just pull back, line up the arrow with the center of the target and let loose. Piece of cake."

Erica tried to follow Ty's instructions, but to no avail. She just couldn't hold the arrow and pull it back without it falling to the ground.

Ty did his best not to laugh, but he wasn't successful. She heard him snickering.

"Ha ha. So you think this is funny?" She smirked. "How about you put an apple on your head and give me some incentive?"

Ty returned the smirk and shook his head. "Here, let me show you. Now face the target with your hand on the bow and we'll try again." She did as he asked, and then he picked up an arrow. "Now, don't take this the wrong way. I'm going to put my hand under yours and reach around you and put the arrow in place and help guide it back."

He had to get close when he reached around her to put the arrow in place. Her tantalizing scent was the first thing he noticed. Then he felt her body next to his. The way her hair felt against his face. He had been becoming attracted to her for a while, but this seemed to bring all those feelings to a head. It was as though he were paralyzed with desire in the moment. He knew she felt it, too.

The mood broke when they heard something behind them.

"Thought I'd find you two here." It was Ethan. "Hate to break it up, but the sun's about to go down. We'd better get to work."

CHAPTER 42

WALTER MINE SHAFT
LUDWIKOWICE-MILKOW, POLAND

ETHAN AND CREW HAD been scrambling throughout the night to get the power connections to the Bell deep down in the Walter Mine shaft. Now Ethan had returned to the surface to regulate the water pumps and turn on the power supply to the Bell.

The Nazis' power source had been drawn in from the nearby coal power plant, but that had been blown apart when the Allied forces regained control of the area in 1945. Luckily for Ethan, though, the power cables still were intact and ran deep into the shaft to where the first Bell had been tested and then to the secret room with the second Bell. The only thing they had to do was connect them to live wires at the surface and they would have all the power they needed.

Since the secret room had been sealed off airtight for the last seventy-five years, the corrosion was hardly a factor, and only minor adjustments needed to be done before the Bell was ready to try.

"The workers had this thing ready to go," Ivan said to Ty. "Looks like it should be ready for the first test."

"I'm ready," Ty said as he turned to the Bell.

"Okay, Ty, remember, all you have to do is think of where you want to be, in time-space, or wherever. That's all you need to do. Just remember this is only a practice run. Try not to manipulate anything that could have repercussions of any kind. Please, please don't try to do something like save or warn you or your dad before all this happened! The downstream effects could be disastrous! Just remember, your final mission should fix all that anyway. You need to gradually prepare your body and soul for what it's going to be experiencing. Got it?" Ivan was stern.

He gave the professor a slight grin. "Yeah, yeah, I got it. Thanks, professor … for everything."

"And one more thing. Don't forget you may experience a little amnesia, but it gets less with each time. At least that was my experience, and I heard the others say the same."

Ty could feel Erica's gaze. He turned to her.

She forced her way past Ivan. "Here, Tyler. This is for good luck."

She kept her eyes on Ty's as she leaned in and gave him a kiss, then slowly backed away. "Don't forget to come back."

Ty had never felt like this before. Sure, he thought he had feelings for Celeste at one time, but this … this felt amazing.

"I won't. You can count on it."

"All right, you guys, we have a job to do," Ivan said as he looked at his watch. "Okay, Ty. We only have these two canisters of mercury for now, so we'll use them for two practice runs, just so you can get the hang of traveling through time. When the next two arrive, it'll be for all the marbles, so we don't have much room for error."

Ty nodded and backed slowly into the chamber, keeping his eyes on Erica. Ivan gave an approving nod to Ty, then slowly shut the door once he was inside and swung the handle. Just before he could secure the latch, though, he jerked and opened the door again.

"Hold on a minute, Ty. It's been so long, I almost forgot." He rushed past Ty and opened the trap door on the Bell, then reached in and grabbed something. "You'll want this. I call it a time barometer."

In his hand was a device that resembled a common wristwatch. On the face of the watch were what looked like shards of the same material the stone was from. There were several triangular pieces splayed across the face, resembling petals on a flower.

"Give me your arm. You'll only need to wear this if you plan on being gone very long. The charge on this will gradually fade with time. Once the last chip has lost its glow, the stone will have lost its usefulness and you'll be stuck in that time."

"Whoa, hold on a minute, professor! What do you mean 'stuck in that time?' I thought time was just a change in vibration. Why would it matter how much *time* has passed?"

"It is, but you must remember the stone is only like a battery, and when the charge has zeroed out, it will no longer be able to match the frequency of your thoughts. Think of it as a bell that's been struck—it will eventually stop vibrating. All the chips on the watch are of different thicknesses, and when there is only one left glowing, that will indicate the last travel you'll have without re-charging it."

Ty took it and looked it over. "Useful information, professor. Thanks for sharing."

"Forgive me. It has been a long time and I was only a boy."

"No problem." Ty smiled.

"Be careful, my boy. We'll see you soon." Ivan retreated and closed the door.

Ty sighed. *What the hell am I getting myself into?*

The hum of the Bell broke his train of thought as it idled on low while he stared out the small viewing port at his comrades. He turned to the control panel and slowly turned up the power to the maximum. The hum of the machine grew in intensity. After giving a slight two-finger salute, he reached into the satchel and took out the mysterious stone. He turned to face the Bell as the hum grew louder.

Raising the stone in front of him with his right hand, he closed his eyes and thought of a time in the not-so-distant past. The Bell began to buzz and glow an ominous blue. Ty stood there without moving while holding the stone, which began to show a greenish aura. His initial thought had been to get away from the Nazi antique, but then a calmness seemed to settle over him that was indescribable.

It went quiet. The tranquility he felt was amazing, so surreal. He opened his eyes and he was in ... an old library? But why was he here? And where exactly was here?

The fog began to lift. He knew this place. Several people sat at tables scattered about.

Is this ... the library?

Then he recognized everything. This was the library he had frequented many times, but why was he here? Just then, the light overhead blew out with a pop.

As he stood there next to the wall behind the tall bookshelves, he saw the closest patron sitting at a table turn and look almost right at him. He slipped farther into the shadows as the young man got up and came closer. Then it all came back to him like a blow to the head.

I remember now—that's me! It worked. I'm really here!

He watched as his former self came closer. His gaze was fixed—a book on the top shelf had his attention for some reason. So much so that Ty knew he wouldn't see him.

His former self stood on a step stool and reached for the book that seemed to be mesmerizing him. With his outstretched hand, he grabbed it, but then the stool tipped and he came crashing to the floor with the book and several others that it had been tightly packed with. Ty quickly picked up the book his former self wanted and ducked behind the next row of shelves while the librarian came running over to see what had happened.

"Tyler, are you all right? You know I'm supposed to do that," Ty heard her say as he walked on the other side of the bookshelf and slowly proceeded into the open.

That voice! I recognize that voice! Is that … Erica?

He quickly came to his senses as they were preoccupied with picking up the scattered books. Ty went unnoticed as he walked past the desk his former self had been seated at.

He stopped and opened the Bible that was on the desk. "I remember now. Numbers mean something!" He flipped to Numbers … Numbers 13:33. Then he casually continued toward the door, glancing at the title of the book in his hand his former self had been so interested in, *Proof.*

Proof of what? He tossed it into the book return and left the building.

CHAPTER 43

ABANDONED MINE SHAFT
LUDWIKOWICE-MILKOW, POLAND

TY TOOK THE STONE out of the bag and focused once again. This time it was on the present, or what had been the present only a few moments ago. He still couldn't believe what had just taken place. So it was his future self that caused the experience at the library several weeks ago? What he had just witnessed was exactly how he had remembered it.

It seemed as though his soul started to vibrate. He could faintly hear the sound of bees, which grew louder and louder, and then … he opened his eyes. He was back in the cave as the Bell buzzed with life and the stone emitted the familiar glow.

Oddly enough, the travel back had caused no amnesia, and he instinctively reached to turn down the power, causing the Bell to lower its hum back to an idle.

"It worked! I was there!" Ty was filled with excitement. "Things are a little foggy, but I remember being there!"

The door swung open and he could see the relieved look on

everyone's face. Especially Erica's. She threw herself into Ty's arms.

"You're back! When I saw you vanish, I … I thought I might never see you again." She looked into his eyes as she slowly backed away. "Sorry, you guys. This is all just so crazy." She paused as she stared at Ty. "Do you feel okay?"

"Yeah, I feel fine. Why?"

"You look … different somehow."

Ivan looked closer. "Oh yeah, I remember now. Do you feel all right?"

"Never better. Why?" Ty scanned the faces of his comrades. "What's wrong with you guys?"

"It's the effects of the travel," Ivan said. "Every time one travels to another time, it seems to age the body ever so slightly. It's not enough to worry about, just a little side effect."

"Jesus. What other little bombshells are you gonna drop on me? Will I eventually come back as an old woman? I mean, I am carrying a purse now."

Ivan took the stone out of his hand and slid it into the bag. He looked Ty in the eye. "Not as far as I know. Now don't forget to put this in the bag every time. It'll hold its charge longer inside."

"All right, you guys," they heard Ethan say over the radio. "Get back to the surface and we'll debrief and get a little rest before we go again."

JUGOW, POLAND

TY'S RUNNING THROUGH A jungle. He's wearing rather odd clothing. His attire looks to be from an era even before the ancient Egyptians. Sumerian perhaps? Not running from something but looking for someone … or something. He suddenly stops—he's found it. It shimmers so much it lights up his face.

"Tyler." Erica gently shook him. "Ethan sent me in to wake you. It's time to try it again."

"Damn, that was a weird dream." Ty rubbed his eyes as he leaned up, slowly coming back into the waking world.

"Oh yeah? What about this time?"

"I'm not sure. It's like I was looking for something, but … I just don't know. Nothing seems to make sense anymore, but at the same time, everything makes perfect sense. Does that make any sense?"

"Yeah, no sense, not really." Erica smiled as she looked into his eyes.

"When this is all over, any chance you might go out to dinner with me?" Ty asked.

"Hmm." Erica appeared to pretend to think about it. "I suppose there's a chance."

Just as he reached for her hand, there was a loud knock on the door. "Time to move, you two." It was Ethan. "We've got a lot to do."

WALTER MINE SHAFT
LUDWIKOWICE-MILKOW, POLAND

ALL RESTED UP AND ready to go once again. This time he was going to try to change something minor. Nothing that would have global effects, yet something of some significance.

He closed his eyes and fixed his thoughts on a time in the past. A time not too far removed that had been high in his thoughts.

This time it was easier. As the Bell started to glow and buzz, he knew it would only be a few more seconds until he entered the time and space he was concentrating on.

This is crazy. Time travel is actually possible!

Then he noticed that something was different. The temperature had changed and the sounds had changed. The buzzing was gone, too.

He slowly opened his eyes and his jaw dropped. He was standing on a street somewhere in a neighborhood. A car honked and he realized he was in the middle of the road and instinctively jumped to the sidewalk.

Where am I? He looked at the glowing rock in his hand and then at the bag in his other hand. Memories began to fill his head as he stuffed the stone into the bag and started to walk down the sidewalk. Then a thought hit him. He had to hurry.

Looking all around, he saw a couple walking their dog, then a boy riding his bike. He picked up his speed and continued to look for something. But what was he looking for?

Somehow he knew time was running out and he picked up his pace even more. Ahead was a moving van parked next to the curb. There were two young men carrying the last piece of furniture into the house the van sat in front of. He knew this was it. He needed transportation now.

Ty watched the men disappear into the house and checked the driver's door—unlocked. He jumped in and fumbled for the ignition. He was in luck—the key was still in it.

He turned the key.

Nothing.

"Hey!" someone shouted from the house. "What the hell do you think you're doing?"

He could hear footsteps getting closer. Frantically, he looked the dash over and tried again. This time he pushed in the clutch and it started. He jammed it into gear and dropped the clutch, and the tires chirped as he sped into the street.

There was a fog still partially clouding what he needed to do, but luckily, his mission was starting to come into focus. He swerved through what little traffic there was and proceeded up the on-ramp with the gas-pedal pushed to the floor. He looked to his left.

There they are. I have to head them off.

Perfect timing for getting in front of the first of two black SUVs and cutting it off. But just then he noticed he'd come up on a slow-moving car and had no choice but to swerve into the left lane to miss it. Instead of getting in front of the first SUV, he cut in between them, almost hitting the second one.

"Shit!" Ty shouted as his entire plan was now a shambles. He skidded to a stop on the left side of the freeway.

As he opened the door, he could see the second car had also came to a stop. *I can't let them see me.* He grabbed the bag and bolted out of the van and into the night.

CHAPTER 44

THE STRANGE OCCURRENCES ACROSS the globe had spurred NATO and several other world alliances to band together to see what kind of threat—if any—they were dealing with. The forces were scrambling to try to get a jump on where the creature would show up next, and this time they were in luck. Only a few kilometers from RAAF Base Townsville, Australia, there had been a sighting. Now they had a chance to zero in on the thing and see it up close.

For some reason, this was the second time it had appeared in this particular area. Only this time it stayed longer than it had in any of the previous spots where it had been sighted. This was a region that had been rife with legends and myths of strange things happening as far back as human history in the area. The creature had been sighted close to the mysterious pile of granite boulders known as Black Mountain, and this time the military had enough time to greet it.

The general's tone over the radio was stern. "Take the shot while you can."

The F-35C Lightning II had circled back around the creature and was now directly facing it.

"But, sir, whatever this thing is, it's not being aggressive in any way," the pilot said, watching in awe. "Not only that, it doesn't look like anything we should be firing a missile at."

The response he heard from the general in his headset was crystal clear. "Are you running this show, Major!? Because the last time I checked, you were to take orders from me! Now give that goddamn thing both barrels!"

God help us all. The major hesitated for a moment and then slowly squeezed the trigger.

The creature stood before the massive mound of black granite boulders as the missile was fired at it, followed by a second.

Major Nelson cringed at what should have been the moment of impact, but to his surprise, the thing didn't even flinch as the warhead passed completely through and out the other side. The major sighed with relief, but then the missiles exploded on impact into the mountain of granite directly behind the creature. The blasts sent numerous car-size boulders flying into the air and plummeting to the surrounding area. Several of the boulders landed on the squadron of tanks and personnel carriers in the background that had just arrived.

Then something caught his eye as the dust settled. A bluish glow emanated from underneath the granite blocks at the bottom of the newly formed crater.

"What the…" The major stared at the eerie sight below.

Whatever it was, it also had the attention of the creature, which seemed focused on the glow as well.

"Well?" the general said over the radio. "What's the prognosis, Major?"

He remained silent as he noticed the glow getting brighter.

"Major! Goddamn it, answer me!"

The general's booming voice brought him back to the task at hand. "Uh, nothing, sir. They both passed right through it like it wasn't there. It didn't even flinch."

"Then give it the other two, pronto!"

"Sir, I really think—"

"I don't care what you think, Major! That's an order!"

The pilot reluctantly fired his two remaining warheads. Again, both passed completely through the thing and blew more boulders out of the first crater, making it even larger. And again, it drew the same reaction from the creature, but now it was already focused on the lowest point in the newly created void in the earth. The blue glow was now even brighter than before. Then a boulder started to move ever so slightly, followed by another.

What the … What on earth is moving those rocks?

The movement of the blocks of granite became more apparent.

What is that? Is … is that a hand?

From under one of the boulders came what looked like a large hand. It moved slowly at first, then became more and more aggressive in moving the boulders that seemed to be imprisoning whatever *it* was.

GIZA PLATEAU, EGYPT

REPORTS OF THE EVENTS in Australia had leaked, and, of course, Ashworth was well abreast of what was going on. The time was now, and he was ready. He had made the necessary preparations, and it was time to go to the transformation chamber. Only a few in all of history had experienced what was about to be bestowed on him, and it felt good. Enoch had been the first, and now he would be the last.

The final piece of the puzzle was complete. The Great Pyramid shimmered in the moonlight with its white casing stones and magnificent emerald green capstone. The ancient wonder almost looked as though it were alive, and Ashworth knew that it soon would be.

The capstone had been carefully placed on top with a Boeing CH 234 Chinook helicopter. How the ancients were able to place the fifty-ton capstone had been a mystery, but he really didn't care. Once he had learned the pyramid's secret, he knew how to make it whole once again.

Ashworth rose from his chair. He was wearing a robe that was thought to have belonged to the mysterious Egyptian king Akhenaten. It was found in the chamber with the hidden tablets under the Sphinx's paw.

He stood in his mobile quarters not far from the ancient structure and stared in awe at the sight, then picked up his phone. "Hanson … it's time."

Without taking his eyes off the gleaming wonder, he walked out the door into the night as a black Land Rover pulled up and came to a stop.

Hanson was quick to get out and open the back door for his boss.

"This will truly be a night to remember, sir."

"Indeed, old friend. Indeed."

To be the first in millennia to use the ancient machine for its true purpose was the most exciting, ambitious dream he'd ever had—and now the time had come.

Ashworth looked at his trusted employee. "Is anyone suspicious as to what will be happening here tonight?"

"No, sir. The only one I was even concerned about was Colton, but I sent him to help at the water ditch entry point by the river just to be safe. There's something about him I don't like. Maybe he's not as dumb as he comes off."

"He did me a great service. For him to be able to gain the trust of the boy was paramount, even if he let him live."

"Yes, sir. Now no one else will ever know the contents of those last two tablets."

"I trust everyone is in place to turn on this wonder at my command?" Ashworth asked.

"They are, sir. It will still take a few minutes for the water to fill in the voids under the pyramid after you give the signal, but that's to be expected."

"Excellent. Most excellent"

CHAPTER 45

BLACK MOUNTAIN, AUSTRALIA

AZAZYEL SHOOK THE LAST of the dust of time off his pre-mortal body as he rose to his feet. It had been centuries ago when he was imprisoned in this godforsaken desert, and the experience had not been a pleasant one.

He looked around to see the pile of rubble remaining that had been blown about by the human's weapons of war. Then he saw the one. Or so he thought. The one who had sentenced him to the life of misery he had endured for millennia.

Azazyel immediately bowed down to the Creator. "Forgive me, my Lord. I have indeed learned the error of my ways and beg you to let me once again walk by your side."

The silence seemed to last another eternity. When he slowly looked up, his Lord stood there motionless, staring at him.

Has it been that long? Is it possible he has forgotten me in this pile of rocks?

"My Lord, please let me make it up to your greatness and the humans. I have sinned a grievous sin and am begging for your mercy."

Nothing. Not even the slightest gesture.

Something is wrong. The Creator is … somehow different.

Azazyel looked up to see the warplanes above. Then he noticed there were more weapons of war on the ground. None of which seemed to faze the Creator as he stood there staring. Staring as though he were lost.

What is wrong with the Creator? Surely he let me out of my prison for a purpose.

"Jehovah, it is I, Azazyel. Do you not remember me after all these years?"

Nothing.

Then he noticed something out of the corner of his eye. A projectile from one of the flying machines was heading right for him, leaving a trail of fire and smoke in its wake. Then two more followed in its path.

He stepped back and watched it explode next to him, sending enormous boulders into the air and blowing him across the debris into a pile of black granite. Lying there stunned, he saw another one headed straight at him.

His instincts took over this time, he leapt to his feet. With a wave of his hand, the first warhead blew up and ignited the two that followed. The result was a huge fireball that engulfed the immediate area, causing the flying machine to burst into flames and plummet to the ground.

He looked back to see that the one he thought was the Creator was gone.

The others—I must find the others. Samyaza. Where is my leader? I can feel that you are near.

Then he heard it. Their cries were faint, but he could feel their existence. He closed his eyes and focused. He could feel their presence somewhere in the outer reaches of this realm. He knew he must find them and free them from their prison.

He heard their cries yet again. He could sense them, but he knew not where they were, so he fled south toward the interior of the great continent. The cries grew more intense as he went.

Where are you, my comrades? Where would the Creator have sentenced you to live out your days on this planet?

He came to a stop. In front of him was an extremely large exposed rock. The red-toned monstrosity jutted over a thousand feet into the air above the surface, covering an area of more than two miles. A perfect barrier to keep a being of his stature imprisoned. As he focused he could hear moans of agony. He could sense he was closer, but the enormous boulder was not the gate that kept the others at bay.

Azazyel was becoming more and more familiar with the abilities he once had. Even when the fallen ones had been in human form, they had realized long ago that all was possible. He stopped and concentrated on the faint cries. He stood on the great rock in a meditative state, focusing on the location in which he was searching for. Then he vanished.

WILKS LAND REGION, ANTARCTICA

IN AN INSTANT, AZAZYEL was standing in a frozen wasteland. Nothing but flat barren land covered in snow and ice as far as the eye could see. This was where he'd heard the cries. Deep under the frozen expanse of where he stood, the wails of agony could be heard faintly in the wind. But they were loud to Azazyel. He knew they were here.

He concentrated on vaporizing the frozen ground at his feet just as he had disintegrated the human's weapons earlier. Nothing.

What is this?

He tried again only to attain the same results. He turned around to see an exposed rock in the distance behind him. With the wave of his hand, it burst into atoms.

The Creator has somehow manipulated the matter that has impris-oned us all these years. By what method was I released?

He turned his focus to the past, and then he saw it. *It was the human's weapons that released me. They are not bound by the same chains that we are for some reason. Free will. They know not … I must go back.*

CHAPTER 46

JUGOW, POLAND

TY AND HIS COMRADES sat in the back booth at a local pub. The rest of the red mercury had just arrived, and Ty had a bad feeling about his last travel through time. To make matters worse, Ethan had just informed them of the NATO alliance clash with an energy creature on Black Mountain in Australia. Time was running out.

"I just don't have a good feeling about this," Ty said, rubbing his forehead. "I was foggy again, and it seemed to take longer than the first time to snap out of it."

Ivan raised his head as he stirred his drink. "It might have been because it was more of a traumatic event. No way of knowing for sure."

"Whatever the case," Ethan said, "it was still a success."

"It can be unpredictable, Ty. If Kammler had only a few more days, we would have known everything there is about this experience, but the bombs just came too early. Don't get me wrong—those Nazi bastards got what they deserved, but just a couple more days and we would have known so much more."

"That's neither here nor there," Ethan said. "The red mercury just arrived, but there was a minor problem."

Ivan jerked his head around. "Problem? What problem?"

"Settle down. We'll still be all right. It's just that only one canister was in the package. We can still move forward with the plan."

Ivan sighed and took another drink.

"Aren't you guys listening to me?" Ty said. "I failed! I tried to change something and was unable!"

"No!" Ethan raised his voice. "It wasn't a failure at all. You may not have saved Tom, but you saved the rest of us! Can't you see that? It was a success. We'd all be dead right now had it not been for you! You've already changed everything!"

Ty nodded and stared out the window. "Maybe you're right. Maybe that's all I was meant to do."

"Good. I know you don't need the extra pressure, but with what's taking place in Australia, it's only a matter of time before all hell breaks loose. Now let's get back and get some rest before the sun goes down and then do this one last time." Ethan stood up. "Everyone ready?"

All four looked at one another and nodded. It was time.

ETHAN'S ALARM WENT OFF at 10 p.m. sharp. The sun was long gone and it was time to do what they had traveled around the world for.

"All right, everyone," Ethan said in a loud voice to wake the rest of the crew. "Time to get moving."

The small cottage they had rented only had two bedrooms, so he could immediately see he was not the first one up as he usually was. Ty's and Ivan's beds were empty.

"I give up. Where is everyone?" He crawled out of bed and went into the hall.

The door to Erica's room opened and he wasn't too surprised to see Ty walk out a little sheepishly.

"You ready for this?"

Ty took a deep breath and nodded. "Yeah, I'm ready."

"Have you seen Ivan?"

Ty shook his head. "Not yet."

"He must be out getting some air. See if you can light a fire under Erica and I'll track down Ivan."

"I heard that. No fire needed," Erica said, blushing, as she followed in Ty's footsteps.

"Good." Ethan left well enough alone and went into the kitchen.

He looked around the room. Nothing of Ivan's was in sight. His tan coat and red hat from the rack were the only ones missing.

Where are you, Ivan? We've got to get going.

Ethan put his coat on and stepped outside, hoping to see Ivan on the porch. Nothing. Not only was Ivan nowhere to be seen, but their rental car was gone as well.

WALTER MINE SHAFT
LUDWIKOWICE-MILKOW, POLAND

IT WAS TIME. THIS was what Ivan had waited for all these years. His chance for revenge. He'd vowed long ago that he would get even with those who had killed his parents and turned his life upside down.

All these years. Now it's my turn, you goddamn Krauts!

Ivan grabbed the door to the secret chamber that housed the Bell and pulled it shut. He rotated the latch just as he heard his name.

"Ivan! Don't do it!" Ethan shouted from down the mine shaft as they watched Ivan latch the door.

"Professor, please!" Ty came into his view first. "Please, professor. Whatever you're planning, I can fix it when I go."

"It's true, Ivan." Ethan was now in view through the small viewing port, too, but they were barely audible now that the door was shut. "What we have planned will fix all our problems, including yours."

"Sorry, Ethan, but I have a score to settle personally."

"Please, Ivan. Think of the rest of the world. We have a chance to make everything right."

"I've waited my whole life for this moment. This is my chance to even the score."

Ivan pressed the "start" button and the Bell began to hum, drowning out the beating on the door by Ty and Ethan.

As the vibration grew louder, Ivan reached into the handbag and pulled out the cone. Holding it in front of the machine, he closed his eyes.

The thumping on the door grew fainter and fainter as he concentrated. The last thing he heard was "Please, professor. Don't take away our only chance!"

TY COULD FEEL THE vibration of the Bell throughout his body. The familiar buzz grew louder as the power continued to increase with Ivan standing in front.

"Erica!" Ethan yelled into the radio. "You must shut off the power now!"

"What? You're breaking up, Ethan. Speak up, I can't hear you!"

"Cut the power now!"

Ty looked back into the room and pleaded one last time. "Please, professor. Don't take away our only chance!"

The cone began to glow as the vibration grew more intense. Ty watched hopelessly as Ivan became translucent. Then he was gone.

Ty and Ethan watched in horror as the Bell began to slow.

"It's off," Erica said over the radio.

She had only been a second too late, but that was enough. They were both speechless—their chance was gone forever.

"Hello? Ethan, Tyler. Is everything all right?" Erica's voice crackled over the radio.

Ethan slowly put the radio to his mouth. "No. No it's not. We'll be up in a minute."

Ty had been working the latch and finally got it open, but it was far too late. Ivan, the stone and the last of the mercury were long gone.

TY AND ETHAN HAD come back to the surface. Their faces were long, as was Erica's.

"It's not your fault, Erica." Ty and Ethan had already stressed this, but their sentiments didn't seem to make her feel any better.

"If I had only been able to hear better with all the background noise. I thought I heard 'cut the power' but just wasn't sure."

Ty gently grabbed her hand and pulled her into him. "Even if you'd cut it then, it would have been too late. He was just too far ahead of us."

"Who would have thought he was going to pull that?" Ethan said. "I guess if it weren't for him, we never would have gotten this far anyway."

"So, what do we do now?" Erica asked.

"Nothing." Ethan had finally given up. "There's nothing we can do now. We've lost our last chance."

Ty's eyes grew wide as he froze in his tracks and listened. "Wait a minute—nothing's changed!"

"What?" Ethan asked.

"Nothing's changed!" Ty slowly spun his head around. "I mean, look around. Do you see anything at all that's different?"

"I'm not following you, Ty."

"If Ivan had gone back to stop the Nazis, why would everything still be the same?" A grin began to grow on Ty's face. "Everything in the mine shaft was exactly the same. And so far, everything I've seen up here is the same as it was, too."

Ethan and Erica both perked up and looked around.

"He's right! I don't see anything either! Do you, Ethan?"

"Actually, no." He plucked his phone from his pocket and pulled up Google News. He smiled as he looked up at Ty and Erica. "All the news headlines—they're the same stories that were there earlier."

He pecked away some more in his phone. "Hitler's death is still the same. The outcome of the war hasn't changed. The world is the same as it was!"

"So, what does that mean?" Erica asked. "Do we still have a chance?"

Ty threw his arms in the air. "It doesn't matter. We're still screwed. "Ivan was probably killed as soon as he went back. The mercury and cone are gone forever."

CHAPTER 47

WALTER MINE SHAFT
LUDWIKOWICE-MILKOW, POLAND

THEY HAD SEARCHED THE alcove housing the Bell over and over and nothing was there that would make the thing work again. Sure, they could get some more red mercury in due time, but without the mysterious cone, nothing was ever going to happen.

"Damn it!" Ethan snapped. "We were so close! We almost made it!"

"Yeah, still hard to believe I never saw that coming." Ty shook his head and stared at the Bell. "He was one hell of an actor."

"I wonder what his plan was?" Erica asked.

"Who knows?" Ty paused. "I don't think he was prepared to be thrown back into Nazi Germany. Maybe he just orchestrated another failed attempt on Hitler's life. Lord knows several have had that fantasy."

"I've seen enough," Ethan said as he turned to leave. "Let's get back up to the surface and see where we can go from here."

"Might as well." Ty turned to start the arduous venture back to the surface. Still perturbed by the chain of events, he kicked a half-rotted wood support beam that had fallen to the floor years ago.

"Hey! What's that?" Erica said from behind.

"Just frustrated," Ty replied. "I should've seen this coming."

"No. Not that." Erica had stopped. "What's that?"

He turned around to see what she was talking about, only to see her pointing to the timber he had just kicked.

"It's just an old support timber," Ethan said as he looked to the ground. "Must be another caved-in offshoot there."

"Would you dumb-asses look a little closer?"

Ty and Ethan looked at each other, and Ty shone his flashlight where she was pointing. There was something else there, all right. Something red.

He knelt and started pulling rocks from the area. Erica and Ethan moved back while he played the part of a human backhoe, exposing the object a little more with each toss. Then he abruptly stopped.

"What is it?" Ethan stepped in a little closer.

Ty was speechless for a moment. "I don't think it's a what but rather … a who."

"What?" Ethan came closer.

"Yeah, it looks like a skeleton." Ty carefully pulled more dirt to the side. "Maybe one of the Jewish workers?"

"He sure isn't dressed like I imagined they'd have been." Ethan knelt next to Ty.

"Look." Ty moved the remnants of a red hat on its scull and pointed. "There's a hole in the back of this poor guy's head. Could've been an execution, all right."

"There's something familiar about that coat and hat," Erica said as she moved closer.

Like a ton of bricks, it hit them all at once. For a moment, no one spoke, yet they all knew who it was.

"What the hell? Ivan?" Ethan stood and stared at the bones.

Ty noticed something under the seventy-five-year-old corpse.

With respect and care, he moved the bones of his old professor to the side.

"Something must have gone wrong." Ethan knelt next to him again.

"I don't think so," Ty said as he finished moving the last of Ivan's ribs. "Remember Ivan said that in 1945 the Nazis had a stockpile of red mercury in one of the other tunnels? Well, I think someone had a change of heart."

Clutched in one arm were three canisters. Two were shattered, but the third was intact and full of red mercury. And in the skeletal remains of the other arm? The bag of explosives and the mysterious handbag.

CHAPTER 48

IT WAS AS IF time had not moved and he was back at the pile of rubble where he had been chained for millennia.

It had been centuries since Azazyel had walked the face of the planet, but he could recognize his influence on the humans as they displayed their weapons of war.

I can see I taught you well, my trusted pupils. Now it is time for you to return the favor to me.

THE CREATURE WALKED TOWARD the closest tank that had its massive barrel pointed at him. It was only a split second before the projectile came out and was on its way.

The warhead exploded and the mysterious being went down. The creature lay there for only a moment before picking up a boulder with ease and hurling it at the closest tank, knocking it on its side as if it were a toy. Like a wounded duck, the creature limped toward the line of tanks, taking machine gun fire as it went, but it was able to slip behind the line and move south toward the interior of the continent.

The thing picked up speed and then even started to take to the air when several more warheads from an Apache attack helicopter came his way. It was able to dodge the first two, but the third exploded close enough to knock it back to the ground. Like Rocky Balboa, it again picked itself up and slowly staggered back into the air. The creature picked up speed to the point where the only things that could keep up were the three fully loaded F-35s.

Time and again, warheads were fired at the moving creature, but it continued south like a wounded animal trying to get away.

The chase continued across the entire continent of Australia and out over the Indian Ocean, where it appeared to take a direct hit from an AIM-120 advanced medium-range air-to-air missile. This time the creature plummeted into the ocean only to shoot back into the air and continue on a southward track.

MAJOR MASON HAD BEEN flying the F-35C Lightning II for the past three years and had never had any encounters such as this. All the way across Australia and the southern Indian Ocean, and now their target was getting closer to the coast of Antarctica. With reinforcements hot on its tail, he was nonetheless skeptical of the outcome after witnessing the several hits the creature had taken along the way only to shake them off and get up and keep moving.

Then, finally, it was as if it had had enough and could no longer move. It slumped to the ground on the frozen landscape in the Wilks Land Region of the southernmost continent on the planet.

"Sir." Major Masson transmitted back to base. "Whatever it is, it seems to have stopped."

"Well, it must be dead by now!" The general barked.

"Not sure, sir. It looked like we wounded it back by Black Mountain and we've hit it numerous times since then, but it just kept limping its way to where it is now. And I haven't seen it—wait, I think it just moved again!"

The creature appeared to be mortally wounded, but it slowly raised itself to its knees and slowly limped to a crevasse in the icy surface.

"It's still alive, sir. I don't know how, but it is. Wait a minute—it just jumped into a crack in the ice! It's gone!"

"It's time for the big guns. Stand down, Major. I have two B-2s overhead loaded for bear, and what they're packing, it can't hide from. Iceman One and Iceman Two, are you in position?"

"Yes, sir," Iceman One reported back.

The two B-2s were flying at twenty thousand feet above, each carrying two of the largest non-nuclear bombs in their arsenal. Known as the Massive Ordnance Penetrator, or MOP, the GBU-57A/B was designed to penetrate deep into enemy fortified bunkers and annihilate everything in their path. At thirty thousand pounds and over twenty feet long, the Boeing-made bunker-buster was even larger than the Mother of all Bombs used in Iraq in the ousting of Saddam Hussein in the early 2000s.

Each B-2 was capable of carrying two of these monstrosities. High above the spot where the creature in distress had just disappeared were two of the flying wings, which had just been given the green light to drop their payload.

Major Masson circled at a safe distance in his state-of-the-art fighter and watched as the event was about to unfold. Then an odd feeling came over him. Something wasn't right.

Then he heard a faint voice, or he thought he did. *Azazyel? What the …*

"Who said that?"

"Who are you talking to, Major?" the general snarled.

"Somebody said … Azazyel. Just wondered who."

"You're hearing things, Major. I'm monitoring the same freq as you and nothing like that came over my end."

"General, there's something strange about this whole thing. I think we should hold off on any further attack."

"Hold off? Tell that to the families of the brave Aussies that thing just killed! This thing is extremely dangerous, Major, and we have to destroy it now!"

"Something's not right. I think we're being set up."

"Set up? How?"

"I'm not quite sure, but I get the feeling that—"

"You're getting a feeling? Major, when I get paid to give a shit about your *feelings*, I'll do so gladly, but in the meantime, stay the hell off the radio!"

"But, sir—"

"Enough! Iceman One and Two, deliver your loads and let's wrap this thing up!"

"Yes, sir," they both acknowledged as their bomb bay doors opened over the snowy landscape below.

The major watched as the four behemoths plummeted to the earth from above. Then he saw something—the creature's hand. The creature reached up out of the crevasse and pulled itself to the surface. Then it looked to the sky. Just before the MOPs were at their target, it turned to look at the major one last time, and with the hint of a smile, it vanished before his very eyes.

CHAPTER 49

JUGOW, POLAND

ETHAN HUNG UP HIS phone and blankly stared into the distance.

"What now?" Ty asked.

"Talk about everything happening at the same time. Looks like we've got another problem to get ready for."

Erica shook her head. "Jesus. As if we need more pressure now. What's going on?"

Ethan tapped his pen on the table for a few seconds before he answered. "When the Dead Sea Scrolls were first discovered, archaeological treasure hunters flocked to the area in search of the next big find. Fortunately, the Jordanian government kept most of them at bay. Then in 1952, an archaeologist uncovered one of the most mysterious of all the ancient texts, the Copper Scrolls."

"Yeah." Ty's eyes lit up. "I read those were found there. I never got a chance to really look into them much, though."

"Well, that may have been a good thing. You might've gotten sucked into a whole other rabbit hole. Not only was the material obviously different from the other scrolls, but so was the writing. Written in an encrypted language that's still not fully understood, the Copper Scrolls appear to be a treasure map for countless treasures taken from Jerusalem, notably King Solomon's Temple. Gold, silver and many sacred objects, and maybe even the Ark of the Covenant.

"Even though the Ark wasn't specifically mentioned in the Copper Scrolls, the Babylonians had a detailed list of everything they took, and there was no mention of the Ark. That makes us think the Ark was hidden away before they got there. The last time the Ark has been seen was before the temple was destroyed. So it's very probable it was taken out and hidden with the other treasure."

"Holy crap, Ethan. You're talking Indiana Jones shit now. I've always been fascinated by those biblical artifacts, but what's that got to do with us?"

"Well, there'd been rumors of numerous well-connected, high-paying collectors and one we've had our eye on, Benton Ashworth, that were trying to do whatever they could to get their hands on the Israelites' most prized possession. Of course, the Israeli government did what they could to keep them from looking for it. Still, there was concern that someone would finally become successful and find it. Thank God the Secretary-General of the UN at the time was deeply interested in all things mystical. I truly believe he understood the full power of the Ark and did what he needed to see it didn't fall into the wrong hands."

"The wrong hands being?"

"Most likely Ashworth. There are those that believe the biblical texts regarding the Ark. The Israelites were able to destroy entire cities with the aid of its mystical force, and anyone with a lust for power would go to extreme lengths to possess it. And Ashworth fits the profile."

"So, if you're saying the Secretary-General of the UN got to the Ark first and, I assume, have it under lock and key somewhere"—Ty rubbed his chin—"then it must be safe, right?"

"Well, for years it was, but we've been looking for it for a long time and believe we've found where it's been hidden away. To make a long story short, it wasn't long after the discovery of the Copper Scrolls that Dag Hammarskjöld, then Secretary-General of the UN, was responsible for having a six-and-a-half-ton rectangular block of iron ore put on display at the UN building in New York. It's in what's known as the Meditation Room. They call it the Stone of Light.

"It just so happens the measurements given in the Bible of the Ark of the Covenant are just slightly less than the Stone of Light. We know it could be just a coincidence, but a couple of days ago the security cameras caught a covered object about the same size being loaded into a van in the parking lot at the UN building."

"You're saying the location of the Ark of the Covenant was in the Copper Scrolls? Then Hammarskjöld found it and hid it somehow in the chunk of iron ore? And someone's stolen it?"

Ethan nodded. "We think so. The Meditation Room at the UN building has just been closed off for some repairs, but I'd bet my bottom dollar that when it's reopened, the stone will be gone."

"Again, though, what's this got to do with us?"

"We think our mystery man, Ashworth, is behind the project that's been going at the Great Pyramid right now. There's no doubt the pyramid was not a tomb. Your theory of its being a machine is all too probable. The renovation project that's been underway is much more than that. We think it's being retooled to be operable once again. To make that happen, it has to have the same white limestone casing covering the outer surface. There also needs to be a water channel reopened to fill the cavities below. Then come the last two keys to make it work. A capstone of a very special unknown material needs to be placed on top. We just found out that's now in its place. So, this leaves the last piece of the puzzle that we think he's been looking for. Any ideas what that might be?"

Ty had put in several hours studying the Great Pyramid, and he'd come across just about every wild theory involving what it may have been and how it worked. It didn't take him long to put the missing piece in its proper place.

"So, the coffer in the King's Chamber really was built to hold the Ark of the Covenant? Or at least what's inside the Ark?" Ty thought for a moment. "If that's true, then whatever's inside the Ark was first used in the pyramid long before the Israelites had it."

Ethan nodded. "It looks that way. The dimensions of the coffer are a perfect match with the Ark. If Hammarskjöld knew the true purpose of the Great Pyramid and didn't want to see it in operation ever again, keeping the Ark hidden would be one surefire way."

"But why not just hide the Ark underground someplace where it could never be found? I mean, if he really wanted to hide it, disguising it as a square rock in plain view at the UN doesn't seem like the best plan to me."

"On the surface, I know it looks that way now, but I'll bet just about everyone who ever went looking for it never thought in a million years to look there. I personally think Hammarskjöld had very high morals and didn't think the Ark should be kept hidden from the people. So what better way to fulfill his objectives than hide it in plain sight where the world's leaders would have full access to it? Unbeknownst to them, of course. I can't say that was his reasoning for sure, but from what I've read about him, well, it makes sense to me. Besides that, from what we know about Ashworth, he's resourceful enough to have found it even if it was buried somewhere."

Erica was shaking her head and rolling her eyes. "Wait a minute. Back up a little here, please. You're saying Hammarskjöld was able to get his hands on the lost Ark of the Covenant based on what was written in the Copper Scrolls, then hide it inside a phony block of iron ore on display at the United Nations building?"

"I'm afraid that's a strong possibility. Ashworth has done his homework over the years and finally figured it out somehow." Ethan paused for a moment. "One more thing. I've been in the Meditation Room and stood next to the Stone of Light. I had the strangest feeling all of a sudden. I swear to God, the hair on the back of my neck stood up."

"As nuts as this sounds, let's say it's all true for a minute." Erica was focused on Ethan. "So just what does the Great Pyramid do?"

Before Ethan could speak, Ty stepped in. "It reverses the process the fallen angels went through to become human."

Erica squinted as she stared at Ty.

"Oh, I know, it sounds crazy as hell, but I remember reading about Enoch. He was on the planet at the time when all this shit with the fallen angels taking human women for wives and having their giant offspring was going on. After some time went by, the Watchers knew they'd made a mistake and conferred with him. They asked him to talk to God about letting them come home, but God didn't want them back. There were some legends that said Enoch was the architect of the Great Pyramid. He sympathized with the Watchers and tried to help them."

"You mean he went against God's wishes?" Erica asked.

"Well, who knows how exactly it all went down? Then there's the Book of Giants, which is even more bizarre. The Watchers may also have been manipulating genetics of different living things and created the creatures of lore in several myths around the world such as mermaids. The Great Pyramid may have been used to reverse those changes as well, but if any of this is true—"

"Then somebody with enough power and money could fire up the damn thing again and turn himself into a—"

"Yeah," Ethan said, "something we'd just as soon not see on the planet again. Having to deal with Himmler's creation will be bad enough, but even more of them?" He paused, then turned back to Ty. "It's time to get the Bell ready."

CHAPTER 50

THE SIGNAL CAME IN and it was time. Several workers began pulling on the large rope that was fastened to the rectangular slab of red granite that had been acting as a dam to the channel from the Nile. With each hoist, the slab rose out of the channel a little more, allowing the water to fill the ditch that went straight toward the newly refurbished ancient wonder. It had been centuries since water had filled the passage, but it was as though the life-giving fluid had been waiting for this moment to fulfill the destiny of the ancient machine.

The vibration from the water in the caverns below was the last ingredient to make the Great Pyramid work. It began to come alive. The white casing stones became a vivid, shimmering white; it was almost blinding. The mysterious capstone started to pulsate like a human heart. All the work that had been done had literally resurrected the ancient wonder.

INSIDE THE GREAT PYRAMID

ASHWORTH COULD FEEL THE power of the pyramid as it started to vibrate as if there were an earthquake somewhere in the distance. Dust from the millennia began to find its way out of every crevice in the structure, producing a mist of silt in the room.

The power—it will soon be mine! Ashworth raised his arms to embrace the coming transformation.

As he closed his eyes to welcome the process, he felt something. Something that didn't seem like what he'd expected. His breathing became obstructed as the life force seemed to drain from his body. There was a sharp pain in his throat. He opened his eyes and tried to scream, but a large hand with an iron grip was obstructing his mouth.

He tried to turn, but the unseen power held his head firm. Then he felt a warm sensation that trickled down his throat and consumed his lower torso. His vision started to fade, as did the force holding him fast, and he slumped to the surface.

As he lay on the floor, he tried to focus on a blur looming over him. With his last breath, he realized the blur was Butch Colton.

WILKS LAND REGION, ANTARCTICA

THE MAJOR STARED AT the total destruction of the once-frozen site. The Wilks Land region in Antarctica had been a mystical place since Operation High-Jump back during World War II. The frozen continent was riddled with conspiracies of the Nazis searching for something buried deep beneath the sheets of ice that encased the bottom of the world.

It had been well-known that Hitler was fascinated with the occult and lost relics of lore. Atlantis, the Holy Grail, the Ark of the

Covenant and even the fountain of youth were among the objects of the many expeditions he sent his men on over the years. But what could possibly have been so intriguing to him on this frozen continent? Could the gravitational anomaly at this exact spot that was discovered in 2008 be involved somehow? Now a crater the size of two football fields exposed the rocky earth below the ice sheet.

"Well, Major?"

He looked over the rubble with a bitter taste in his mouth. "There doesn't seem to be anything moving down there now, sir."

"I expected as much. You play with fire and you'll get burned. Now, let's get everyone home."

"But how could we have been hitting it over and over again while it limped its way here and fell into the crevasse, yet it was still able to crawl out and get to its knees right before the last assault? It just seemed too convenient when it stopped. Almost like it was baiting us."

"Baiting us? Who's still breathing the air and who's not?" The General yelled over the radio.

The major shook his head as he looked over the gaping hole. "Sir, I know something's not right. Whatever that thing was, I could have sworn it looked right at me and smiled, then vanished before impact."

"Get over yourself, Major. Of course it vanished. We hit that son of a bitch right in the mouth and blew it into the next millennia! Now turn your ass around and bring back my airplane!"

"Yes, sir." He looked the crater over one last time before turning his state-of-the-art fighter jet around to leave.

Something bad is coming ... I can feel it.

AZAZYEL STOOD THERE AND watched the frozen dust settle after the humans had taken their war machines back to where they had come from. He could feel the presence of his comrades and knew it would be soon that he would be reunited with them.

Samyaza, my leader, you are near now. It is safe to return.

Looking over the newly formed crater, he saw movement. From under the scattered boulder fragments, forms began to emerge. Beings forged of pure energy in its most unadulterated form.

The chiefs of the two hundred were the first to rise up; Samyaza, who was their leader, Urakabaraneel, Akibeel, Tamiel, Ramuel, Danel, Azkeel, Saraknyal, Asael, Armers, Batraal, Anane, Xavebe, Samsaveel, Ertael, Turel, Yomyael and Araxyal. They and the remainder all pulled themselves from the earthly dungeon that had imprisoned them for millennia. They were free at last.

CHAPTER 51

GIZA PLATEAU: THE GREAT PYRAMID

THE INTERIOR OF THE Great Pyramid was shaking as though it were sitting on top of an ancient volcano about to awake. Butch had only felt fear a couple of times in his adult life, and his instincts wanted him to get the hell out of there.

He had slipped into the Subterranean Chamber when his coworkers were beginning the process of letting the waters of the Nile infiltrate the cavities under the ancient machine. All he had to do once inside was wait for Ashworth. From the descending passage, he had the perfect view and wouldn't be seen.

Ashworth had taken the life of Grant's youngest son, and Butch had to make it right. Doing away with Ashworth had been the only way. An eye for an eye.

He slid Ashworth's limp body out of the way with his foot and stood upright in the alcove in the Queens Chamber. The same spot where Ashworth had been standing. The vibration was increasing and he knew he had to get out, but he couldn't move. A force of some kind engulfed him and rendered him helpless. It seemed that whatever Ashworth had planned for himself would now be Butch's fate.

What the hell is happening?

The halo of silt that had been waiting for ages to be released started to clear and then settled on the floor. The rumble of the ancient machine slowed and began to sound like an angry hornets' nest.

Then Butch started to feel something, something indescribable. But it felt good, *real* good. He opened the palms of his hands and stared at them. They were becoming ever so slightly translucent.

What's happening to me? It … it feels amazing!

The buzzing was constant now, but he was gradually changing … evolving … transforming. Transforming into something of the spirit world. The exact reverse of the transformation the Watchers underwent on top of Mount Hermon centuries ago. He was becoming … a Watcher!

What fear he had felt was now gone. He had never felt so in touch with the elements around him, so powerful, so alive!

"Amazing!" Butch shouted in a powerful voice.

The transformation was complete. The last of his physical body was gone and his essence pulsated with pure energy now. A thought form like those that Edgar Cayce said had come to the planet at the beginning of time. A being second in power only to God himself.

Soaking up the tranquillity of the moment, he raised his arms above his head and embraced his new form. Then, with a loud roar and a brilliant blue flash, he was gone.

WALTER MINE SHAFT
LUDWIKOWICE-MILKOW, POLAND

TY AND ETHAN HAD just finished carrying the last of the equipment into the tunnel that housed the Bell.

"The bow and quiver full of arrows, the sword—what the hell is all this?" Ty said as he held up the strange gear.

"You'll need to look the part, Ty. Trust me, it's the appropriate attire for the time you'll be in. As far as we can tell, anyone wearing this had free rein back then, so put it on."

"What? You Googled what the people wore then?" Ty said as he donned his new clothing.

"Funny, but actually, yes. The ancient Sumerian carvings are all over the Internet, which spared us from museum hopping around Iraq. It was pretty clear that anyone of extreme importance wore this kind of clothing."

"I still don't even know what the backup plan is. You said you'd fill me in when the time was right. When might that be?"

"Trust me a little longer, would ya?"

Just then, Erica's scratchy voice came over the radio. She was barely audible, so he held it up to his ear. "Ethan, a text just came in for you. 'Antarctica, Black Mountain all are blown ... Azazyel and the rest are free.'"

Ethan froze, his face white. "It's happening!"

"What is, Ethan?"

"It's time, Ty. You have to go now!"

"Now? I mean ... we need to go over things more. I thought there'd be more time. Hell, do we even know if these explosives are going to work after being down here with Ivan for all these years?"

"I thought there'd be more time, too, but we have to get moving now. You'll have all the time in the world once you get going. But if you stay here any longer, they'll know they have to stop you. Those explosives have been in the waterproof Kevlar bag the entire time, so they'll still be good."

Ethan pulled a small notebook out of his pocket and pressed it into Ty's hand. "If plan A fails, plan B is written in here. Don't look at it until you know you're going to need it. Trust me, Ty. If you read it before then, the Watchers will know what you plan to do and stop you before you get the chance."

"But Erica … I have to—"

"She knows. I'll tell her, but you have to go now, Ty."

Ty grabbed the radio from Ethan's hand and put the mic up to his mouth. He keyed it, but no words came out. He stared at Ethan, then gave it back.

"I hope you know what we're doing. You do realize how crazy this idea is, don't you?"

"I do, but we have to try. It's our only chance." He pointed to the notebook in Ty's hand. "Then it's plan B. God only knows what that will do to humanity, but there's a good chance it will stop this insanity from taking over the planet ever again."

"Okay then." Ty quivered a little. "You're right. We don't have a whole lot of choices, and I do trust you."

"Wait, Ty. I almost forgot."

Ethan reached into his bag and pulled out an object wrapped in a cloth. "I just got this today, and you may need it," he said as he unwrapped the mysterious object and held it out to Ty.

Ty looked at the relic in Ethan's hand. It was the same dagger he had seen in Victor's basement only a few weeks ago. "I … I remember this. Not just from Victor's museum but somewhere else. Somewhere long before then." He looked at the long sword in his sheath and then back at the small dagger. "What makes a little dagger so special when I have this?"

"Legend is, it was forged from a strange material that was capable of killing the Nephilim. If it could kill them, then you should—"

Erica's voice cut in over the radio. "Ethan, we have a problem!"

"What is it, Erica?"

"It's the pump up here. I saw a flash and heard a loud noise, then it just stopped! I think maybe something outside was hit by lightning! Wait … there's another flash! You guys need to get out of there!"

"Lightning? It's the middle of winter. Are you sure about that?"

"There was a bright bluish flash outside right before the pump quit, and just now there was another. What else could it be?"

"That wasn't lightning, Ty. They're here—you have to go now!"

They looked at the floor of the tunnel and could see the water beginning to rise. The submersible pump wasn't enough to keep the water level down. It would only be a matter of seconds before it would find its way through the open door to the room that housed the Bell.

Ty froze only for a moment as he pondered the situation. Then he snatched the dagger from Ethan's hand. "You take care of her until I get back."

Ethan just nodded as Ty sheathed his sword and slid the dagger into waistband and entered the chamber, latching the door behind him.

"Okay, Erica," Ethan said into the mic, "we need to power up now."

"What? You have to get out of there now!"

"We have no choice, Erica. It's now or never! Now please turn the power on before it's too late!"

He stared at Ty as he spoke, and then Ty turned to face the machine as the familiar buzzing grew louder. Standing there dressed like a Sumerian god with the stone in one hand and the handbag in the other, he disappeared one last time.

CHAPTER 52

THE DILAPIDATED POWER PLANT looked as deserted as it had probably been since the fall of Berlin decades ago. A slight hum emanated from the bushes next to a small building surrounded by rubble.

Out of the clear blue winter sky, a blue flash followed by a loud pop broke the silence. A blurry glowing figure stood in its wake as the dust settled. It was Azazyel.

Like a wild animal released from a life of confinement, he seemed to take in the moment of his new surroundings—the sky, the trees, the aroma of nature. Then he turned to bushes from which the hum came. He was on a mission.

Azazyel waved his electric arms and the vegetation turned to powder and fell to the ground, exposing the purring water pump. With another wave of his arms, the pump was atomized and a pool of water flowed out of the now-exposed output pipe.

He then focused on a thick electrical cord that followed the water pipe into the small enclosure. Just as he began to raise his arms, another blue flash exploded behind him, causing him to turn and look. Standing only a few feet away was an eerie sight: the spit and image of himself.

"Let me guess, you must be Azazyel." the new creature said in a gruff tone.

"You are not one of us. From where do you come?"

The newcomer opened his palms and emitted a blast of energy that blew Azazyel out of the rubble and into the open field outside the border. Seemingly stunned by the blow, Azazyel picked himself up only to be hit by another blast of the blue plasma force.

"What do you want of me?" he asked. "Has the Creator sent you?"

The newcomer was silent but let loose with yet again another blast, even more powerful than the last. Azazyel was on guard this time and dodged the pulse and returned with one of his own, knocking the newcomer into a pile of broken concrete.

"Why do you wish to harm me?" Azazyel questioned the newcomer. "Of course, you must know you cannot. Or have you not figured that out yet?"

The newcomer picked himself up and shot into the air, just avoiding another blast. Hovering above Azazyel, he let loose with a burst that pushed the fallen one several feet into the earth.

"Oh yeah? And what makes you think I'm trying to hurt you?" he said as he floated to the ground farther away from the concrete enclosure.

Azazyel pried himself from the ground and stood as though he were trying to connect to an invisible mental force in the air.

"Ah … I see who you are now and why you are here." Azazyel turned his sights back to the power cord that ran into the ground.

"You're a little late for that now, buddy," the newcomer said. "The time has passed."

Azazyel looked at him and laughed. "Not bad for just being born, my friend, but believe me when I say your friends' attempts to stop us will still fall short, for it is they that are too late. It is already written."

The newcomer expelled a large ball of plasma to send Azazyel flying to the turf again.

"It's written, huh? Too bad I don't read."

Azazyel shook himself off one last time. "You are new to this realm and will be no match for all of us."

"Is that right? What makes you think I'm alone? I may have a friend soon."

Again, Azazyel took a spiritual breath to acquire answers. "Ah, yes. You mean the other that is here who does not belong. The one who is equal to the Creator. Tell me, my new friend, what makes you think it will heed your wishes against us? We have done nothing to wrong him."

"We'll see about that … *friend*." With that, the newcomer vanished.

AZAZYEL LAUGHED IN THOUGHT as the newcomer vanished from sight. *Very impressive, my new friend. Very impressive. I know not how you were tipped off to my mission, but that is of no consequence now.* He pondered the thought and a slight sneer came to his face. *A very bold being indeed, yet you are no match for all of us.*

Just as he was about to transport himself back to the others, he felt another presence, a vibration he had not felt since he was in the physical form centuries ago. He turned to see a beautiful woman step out from the small building inside the rubble pile. His gaze became focused on the female. The beauty of an earth woman was the catalyst that had sent the heavenly beings down the murky path that ended up with their imprisonment deep in the frigid confines of the planet so long ago. Yet as he stood there focused on the lovely woman, thoughts of lust poured through his soul as it had at the dawn of humanity.

Then another thought came to him. Yes, he could take the beautiful woman for himself, but he had a better plan. One that would surely gain the trust of the new Most-High.

CHAPTER 53

MOUNT HERMON, ANCIENT LEBANON

TY OPENED HIS EYES as the buzzing in his head slowly faded. *Where am I?* He was standing on top of a high mountain, with a sea visible in the distance. He slowly turned to the sites on all sides as he tried to remember something. There was a vast desert opposite the ocean as far as the eye could see. A lush green area lay between, and he noticed what looked like a small village at the base of the mountain.

What is this place?

He looked at the cone shaped stone glowing in his hand, then at the bag in his other. In a motion of reflex, he put the stone in the bag and saw the dagger in his waistband. He pulled it from its resting spot and looked it over closely.

This is important. But why?

In a sheath on his side was a long sword that glistened in the sunlight as he extracted it and inspected it from its handle to its razor-sharp tip.

The sandals on his feet felt foreign but were surprisingly comfortable. After sliding the sword back into its sheath, he felt the quiver slung over his right shoulder and the bow on his left.

Something was gnawing at him. *There's something missing, but what?* Then the fog started to lift. His memory came flooding back in an instant. He was here to stop the Watchers!

Ty scanned the area around where he stood. *Where is it?*

The duffel bag with all his weapons and explosives was missing. He scanned the entire area on the mountaintop—nothing. For some reason, they didn't make it.

I need that bag. It has to be here!

He looked at his time barometer. Only one travel left. He had no choice—he'd have to go back now and try again.

He pulled the shimmering stone from the bag. Just then, a glow from above caught his eye. Whatever it was, it was growing larger, as if it were getting closer. Mesmerized by the beautiful sight, he watched as it slowly descended.

It's them, the Watchers! The fallen angels are here! He looked around. *I have to find a place to hide.*

Several yards away was a boulder. It was the only thing close enough to hide behind. He made a dash for it as the descending light became brighter. Running as fast as he could, he made cover just in time as the glow intensified. The fallen ones were here.

Individual forms began to appear as they settled onto the top of the mountain one by one. This was an event he had dreamed about—the fabled fallen angels making their grand entrance into the world for the first time.

Several seconds passed as all two hundred of them planted their spiritual feet on the surface of the earth. One stood out from the rest and drew the other's focus. No words were spoken, but he could tell they were communicating with the one who was obviously their leader.

I remember now ... Samyaza! The leader of the Watchers!

The Watchers stopped what they were doing as though they were listening for something.

Did they hear me?

Ty gently pushed his thoughts from his mind and focused on his heartbeat. It worked—after a few moments, they were back to whatever it was they were trying to decide. One in particular seemed to be pleading his case for something. Something that sparked a debate of some kind.

Several minutes went by, and the mood changed. The spiritual beings knelt on the ground as though a prayer were being offered … or an oath being taken.

Then something mysterious and magical happened. The sheen of the creatures intensified to an almost blinding blue light, as though a supernova were coming to life before his very eyes.

A thought emerged in the recesses of Ty's mind. *The transformation. Soon they'll be human. Human and vulnerable.*

Without the benefit of the duffel full of explosives, the deck was stacked against him, but there still might be a chance. They would make the transformation soon, and that's when he would have to strike. He was far outnumbered, so he had to figure out another way.

Just then a voice invaded his thoughts. *Cut off the head of the snake and surely it will perish.*

Ty looked at the dagger in his belt. Was this the purpose of the mysterious dagger? How could he take out their leader and escape with his life?

The tip of the bow that was strapped over his shoulder scratched the earth out of the corner of his eye. He quickly scanned the rest of his strange wardrobe. The sheath that housed the dagger was bound to his waistband with a leather strap.

Several years of meditation practice helped him keep his thoughts as quiet as possible. He unwound the strap, releasing the sheath, and quietly pulled an arrow from the quiver over his other shoulder. With the leather strap, he securely fastened the dagger to the end of the arrow and slowly and quietly took the bow from his shoulder.

The fallen ones were now gathered in a tight group as the magnificent, brilliant, blue-green radiance intensified. The illumination grew to an immense magnitude. In the matter of a few seconds, it was so bright Ty had to look away. Then the light was extinguished.

Ty couldn't believe his eyes. The fallen ones stood in the same spot, but now the ominous spiritual glow that had engulfed them was on the ground at their feet. It had happened—they were completely human. Now was the time.

Ty placed the arrow mounted with the dagger in his bow and patiently watched. It must be clear who was their leader.

Show yourself, Samyaza!

AZAZYEL LOOKED HIS NEW form over closely. *Ah, to be of human form. Everything seems so different. So much to feel.*

The rest of the two hundred milled around, checking out their new physical bodies as well. For the first time in their existence, they knew what it was like to be flesh and blood.

"We now feel the same things as our master's favorite creation." Azazyel looked to the sky, then at his comrades. "And now we shall take the daughters of men!"

"Ah, yes, my faithfuls." Samyaza stepped forward next to Azazyel and turned to face the group. "I fear that you may perhaps be indisposed to the performance of this enterprise. And that I alone shall suffer for so grievous a crime."

Azazyel turned to Samyaza. "We all swear and bind ourselves by mutual execrations that we will not change our intention but execute our projected undertaking."

Samyaza stretched his arms in the air and addressed the crowd.

"Come, let us select for ourselves wives from the progeny of men, and let us beget children!"

The mob of transformed angels cheered like a charged platoon ready for battle. The mood was set and the moment was now. They would have reign over this world and all those who inhabited it.

Azazyel could feel the energy pulsating through the horde and a smile crept across his face. Then he felt something else. Something that wasn't right. He spun around and reached in the air and quickly closed his hand around the incoming projectile, stopping it just inches from Samyaza's head.

CHAPTER 54

MOUNT HERMON, ANCIENT LEBANON

TY HAD BEEN RUNNING as fast as he could down the mountain. What had gone wrong? His aim had been true and he had been only a split second away from achieving his goal. The only answer he could come up with was that these beings harbored a mastery of the physical world they now resided in. Had this entire plan been nothing more than a desperate futile attempt from the get-go?

He had to get to the village below and warn the people of the impending doom coming their way. Even if he succeeded, was it possible to change events from the past? The obvious answer was "no," and nothing he'd seen so far suggested anything different.

Ty slowed down as he approached the bottom of the mountain. He had been running the entire time and was hardly winded. A transformation of some kind must have happened during the last time travel. He could tell he was stronger than before. A more perfect version of his former self.

A little pond glistened just outside the small village to which he was headed. He knelt down for a drink but froze in his tracks as he noticed his reflection. He put his hands to his face. His once-clean-shaven face was covered with a thick beard.

What's happened to me? Am I even the same person I once was?

Most of his past he could now recall. The memory of how and why he had got to where he was seemed so far away, yet he knew it had only been moments ago.

Ty slowly stood up and walked into the village. Now he understood why Ethan had supplied him with the clothing he had on. Judging by the other men, he would surely be considered upper-class. And his stature surpassed that of all the others.

The people stopped what they were doing and beheld his presence. A small boy even dropped to his knees.

What the … Do they think I'm some kind of god?

"People, people, please listen to me." He turned and looked up the mountain. A cloud of dust could be seen slowly descending. He pointed to the site and looked back at their bewildered faces. "Those coming are evil. You must leave now!"

They whispered to one another, and then it hit him. *Shit! They don't speak English! I'm speaking gibberish to them!*

There was nothing he could do. If he stayed to confront the two hundred, surely they would kill him. He had no choice.

He retrieved the small notebook Ethan had given him from the bag and opened it. His face went blank as he stared at what he had just read. His eyes glazed, he looked back up the mountain to see the dust cloud getting closer. He knew he only had one option left… he had to go now.

He reached into the handbag and pulled out the stone. The intensity of the blue-green tone matched the indicator on his wrist. He had only one travel left.

Holding the stone in front of his face, he closed his eyes and concentrated. The now-familiar buzz began to grow as he stood still—until he vanished.

CHAPTER 55

DAN AND SELENA WERE immersed in their study at the old public library not far from headquarters at Langley. They'd only been back from Argentina for a few days, and their time had been eaten up by numerous debriefings and filling out enough paperwork to fill a small warehouse. To make matters worse, none of their superiors had any sympathy for their story.

Idiots. Dan shook his head. *With all the reports of some energy being showing up around the planet and that mysterious showdown in the outback and then Antarctica, they still don't give our account any credibility?*

In the little free time they'd had in between being drilled for information, they'd been poring over all the ancient texts they could find that referenced fallen angels and giants.

"Look at this, Dan." Selena kept her head in the old book while she motioned to him. "'Bind Azazyel hand and foot, and cast him into the darkness: and make an opening in the desert, which is in Dudael, and cast him therein. And place upon him rough and jagged rocks, and cover him with darkness, and let him abide there forever, and cover his face that he may not see light. And on the day of the great judgment, he shall be cast into the fire.'"

"Dudael? Is that a real place?" Dan asked.

"Let me look." Selena plugged away on her iPad. "Looks like maybe east of Jerusalem … or maybe a region of the underworld?"

"Have there been any sightings of this thing near Jerusalem?"

"I don't think so." She paused and looked up at Dan. "What do you suppose it means by *underworld?*"

He thought for a moment. "Of course, hell comes to mind, but most theologians don't put much stock in that being an actual place. If all these events happened here on earth, then it would have to be a physical location on the planet somewhere … but where?"

"Let's think outside the box for a minute." Selena grabbed the atlas and flipped to the world view. "Underworld, under … not down under … Australia?"

"Hmm … maybe." Dan raised his head from the book and stared out the window. "Well, we do know the thing showed up in Australia, which set off a little skirmish, but why would it have been there? It's been seen all over the world at different mysterious places, but why Black Mountain in Australia?"

Selena jerked her head up. "Did you say Black Mountain?"

"Yeah, that's what my source told me. Why? What's so special about that place?"

"Desert, jagged rocks … I went to Black Mountain when I was in college and it sure sounds like it fits the description." Selena almost shuddered as she spoke, "Let me tell you, that is one creepy place, too."

"So, if that really was the place God imprisoned—what did you say the name was? Azazyel?"

"Yeah, Azazyel." Selena answered then asked. "Then what about the others? I mean, there were supposedly two hundred of these things, right?"

Dan took his glasses off and set them on the table before he answered. "Yeah. Well, there was the same scenario in Antarctica. Some energy being, then lots of bombs dropped. It was somewhere around the Wilks Land Region, which is odd, because that place has been in the news lately due to a weird gravity anomaly there."

Selena bit her lip as she tapped her pen on the open book. "Are you saying that's where the others were buried?"

"Maybe. A lot of conspiracy theorists believe it. Bad thing is, by the time we find out if this is true or not, it'll be too late to do anything."

"But Black Mountain? I'm telling you, I got a real bad feeling about that place. I felt a presence of some kind there. Something evil. Must have been a good reason to blow up a national landmark like that, but it still doesn't make any sense. If Himmler's lair was blown up … I mean, we both saw the hole after the blast."

Dan turned to Selena. "So, you think this is something else? Do you really think Azazyel and the others are real?"

"Look, I didn't believe any of this at first, but when Grant and his son never came back, then that odd explosion … Something weird is going on. And there was something about Larson's kid that I just can't quite put my finger on."

"Yeah, I felt it, too," Dan said.

"I think we need to at least find someone who will listen and give our story some consideration. If these fallen angels are real, then we need to do our part to see they stay put."

"I agree. History doesn't need to be repeated in this case."

"So, who do we know that'll listen?" Selena asked.

"I know someone. Someone who owes me a favor."

THE PENTAGON
ARLINGTON COUNTY, VIRGINIA

THE GENERAL HAD BEEN on the phone with the president all

afternoon about the new offensive efforts in Australia and Antarctica. Nothing had made any sense. The general had been certain the final strikes at the unknown entity were more than enough to solve the problem. Whatever it was that had been roaming around the planet must have made a stand at Black Mountain before it fled to Antarctica. Luckily, the four MOPs were enough to put an end to its campaign.

Just then his secretary buzzed in. "Sir, there're a couple of field agents from the Central Intelligence Agency here to see you. A Dan Clancy. He said you're expecting them."

"Yeah, send them in."

THEY HAD PLEADED THEIR case for over an hour, but the general wouldn't have anything to do with it. Even though Dan had played football with the general in college, he couldn't convince him of their theory's credibility. Maybe it was because he was having a hard time swallowing it himself.

"Sorry, Dan, but do you know how it would sound if I went to the president and told him I thought there were angels and demons getting ready to storm the planet? He'd have me committed and I'd deserve it!"

"You have to admit something weird is going though, Max. With all the reports of some energy being showing up and then vanishing in all corners of the earth ... I mean, that's just inexplicable."

"For Christ's sake, Dan, it's most likely something the Chinese are working on. You're as far gone as one of my pilots. Maybe not quite that bad yet, unless you're hearing things, too. Azazyel ... Jesus, man, what gibberish."

Dan and Selena shot each other a glance. "What did you say?" Dan asked.

"I said, it's most likely the Chinese—"

"No, not that. Did you just say … Azazyel?"

CHAPTER 56

THE VIOLENT BUZZING STOPPED and silence ensued as Ty opened his eyes to a beautiful setting. The peace and tranquility were almost overwhelming. In the distance was a waterfall flowing into a small pond that glistened with a turquoise sheen. Surrounding the area were trees of all sorts. They chattered with life thanks to numerous songbirds.

Instinctively, he put the now lifeless stone in the bag he was carrying, and then it hit him. *Where am I?*

He looked around at the lush jungle, then turned his sights to the sword sheathed on his side.

What is this? Why—

He noticed his reflection in the pond. Staring back at him was an even larger and more muscular man than before. And there was something on his face. He reached up and felt the long flowing locks of a thick beard.

What's going on? Who am I?

Then, he sensed a presence. A presence that was very close. One that sent shivers down his spine.

Something broke the silence. A voice … a faintly familiar voice yet still unlike any other. It was cold and eerie, but the most disturbing thing was that it seemed so calculating. So very calculating. "Enoch."

He wheeled around only to see nothing. "Who's there?"

"Ah, the better question is, who are you?"

Ty spun around again, only to see more of the same.

"Do you not recognize me?" the voice asked. "Surely you need not see me to remember?"

I must be hallucinating.

"Hallucinating? Do you really think I am a hallucination?"

Then Ty remembered something. He was on a mission, but for what?

"Ah, you are starting to remember your true purpose," the voice said with a hiss. "Are you sure you want to proceed?"

In the blink of an eye, Ty's sword was out of its sheath. He spun around again and still he was alone. "Get out of my head and show yourself! Why do you hide from me?"

"Hide from you? I am here to guide you."

"Guide me? To what?"

"Why, to your goal. The goal you have traveled so very far to attain. One that I can assure you will be futile."

Ty tried desperately to see where the voice was coming from, but there was no one in sight. It almost seemed like it was coming from his own mind. But that wasn't possible … was it?

"Do not try so hard to rationalize my existence. Do you not recognize where you are? Has it been that long … Enoch?"

"Why do you call me that?" Ty yelled as he spun around again, only to verify his solitude.

"Ah, you do not remember the start of your cause? Your futile attempt all those years ago to cleanse the earth of the abominations you helped to create?"

"What the hell are you talking about? I've never been here be-fore!"

"How would you know?" the voice said. "You don't even know who you are. But I remember. I also know that someone very close to you is stuck in this time. Would you like me to lead you to him?"

"What? What are you talking about? Show yourself, whoever you are … now!"

"Is your memory coming back some? Are you not looking for someone in your current life?"

Ty paused as more memories trickled back into his mind. Jumbled memories from a time far away.

"You are beginning to remember … Yes, for it is true. You are not alone."

CHAPTER 57

TY WAS WRESTLING WITH the barrage of memories flooding back into his mind as the strange events unfolded in this new magical place he was in. He was on a mission, but what was it? Could he really be here to try to save the world? If the Watchers had actually returned to the time he just left, the outcome was likely to be dire. And just how was he supposed to stop them anyway?

Of course, the eerie voice from in his head just didn't seem right. Had he been hallucinating? Might that be a side effect of traveling through time?

"Again with the doubts?" The voice seemed to be reading his mind. "Follow the stream to above from where the water falls, to the edge of the oasis. It is there you will find the one you seek."

"And just who is that?" The voice seemed to come from no specific direction as Ty stood with his sword held high.

As quick as the presence had come, it was gone. Either that or the voices in his head had subsided. But the chills he got when he heard the voice made it seem so real. It was something he hoped he'd never hear again, but somehow knew otherwise.

Ty's thoughts came back to his mission. It was as though a word were on the tip of his tongue but he just couldn't think of it. At first he thought he was in a hurry to stop the Watchers, but how was he to do that? And why was he in a hurry if he didn't know what he needed to do? Then a calmness came over him. Whatever it was he came to stop wouldn't happen for years to come. He was in no hurry after all.

Ty brought his focus back to his surroundings, and what beautiful surroundings they were. The thick, lush grass was the greenest he'd ever seen, with flowers of every color sprinkled throughout. Trees of almost every variety sprang forth here and there through the beautiful carpet as far as he could see. Surrounding the valley were rolling hills that gradually turned into rugged yet enticing mountains, giving the valley an odd sense of security. The beautiful color mix had a soothing, captivating effect he couldn't define.

Follow the stream to above from where the water falls, to the edge of the oasis?

Ty scanned the area one last time. He sheathed his sword and, with the handbag in his grasp, started up the stream bank.

IT HAD TAKEN HIM a few hours to make the trek to the top of the mesa above the waterfall. This was truly the most beautiful place he'd ever seen. He stopped numerous times to listen to the birds sing their songs of thanks from the tops of the trees. He'd seen several small animals here and there, and none seemed to be frightened by his presence, just as he wasn't by theirs.

Almost all the trees he had encountered bore some kind of fruit, and all those he'd tried burst with unimaginable flavor that seemed to satisfy his soul to the core. Some of them he was familiar with and some he was not, but the fragrance of all was nearly intoxicating.

He could remember just about everything that had led to his arrival here, but he still didn't know where that was. And though he knew he was far from home, the magical ambience of this place clouded the homesick feeling that should have been overwhelming him.

To the edge of the oasis. I must be almost there.

He could see now that there was an end to this mystical place, for on the horizon was a barren landscape, nothing like the lush grounds he had been traversing.

It was then he noticed something out of place in the distance. An object foreign to the area but something he seemed to recognize.

No … Is that what I think it is?

He hurried his pace. Maybe his eyes were playing tricks on him.

It was slightly corroded and looked a little older than he remembered. And, if he had truly gotten out of the time he'd tried to leave, *that* shouldn't have been here. Yet here it was. Something that had been haunting him for the past few months.

The Nazi Bell!

TY STOOD STARING AT the old relic. It was undeniably Die Glocke, but it almost seemed as though it had been centuries since he last saw it. And which one was it? Might there even have been a third one? But most troubling of all—what was it doing here?

He ran his fingers over the corroded hieroglyphs around the bottom. Everything was exactly as he'd remembered, except older.

Why did the voice think I was looking for this?

His mission here had nothing more to do with Die Glocke— unless it could get him home.

Then he noticed something. Something that looked like a shelter. After scanning the area, he retrieved his sword from its sheath and approached the simple structure. Several ferns from a tree similar to a palm tree had been woven together to form a small hut resembling a tepee.

He eased his way to the opening to look inside. Empty, but it was apparent he wasn't alone. Could this be the dwelling of the being whose voice he'd heard earlier? Something about that thought didn't seem to make sense, but who else could it be?

Ty stepped back and closely scanned the entire area as far as he could see. Then he saw what he was looking for on a nearby ridge. The perfect lookout point. He took one last look around and started his jaunt up the hill.

It didn't take him long to hike to the ridge, but having to drop down the other side so he could make his way to the vantage point without being seen had cost most the day's remaining light. Now he would have to wait until morning to see who was inhabiting the small hut below.

THE NIGHT HAD PASSED swiftly. He was surprised by how well he'd slept while leaning against a protruding root from a large tree just on the other side of the top of the ridge. He was starting to notice the little things, like just how perfect the temperature was, which was a good thing, since his wardrobe was lacking.

The peacefulness was also subduing. He felt as though he didn't have a care in the world right now. Such a change from the past several weeks. There was an air about this valley that soothed him to his core.

He stretched from his slumber, then crept up to the top of the ridge to the spot he'd picked out from below the day before. It was becoming light enough to see any action from the shelter below. Now all he had to do was wait. Sooner or later, he'd see who—or what—was occupying it.

TWO DAYS HAD PASSED and the only life forms he'd seen come close to the little hut were animals. And they were all grass and leaf eaters—not one predator had been in the area. And even stranger, all the animals made a wide berth around the corroded relic that didn't belong here. Why would they be afraid of an inanimate object? And more puzzling, how and why did Die Glocke end up here?

Just as he was pondering that question, he saw movement out of the corner of his eye. Something was moving closer to the hut, and this time, whatever it was looked human!

CHAPTER 58

THE PRESENT: WILKS LAND REGION, ANTARCTICA

SAMYAZA WAS THE FIRST to speak. "Has the time of generations passed? Are we now to face our judgment?"

He looked out at the rest of the two hundred, and then he saw Azazyel. "Azazyel, the Most-High has freed you as well? We must repent so he will allow us back into the paradise we wrongly chose to leave."

"It is good to see you again, my leader." Azazyel knelt in front of Samyaza. "The ages have been long, but now I feel it will be our turn to reign over the humans as we did in the past."

"You would so choose to rebel against the god of the ages yet again? Do you dare risk all eternity even now?"

"You must listen to me, Samyaza." Azazyel rose to his feet. "There is another of the Most-High here, but he is not the same. It was not he who set you free but the children of men. Their weapons of war were able to unlock the earthly chains which have bound us in our prison."

"How can that be?" Samyaza looked to the heavens. "Another one of him?"

"This I know not, yet I have seen him and he knew me not. I could sense his power and it is the same as the god of the ages." Azazyel paused only for a moment before continuing. "There is also another like us here. His motives do not match ours, nor do his means of existence."

"How do you know this?"

"I have encountered him. For I tried to stop the one who tried to kill you, my master, when we first came into this plane of existence on the top of Mount Hermon long ago." Azazyel bowed again to Samyaza. "The one like us knew why I was there and caught me off guard. I was unable to stop the young one from going back to an earlier time. I am sorry to have failed you, master."

"It's no matter, my loyal servant." Samyaza put his hand on Azazyel's shoulder. "His attempt was in vain, as you did save me all those ages ago."

"Yes, but I fear he has more to his plan than we can see."

"Let us worry about him later. Tell me about the almighty one that is here now."

"This one's very being is a new existence to any realm and knows not how anything works here but is slowly learning." He raised his gaze to meet Samyaza's. "If we can form an alliance with this one, we would be unstoppable. The earth would be ours for the taking for all eternity."

"Azazyel, have you not learned anything?" Samyaza questioned him.

"If we can earn the trust of the one who is the Creator's equal, we will be unstoppable!" Azazyel clenched his fists. "The Creator will dare not take on one of the same as him."

"And how do you propose we gain his trust? What is it we can offer to one that can have it all?"

"He does not know he can have it all yet. As for what can we offer, I have already found the perfect gift, my Lord."

Azazyel waved his arms and vanished. A split second later he returned. Only he wasn't alone. In his arms was a beautiful brunette woman in a deep sleep. The woman was Erica.

"We must take our offering to him. I can sense he has returned to the great structure on the banks of the Nile." Azazyel looked at the rest of the Watchers, then back at Samyaza. "I ask you this, my Lord, would you rather repent or have revenge?"

CHAPTER 59

THE LOOK ON THE general's face after he hung up the phone was grim. Dan and Selena had spent the entire afternoon showing him all the evidence they had uncovered in the past few days to support their theory, but it wasn't until he received the new intel about another energy being on the Giza Plateau that he had a change of heart about their claims. Even worse, a satellite had spotted several more creatures in Antarctica shortly after the bombers left.

"I can't believe anything could have survived the blast we hit that thing with down there." The general's face was stone cold as he stared blankly into space. Then he came back to life and picked up the receiver and began to dial. "I'll hit them again with more this time. I'll use the whole goddamn Air Force if I have to!"

"No, Max." Dan reached out and hung up the phone. "Conventional weapons will be ineffective on these things."

"We've already proved that," Selena said.

The general glared at Dan. "We haven't dropped a big one on it yet."

"That still will most likely do nothing except cause radioactive fallout that will spew into the atmosphere and spread across the planet. Damn it, Max, haven't you heard a word we've said?"

"Well, what the hell do you want me to do? Nothing?"

Dan looked at Selena, then back at the general. "What about HAARP?"

"What do you know about that?" the general demanded.

"I know enough to know there have been several earthquakes around the planet linked to it," Dan said.

"HAARP's classified information, Dan. I want to know how the hell you know anything about it."

Dan sprang from his chair. "For Christ's sake, Max! Classified or not, we need to try something. And I'll bet my bottom dollar that the rest of these bastards are going to be showing up in Egypt real soon, too. This is twice they've been spotted there. There's something special about that place to these things for some reason. We need to act now and be ready!"

The general stared at him. "All right, Dan, just what do you think HAARP is anyway?"

Dan shook his head and took a breath. Then he told the general everything he had heard about the secret project in the frigid arctic.

HAARP stood for High-frequency Active Aural Research Program. In the 1980s, an array of antennae for a high-power radio frequency transmitter was installed at a secluded base in Gakano, Alaska. The official response from the government when asked about its purpose was, that it was no more than a research facility. Although the heavily guarded base under the control of the U.S. military led to numerous conspiracy theories that they were doing much more than studying the ionosphere.

The $290 million facility could theoretically manipulate the weather just by heating up a portion of the ionosphere, causing the jet stream to move. Even more disturbing, raising the ionosphere and letting it fall again could cause vibrations to enter the earth that might trigger an earthquake.

In 2010, there was a devastating earthquake in Haiti, and the Venezuelan dictator Hugo Chavez was certain it was caused by a HAARP machine. Could that really have been possible? Had mankind finally figured out how to control the weather? If so, the practical purposes for the military were obvious, and that would answer the question of why the Navy and the Air Force were in charge of HAARP.

To confirm the physics behind HAARP, Dan also told the general that Nikola Tesla had built a small mechanical vibration machine. During an experiment, it almost brought down a steel building he was living in on Wall Street just by hitting the resonant frequency of the steel structure.

The general stared at Dan for several seconds before he spoke. "If there really are these … spiritual beings as you say, what makes you think HAARP could have any effect on them?"

"It's all about vibration and frequency," Dan said. "That's all anything is."

"Jesus Christ, Dan, this isn't Woodstock! We're not going to be able to stop these things with good vibrations!"

"Listen to me for a minute! It's not like that at all! Everything in existence vibrates at a certain frequency. The ceiling in here, your desk over there, even the clothes you're wearing. On a molecular level, they're all vibrating at their own specific frequency."

"So what? What's that got to do with anything?"

"You've seen the commercial where the singer hits and holds a high note, which causes the glass to shatter?" Dan asked.

"What the hell are you talking about?"

"Just be patient, I'm getting to it. It's all about the resonant frequency of the glass. Once the singer hits that exact frequency and holds it long enough, the glass molecules vibrate so much it shatters."

"It's the same thing as with the Hutchinson effect," Selena said. "I read about John Hutchinson several years ago. He basically proved that if the wave length of an external frequency matches that of the distance in separation of the atoms in a material—such as the glass—then the material can be manipulated by a change in the frequency thereafter."

"Talk English, would ya?" the general snapped.

"It's just that if the frequency is raised from there, it'll create a diamagnetic force that can cause levitation of the object. But if the frequency is lowered, the object will start to act like a liquid and can even be disintegrated."

"And you think HAARP can do that to these creatures?"

Dan nodded. "Well, these spiritual beings are made up of something, and that something has a frequency—"

"And once we find out what that is," Selena said, "we can dissolve the sons of bitches!"

Dan looked at the general. "What have we got to lose?"

CHAPTER 60

THE DISTANT PAST

TY HAD STUDIED THE figure at the hut for hours. It had been obvious he was just doing things to survive, and with all the food-bearing plants in the area, that was an easy task. There was something strangely familiar about the human. Whoever it was had a large beard and appeared to be very muscular. Something else odd—the clothes he had on didn't seem to match the time he was in. Which was … when exactly? Ty was still unsure about that, but he could feel he was in the past.

In any case, he didn't get a sense of danger about the man he'd been watching. Not that he felt danger the way he once would have, especially having the razor-sharp sword tucked safely away in its sheath. But now it was time he made contact.

It had taken roughly an hour for Ty to make his way around to approach from the back side of the Bell and the little shelter. He was only a few hundred feet away now, and whoever was here would still have to be inside the hut.

Ty eased closer and quietly slid the long sword out of its sheath.

Although he didn't feel any danger, he wasn't about to take any chances. The faceless voice he'd heard in his head when he arrived in this magical place had sent chills up his spine and left a sense of foreboding throughout his being.

A rustling noise came from the little hut just as he was almost there. With his sword raised and cocked, he edged around the front to look inside. Ty's face went white as his arms slumped to his side and the sword fell to the ground.

"Dad?!"

The occupant stopped what he was doing and snapped his head up. "Ty?!"

Ty stood in disbelief. There was no doubt it was his father—Grant—but he, too, had changed in his appearance. Like Ty, he was more muscular and had a thick beard covering his face. He was wearing—what was left of it—the same attire he'd donned before they sneaked into Himmler's lair back in Argentina. How was this possible? Why would the Bell transport him here?

The split second of shock seemed like minutes, and then Grant shot out of the hut and embraced his son.

"Ty! My God! Is it really you? God, it's good to see you!"

"Dad, I can't believe it's you!"

Grant stepped back to look over his son. "Damn, you look good! I thought I'd never see you again. Where have you been? I looked and looked for you. I scoured this entire place, but there was no sign of you anywhere."

"I just got here. How long have you been here?"

"Just a few days, I think. It took a while before I could remember anything. I'm still a little foggy with things, but I remembered you right away." Grant looked down at Ty's sword lying on the ground. "Where the heck did you get that thing?"

Ty was still in mild state of shock, and it took him a few seconds before he shifted his gaze to the ground. "Oh, yeah." He reached down and picked up the sword. "So much has happened since I last saw you that I don't know where to begin. What do you remember about how you got here?"

"I remember going back to that crazy Nazi's little castle when they caught us. Then right after he showed us his little experiment, everything went black."

"Yeah, that's what I remember, too. We found out later the place blew up. I guess we were just both lucky."

"Have a seat, Ty." Grant motioned him to a small rock outcropping to sit on. "Please fill me in on what I've missed."

THEY SAT THERE UNTIL long after the sun had gone down. Strange, even though the sun had dropped below the horizon, it was still very luminous out. Grant shook his head numerous times as Ty told him of the preceding events. It seemed hard for him to swallow, but Ty could tell his father knew it was true.

"And I thought I'd heard it all at the Agency," Grant said as he stared off into space. "But Butch screwed you over huh?"

Ty nodded. "It sure seems like it."

Grant had a puzzled look on his face. "He'll do damn near anything for the right price, but he'd never wrong me."

"He thought you were dead. We all did. I still don't understand why you ended up here. By the way, have you figured out where we are?"

"No idea. Pretty nice place, though. Plenty to eat, perfect temp. A little lonely, though … till now."

Ty smiled back at his father. "Yeah. At least something's working out well."

Grant's smile left his face. "And your mother? Have you seen her?"

"No. Ethan assured me she was fine but thought it best to not tell anyone of my return until we accomplished what we needed to do."

"Yeah, I suppose he was right. I do miss her … I miss her a lot." Grant forced a smile, then turned his attention to the Bell. "So you say that thing is a time machine, huh?"

"Oh yeah. Works quite well, too. I don't think Himmler had any idea of its full potential, though."

Grant raised his eyebrows. "So is there any way we can use it to get back home?"

Ty laughed and shook his head. "Not unless there's a large current bush around here. I'm not sure we'd want to go back now anyway. I think it's too late. The fallen angels are back, and I blew my chance to stop them."

"You said Himmler's creation might actually be … a clone of God himself?"

"That's what Ethan said. Or something real similar."

Grant's eyes lit up. "Well, if that's the case, there's our chance right there."

"What do you mean?"

"I mean, if it really is a 'piece' of God, then it has to be good. And if it's good, it can do the same thing to the Watchers as God did to them before the flood."

"You mean bury them again?"

"Sure, why not?"

"Yeah, that would be nice, but will it?" Ty rubbed his forehead. "From the sound of it, this 'God' is having a hard time figuring out what it is. It may not even give a crap about what the Watchers are doing."

Grant sat motionless as he appeared to rack his brain for a solution. Then his eyes grew wide as he raised his head and looked at the Bell. "That thing's made of copper, right?"

"Yeah, why?"

"I think I have an idea."

"I'm all ears."

CHAPTER 61

THE TWO MEN HAD been busy for three days straight. Although moving the Bell closer to the stream was a struggle—despite their more muscular new stature—it wasn't the most taxing part of their little venture. There was a natural low spot close to the stream to rest the Bell in, so they didn't have to manually carve out a spot, but mining and transporting the vital mineral needed to make Grant's plan work was by no means an easy chore.

While Grant had been looking for Ty in the preceding days, not only had he found an endless supply of food growing in the area, but there was also an abundance of just about any mineral known to man, including zinc. And it was the zinc that was critical in giving their plan even half a chance.

Ty dropped the last chunk of the key ingredient onto the pile on the clay-lined low spot a few feet from the Bell.

"Now, can we find something a little lighter to pack around?" he said as he wiped the sweat from his brow.

"I thought you'd never ask." Grant smiled. "Follow me."

They didn't have to walk far before they came to a stop. "There you are, my son, the biggest lemon grove I've ever seen!"

Ty's jaw dropped when he saw the brilliant yellow sight. The beautiful oasis had it all. And the lemons dangling from the trees were big, juicy and ready to be picked.

"What a paradise!" Ty said as looked from tree to tree. "I've never seen anything like it. These are the healthiest-looking lemons I've ever seen! Everything here is." He turned to his dad. "Where the hell are we?"

Grant shook his head. "I don't know, son, but I can think of worse places to be stuck."

"Yeah, me too. Well, let's get to picking."

IT HAD TAKEN SEVERAL trips back and forth with as many lemons as they could stuff in their makeshift bags made from palm boughs. All in all, there were several hundred plump lemons filling the space between the pile of zinc and the Bell itself. Now there was one task left to do.

Father and son reminisced about earlier, simple times as they steadily squashed the lemons in the pit with their feet as well as they could. To think Ty's curiosity about the inexplicable stone structures across the planet and the short verse of Genesis 6:4 would lead to this was mind-blowing.

All the legends and folklore he had uncovered appeared to be true now. Witnessing the fallen angels making their grand entrance on the planet was the most spectacular thing he'd ever seen. If only the consequences of their actions weren't so dire, maybe he could have enjoyed the experience.

"Looks like we got damn near all of them, son. Time to see if this is going to work."

"Yeah, the moment of truth. Thank God Himmler had those extra canisters of red mercury in the side compartment of this Bell. There were none stored in the second Bell. Ethan had to have some flown in. It's amazing these survived the trip here."

"Even one of your magical stones was in there. How the Nazis were able to come up with this idea to begin with is beyond me. You said they got the idea from those ancient Hindu texts?"

"According to the professor," Ty said. "They were known as the Vimana. Ancient flying machines powered by a mercury vortex engine of some kind. Seems to me that line of folklore must have actually happened as well." He turned his attention back to the project. "Well, let's let the water in and give it a try. Doubt we'll have enough power to send us anywhere, but hopefully enough for what we need."

Grant kicked the dirt loose that was keeping the stream from entering the shallow pit. A slow controlled flow of water entered and gradually filled the low spot, mixing with the lemon juice and covering the pile of zinc and the bottom of the Bell.

They walked along the bank and stood as close to the Bell as they could without getting in the water. The only sound they could hear was the sloshing of the water in the pit. It wasn't working.

"Nothing? How can there be nothing? The professor said just cutting through the earth's magnetic lines of force in the back of an airplane generated enough electricity to make the Bell disappear into the future twenty years. We should be getting at least something."

"We need more electrons to flow," Grant said. "Let's get more of that zinc in the pile before the water leaks out."

"I was afraid you were going to say that."

WITHIN AN HOUR, TY and Grant had successfully mined enough of the precious element to completely fill the side of the pond opposite the Bell. There was no more room for more zinc in the pond and still be covered with the slurry of lemon water. If this didn't work, they were going to have to start all over by making a larger pit to hold even more zinc.

As Ty stood back to catch his breath, he heard something. There was a soft buzzing coming from the direction of the Bell. Grant obviously heard it, too, as he trained his sights on Die Glocke in silence.

"Look!" Ty pointed to the bag that housed the stone lying on the ground next to the Bell. "It's glowing a little!"

A greenish light was emitted from the open end of the bag and ever so slightly pulsed in time with the faint buzzing of the Bell. Now was their chance.

They rushed over and Grant picked up the bag and retrieved the stone from within.

"I know this was my idea, but it just seems so crazy," he said as he looked over the glowing stone.

"Believe me, I know, Dad. I thought the same thing. Remember, like you said, 'thoughts are things' and anything can travel through time if the frequency of what is traveling is matched up with the frequency of the time you want it to go to, even a thought. You'll have to transmit your thoughts to Butch the same as if you were talking to him and in the exact time frame I told you about. There's no way this little amount of current will send either of us anywhere, but a thought? It should be enough to easily send a thought through time."

Facing the Bell, Grant held up the faintly glowing stone in front of his head and closed his eyes. "All right then, here goes nothing."

CHAPTER 62

MILES GEHRING HAD BEEN based at the Vandenberg site in California for slightly more than fifteen years. In that time, he had never been asked to rush a project through as fast as he had now. Had he not been in the docking room before the scheduled launch, he never would have seen the forty-foot polished gold-plated mirror being folded and placed in the large capsule attached to the satellite.

He had seen several different forms of satellites, which all had their own unique traits, but never anything like this. It then became obvious why the rocket needed for this special launch was one of the most powerful he had ever worked with. The capsule containing the folded gold mirror was huge.

He picked up the landline from his desk and hit the speed dial. "Sir, everything's ready." He cradled the receiver while tapping a pen on his desk. "Okay, as soon as the sun goes down."

GIZA PLATEAU, EGYPT

ONCE THE WATER HAD been shut off, it didn't take long for the pyramid's harmonic state to cease. Hanson stayed hidden from view in the shadows of the Sphinx. Although the Great Pyramid stood silent for the time being, it still glistened from top to bottom as though it were alive. According to legend, the brilliant glow the Great Pyramid emitted when it was first finished in antiquity would have made it visible from the moon. Judging from what he saw now, that was not an exaggeration. The great structure pulsed with an immense energy similar to that of a supernova yet somehow was very pleasurable to gaze upon.

Ashworth's plan had been in the works for several years. For him to disappear without the slightest acknowledgment to his right-hand man just didn't make sense. Could the transformation have erased his memory somehow?

Just then his cell came to life. "Yeah ... It looks like it. Everything went as planned ... That's the strange thing, though. The transformation took—I saw the thing after the pyramid had been on for only a few minutes—but then it just disappeared ... I don't know how anything could have gone wrong. Maybe he had a change of heart with his newfound power ... Okay, I'll let you know."

He slid his phone back into his pocket without taking his eyes off the pyramid.

JOHN GROGAN HAD BEEN based in Cairo ever since the first Gulf War. He had grown accustomed to life on the Nile, with the great monuments always watching over. Being able to witness the restoration of the ancient wonder had been an amazing experience. Then word of what had really happened got out. Now it was as if life had been taken straight out of a science fiction movie. And judging by his current mission, that wasn't going to change anytime soon.

He had received orders to get into place on the plateau for this special operation shortly after reports that an energy being had been seen near the pyramids. With a sealed transport case next to him and his spotting scope nestled to his eye, he was able to see everything that was unfolding on the Giza Plateau. His office had been aware that Benton Ashworth was behind the restoration project, but that was the extent of what they knew. Ashworth had always kept a low profile, but every once in a while his name would come up in connection with high-profile off-the-grid projects. Nothing illegal, but some were quite bizarre.

He glassed the area in the distance for activity. Then the night sky began to light up. At first it was just as though a thunderstorm might be building off in the distance, but then it became more intense.

Looks like it's showtime.

A blue glow began to build at the base of the Great Pyramid. It became more and more intense until he had to squint to keep the spotting scope trained on the area.

Then he saw it. The creature that had been spotted across the globe at various ancient sites. His jaw grew weak as the thing became more defined. It was amazing! Pulsating with energy yet having a vague resemblance to a large human body with arms and legs. But there was no mistaking this for any living thing on the planet he'd ever seen. Its eyes glowed a brilliant yellow as it stood there and began to scan the area.

What's it looking for?

Then the night sky lit up again. He took his eye from the scope to get a bigger view and saw several other bluish creatures materialize between the pyramid and the Sphinx. In just seconds, the numbers increased until there were too many to count.

Somehow these looked slightly different from the first. They were noticeably smaller yet still larger than any normal human. They didn't seem to emit quite as vivid a glow either, but there was no doubt they were an energy being of some kind.

The vibration of Grogan's phone broke his trance.

"Yeah … All set. Just waiting for the word now … If I weren't looking at this with my own two eyes, I wouldn't believe it … Hang on. Let me check."

Grogan took a look through his spotting scope again and put the phone back to his ear. "They're within a three hundred-foot radius now … Yeah, close, but not quite close enough yet. I'll keep watch and give the signal as soon as they are … Okay."

He slid his phone back into his shirt pocket and opened the sealed transport case lying next to him. Inside was an expensive-looking device with "JDAM Laser Guidance" written on the side.

Grogan attached the little laser in the holder on the spotting scope, and it snapped into place as though it had been waiting for this opportunity.

After taking a heavy breath, he put the contraption back to his eye and waited. "All right, you guys—or whatever the hell you are—let's bunch up a little closer now."

CHAPTER 63

THE DISTANT PAST

ALL AT ONCE, THE fog lifted from the recesses of Ty's mind and another memory came rushing back. He knew where he was and what he was here for: plan B. There was no way of knowing if his dad's message got through to Butch or if he honored it if it had, but Ty had to find what he'd come for and complete his mission. One that would alter everything to come—hopefully for the better.

He turned to his father as his head cleared. "I remember now. Why I'm here. I remember."

His dad squinted at him. "Must be big. I don't think I've ever seen that look before."

"Yeah." Ty nodded. "Plan B. The last resort."

"Can you fill me in? Or maybe I don't want to know."

Ty took a deep breath. "Ethan thought that if mankind had never strayed from God's original commandment, maybe he wouldn't have allowed the fallen angels to come to the planet and further corrupt all humanity."

"You mean ... stop the first sin from ever happening?"

"Yeah. It's just a theory, but I think it's worth a try."

Grant stood silent for a moment while he looked their surroundings over. "I'll be damned. So that's where we are."

Before Ty could comment, another thought surfaced. "Hey, Dad, have you heard any voices here? I mean a voice without a physical body, if that makes any sense."

His dad put his hand to his chin and shook his head. "No. Yours was the first one I've heard. And I'm selfishly thankful for that. Why? I'm assuming you did?"

"Yeah. I forgot all about it when I saw you, but I remember now. Right after I got here. I thought I may have been hearing things from the effects of the time travel, but I don't think so. Especially since the voice told me I'd find you here ... or someone I was looking for, which was obviously you."

His dad was straight-faced now. "Did it say anything else?"

"It called me something, a name. A name that didn't make any sense."

"Yeah? What?"

"It called me Enoch."

"Enoch? Like from the Bible, Enoch?"

"Not sure, but that's the only one I know. Another strange thing. Whoever, or whatever, the voice was, it seemed to be able to read my thoughts."

His dad narrowed his eyes and took a deep breath. "Son, there's something you should know. When you asked me to read the book of Noah from the Dead Sea Scrolls, of course I did. But the description of Noah as a baby was nothing new to your mother and I."

"What do you mean?"

"There was always something special about you. We noticed it right from the start. All these dreams you've been having, your exceptional athletic abilities—nothing about you has been a surprise to us."

"What's any of this got to do with the book of Noah?"

"Son, when you were born, everything, and I mean everything about you matched the description of Noah as a child. Noah must have acquired his mystical traits from his great-grandfather Enoch. We knew you were special, just not how special, I guess."

THE TWO WERE RATHER quiet as they trekked deeper into the oasis. Less and less had surprised Ty since this adventure had begun only a few months ago. But what his father told him didn't really sit well. For his whole life he was happy to believe all the traditional beliefs that went with being a Christian, and those didn't include reincarnation. Might he have lived in another life long ago?

Of course, this would explain the feelings of déjà vu he experienced when he was at the Great Pyramid, as well as all the wild dreams he was having lately. Even Erica's hypnotherapy regression now made sense. But why would the voice call him Enoch? He vaguely remembered something about the Sons of Jared, but what was it? Just a few months ago he was a normal college student about to graduate and get on with life. That seemed like several lifetimes ago now.

At least he wasn't alone in trying to digest all the unbelievable events. After his father told him of his special features as an infant, Ty finished telling him about the mission he was on. His dad still seemed far away as he processed what Ty had told him.

"Just when I thought things couldn't become any crazier," his dad said while shaking his head.

"Yeah, tell me about it. What happened to the days when we'd kick back on the couch and watch a sci-fi movie instead of actually living in one?"

His dad laughed. "I wish I knew, son. I wish I knew."

TY AND GRANT HAD MADE their way into the heart of the oasis when Ty heard the voice again.

"Enoch!"

They spun around to see where the voice had come from, only to find this time that it wasn't just a voice—there was an earthly entity with it as well. One that prompted both him and his father to take a step back. The voice was coming from an ugly four-legged serpent of some kind. One that slightly resembled a large Komodo dragon but with the expressive face of an intelligent being. It was the creature from Ty's dreams.

"What in God's name is that?!" Ty stood stunned by the sight.

"Why so surprised? How could you have forgotten the old world and the way it used to be? And that of your previous existence? Enoch! One of the two original Sons of Jared? Would you rather I call you Hermes? Or maybe Thoth?"

"What the hell are you and what are you talking about?"

"They're all one and the same. You! Nothing of this world should surprise you. I am sure you will remember your past soon. Even your earthly father knows it to be true. It was you, Enoch, who tried in vain to help return the Watchers to their heavenly bodies which they chose to forgo with their decision to lie with the daughters of men. You could have done away with them, but you chose to help them when they came to you to ask God's forgiveness for their actions."

"You lie, serpent!"

"Do I? Is this not why you must do what you should have done ages ago to save God's chosen creation? If the Sons of Jared only knew their founding father was a traitor to them. Have you not learned your lesson even yet?"

"What? You're full of crap, serpent! You don't know what you're talking about!"

"The machine you built to transform them back into their spiritual bodies was a commendable undertaking, but going against the Creator's decision should have brought on the death of you along with the fallen ones." The serpent hissed.

Ty stepped closer to it. "Enoch was favored by the Creator! Why do you think he did not experience death but was transformed straight into the spirit world? He was in God's favor!"

"Is that what you think?" The serpent laughed. "He didn't transform you. It was you! You had to test your pile of rocks before you would subject anyone else to undue harm. Poor Enoch, the man with cares and concerns. Have you not learned to let that human emotion go and be what you always could have been?

"Why do you think Noah, Enoch's great-grandson, was chosen for his task to build the ark and save God's creations while the earth was cleansed from the abominations? The ungodly unions of the fallen ones and the humans. The Nephilim!" The serpent narrowed his eyes as his forked tongue slithered out. "It was to clean up the mess you made when you tried to save the fallen ones! When Noah's father saw his son's eyes light up the room when he was a child, he suspected infidelity by his wife with one of the Watchers. But that was not the case. It was because of your altered DNA, Enoch! You had to be the first to try the Great Pyramid and see if it could do what you intended! Even after you returned to human form, you knew you were never the same. Your decision to father children afterward only passed on the Watcher gene even more. The very bloodline your wretched little group, the Sons of Jared"—the serpent spit in the dirt—"so pitifully tried to extinguish thereafter!"

Ty was speechless. Could this be true? Could he really have had an earlier incarnation as Enoch, the first Son of Jared? It would explain his familiarity with the Great Pyramid when he first laid eyes on it only a short while ago. He had been infatuated with the lost knowledge of the ancients, the lost continent of Atlantis, even with the giants of lore. Might this all be an extension of his ambitions from a previous incarnation?

He had to shake off what the serpent was telling him. Even if it was true, he had a mission to do now. A mission that could possibly fix all of mankind's misguided undoings of the future.

"Say what you will, serpent, but stay out of my way or you'll be sentenced to an early life of crawling on your belly by the edge of my sword!"

He pulled the razor-sharp sword from its sheath and held it inches from the serpent's throat. The ugly creature reared up on its hind legs and hissed.

Ty moved his sword even closer. "If you think I jest, go ahead and try me!"

The serpent narrowed his eyes and slinked back. "Ah, so you truly have come to fix your blunder from the past. Do you really think there is anything you can do now to undo what is already written?"

CHAPTER 64

GROGAN HAD BEEN WATCHING the fantastic scene on the Giza Plateau from behind a huge granite block for several minutes now. It was obvious the large group of beings were trying to appease the superior one. All had bowed down submissively to it, but all the while, the larger one seemed to take no notice. It acted more like a child who was taking in its new surroundings and just enjoying the moment.

Then Grogan saw something else. Another life form within the multitude. A human, a human woman.

He zoomed in on the action. *What are you sons of bitches doing with her?*

They had a woman, all right. It looked like they were offering her to the creature as some kind of present.

Grogan pulled out his phone and made a call. "Looks like they have a human hostage. What should we do about that? ... Okay, you're the boss ... Almost. Maybe another ten feet or so is all ... You'll be the first to know."

He slid his phone into his pocket and put the scope back to his eye.

AZAZYEL LAID ERICA AT the feet of the creature and backed away. "This is our gift to you, almighty one."

He was hopeful that his offering of the beautiful woman would entice the creator's doppelganger enough to gain its confidence. If it had the same spiritual qualities as the fallen angels, somewhere in the fiber of its being would hopefully be at least one grain of lust.

The beautiful human women who inhabited the planet centuries ago were enticing enough for all of Samyaza's followers to cut their ties with the Creator in exchange for experiencing humanly pleasures. Surely there was a chance this creature could also be tempted.

The creature looked at Erica in her deep sleep only for a moment before scanning the entire two hundred.

What does it seek? Azazyel looked from Erica to the creature.

"Why does it not take note of our gift?" Samyaza turned to Azazyel. "There is something strange about this one."

"There is indeed, but we must give it time, my Lord, for once we have gained his trust, we will be unstoppable in this realm. With him on our side, surely the Creator will have to bow down to us."

THE SPIRITUAL REALM

BUTCH HAD PROJECTED HIMSELF into the plane of existence outside the physical world. Taking in all the vibrations from the past, present, and future was a glorious experience. He was growing accustomed to his new form. The power he felt was like nothing he could have imagined. It seemed like he was becoming more in tune with his environment by the minute, so much so that he could hear the plants growing while he was in the physical plane. Even the electrons in the atoms made a distinct sound as they rotated about the nucleus. The sense of power was exhilarating. He still wasn't sure how he got the thought to intercept the creature in Poland, but he was sure Grant had somehow sent him a call for help when he had been in Mexico with Ty and the girl. Maybe both were connected somehow. At least he knew his longtime confidant was still alive. But where was he?

There was something else about his encounter in Poland. Something he didn't like about the equal he'd distracted was still needling him to his core. He'd sensed something from within the creature's soul. The being had aspirations much larger than those of anyone—or anything—he'd ever come across in all his years in the espionage world. He'd encountered several powerful sociopaths who had aspirations to overthrow their respective governments, but this thing had bigger plans, much bigger. He could feel it.

That's when he felt something else. An associate of some kind was in distress. The increased awareness of his surroundings was growing by the minute. He could feel that the one in distress wasn't one of importance to him, but she was to Grant's son. And because of that, he chose to intervene. It was time to go back to the physical world. Back to the same location of his magical transformation.

GIZA PLATEAU, EGYPT

GROGAN WAS WATCHING THROUGH the spotting scope as the woman lay motionless at the feet of the impressive energy being when his phone beeped.

"Yeah? … They haven't gotten any closer yet … The main bunch? … Let me look." He zoomed in on the group of two hundred. "Yeah, the big bunch is within the zone. Is that good enough? Don't you want them all? ... Okay, I understand. Is the satellite in place? ... Good enough then. It's a go."

He slid his phone back into his pocket and flipped the guarded switch on the laser attached to the bottom of the scope. He put the contraption back to his eye and carefully placed his finger on the exposed switch.

HANSON HAD BEEN WATCHING the event unfold in front of the Great Pyramid for several hours now. It had been obvious the two hundred were trying to get into the good graces of the larger one. So far their attempt with the woman seemed to have fallen short.

Where's Ashworth?

Hanson took his eyes from the site to scan the area in the background. Then something caught his attention out of the corner of his eye. A red light of some kind.

What the ...

He put his binoculars to his eyes. Off in the distance behind a large chunk of granite was someone pointing a device in the direction of the pyramid, emitting a red laser.

What are you up to?

He turned back to the gathering of the heavenly beings and glassed the area. There it was, a red dot in the middle of the two hundred.

He slowly lowered his binoculars with a blank stare, then turned his gaze to the sky. High overhead was something out of place. It almost looked like a bright star in the blue sky, but if it was a star, why could he see it so clearly during the day?

Just as quickly as he had seen the strange light in the sky, he opened a case and retrieved a long-barrel rifle with a powerful sniper scope attached. Not wasting any time, he ratcheted the bolt and took careful aim. Whatever this stranger was planning, Hanson wasn't going to let it happen on his watch.

GROGAN TOOK A DEEP breath and held the crosshairs on his target. The lone being had never gotten close enough to the others, so it was his lucky day, but the others? Their number was up. Hopefully, the brains on the other end at HAARP knew what they were doing.

He only needed to hold on his target for a couple more seconds and it would all be over. The beam transmitted from the array of microwave antennae in Alaska would bounce off the special satellite that was overhead now and—theoretically—lock on to the creatures and match their resonant frequency. Then their atomic structure could be manipulated just by changing the frequency, or so they hoped.

Just a little longer, you damn freaks. Just a little longer.

Right at that moment, he felt a sharp pain in his lower left thigh.

What the …

He flinched, which caused the laser to drift from its original mark to a spot right in front of the largest of the spiritual creatures—just in time for the sonic-energy beam to hit its new target.

CHAPTER 65

TY HELD HIS RAZOR-sharp sword just inches from the serpent's neck. The creature didn't exactly seem fearful, but it had frozen in place.

"So, you now have a backbone in this body?" the serpent hissed as it backed away from the drawn weapon. "You were so eager to help the fallen ones in your first life."

Ty gritted his teeth. "If I were you, I wouldn't be concerned with that now. Just stay the hell out of my way or I'll spill your guts on the ground here and now!"

"Are you prepared for the aftermath of what you intend to do? Such an undertaking will have everlasting consequences that may not be what you think."

"Oh, there will be long-lasting ramifications. Of that I can assure you. If I were you, I'd be worried about what's in store for your sorry ass." Ty stepped closer with his sword trained on the serpent's throat. "Now stay out of my way or I'll have no choice but to send you back to the dust from where you came."

Ty held his ground and watched the serpent slowly back away from his blade and disappear into the brush. He sheathed his sword and turned to his father.

"You ready?"

Grant looked at Ty, then into the brush where the serpent had disappeared. "Yeah, let's do it. I have a feeling we haven't seen the last of whatever the hell that was, though."

"I agree, but I'll deal with him if we do. Now, let's get going before something else tries to stop us."

GIZA PLATEAU, EGYPT

BUTCH APPEARED JUST IN time to see the sonic-energy beam trap Himmler's creation and start to pull it into the air. At first, the creature looked to be stunned slightly, and for a few seconds, it appeared to be just taking in the experience while it looked around. Then it seemed to become uncomfortable.

He turned to the sky and saw the energy reflecting off the satellite high above, acting like a tractor beam on its target below. Being at a safe distance, he had to see how this was going to play out. Then he saw something else. The creature wasn't alone. A woman was suspended next to the mysterious being—Erica.

Raising his arms, Butch was going to send a plasma blast to try to knock Erica out of the force that held her and the creature in place, but he stopped.

No, that might hurt the girl.

Off to the side, he saw Azazyel raising his arms as though he had the same idea.

You son of a bitch. You don't give a crap about the girl.

Butch threw a plasma burst at Azazyel, which knocked him off his feet and into the side of the pyramid. Several of the newly installed white casing stones came crashing down, with a few flying through the air and almost hitting Erica.

Butch quickly disappeared and rematerialized closer to Himmler's creation and Erica. Azazyel picked himself up just in time to be hit by another blast. This time it was from an angle that wouldn't send any debris toward the one Butch was trying to protect.

Again, Azazyel was blown back, but this time Samyaza turned to see where the blast had come from and sent one of his own back at Butch. He saw the burst of energy from the corner of his eye and slid to the side enough to avoid it, but just as he did, Azazyel got to his feet and sent another blast, which was a direct hit to Butch's chest.

I can't take them all on, but I gotta get the girl out of that beam. And the other—maybe I can convince it to give me a hand if I help it.

Butch picked himself up just as another blast was heading his way. He looked to the sky, then shot up. In the blink of an eye, he arrived at the satellite that was reflecting the sonic-energy waves.

With only a moment to admire the orbiting sheet of gold, he saw a barrage of blue streamers heading right at him. It was the entire two hundred fallen ones, and they were only moments away.

Shit! All you bastards gotta come?

He only had one chance and he had to be quick. Staying out of the beam, he quickly maneuvered around to the back of the satellite and grabbed it. Then it was just a matter of moving it slightly and taking aim at the incoming targets. Piece of cake.

"You want some of this? Then come and get it, you sons o' bitches!"

It was too easy. All of the two hundred were coming at him in a nice tight little group. He took aim with the beam and it was a direct hit. It was as though their life force had been sucked dry. They were frozen in place, and life for them was about to get a whole lot worse.

GIZA PLATEAU, EGYPT

GROGAN HAD ALMOST FORGOTTEN the pain in his leg. The show he had been watching was unlike anything he'd ever seen before. He had positioned himself farther behind the big rock, which must have been enough, since there were no more pieces of fast-moving lead coming his way.

Who and why would somebody be shooting at me?

It just didn't make any sense, but the scene at the base of the Great Pyramid sure took his mind off that for a bit.

Although his aim had been knocked away from the group of two hundred magical beings when the bullet hit him in his leg, he decided to keep it on the lone bigger one because that's where the laser was now aimed. He couldn't believe it was actually working. The creature had been slowly lifted off the ground, and it became obvious it was trapped. Now he just had to hold his aim long enough until it disintegrated.

Then from out of nowhere, a blue blast of energy knocked one from the big group into the pyramid. Pieces of pyramid flew through the air when the creature hit the structure. It had just pulled itself to its feet when another blast knocked it away.

Now he could see where the blasts were coming from. Next to the big creature that was stuck in the beam was another that seemed to match the smaller ones in the multitude. Then one of the others from the multitude returned fire. The newcomer was able to sidestep, only to be hit by a blast sent from the one he had knocked into the side of the pyramid. The newcomer seemed to analyze the situation, then shot straight into the sky, only to have the entire bunch takeoff in pursuit.

The creatures had only been out of sight for a few moments when the immobilizing beam suddenly moved away from the larger creature and the girl. They both fell to the ground as the force that had been levitating them vanished.

What ... what happened? Is this thing working?

Grogan took the scope from his eye and looked it over closely. *This doesn't make any sense.*

He put it back to his eye. He could see the laser on the target but still no beam from above. He reached for his phone.

"It's me. Not sure what happened, but it no longer seems to be effective ... Doesn't seem to be. The bigger one is blasting everything in sight, and it doesn't seem to matter if I paint him or not now ... What? How do you propose to do that? ... I understand. Consider it done, General."

He hung up and dialed, never taking his eyes off the action.

"It's not working. Orders are to shut it off ... It looked like it was going to work at first, but now... nothing ... Not sure why. You know the general better than I do, but I wouldn't wait on it."

He stowed his phone back in his pocket and went back to watching the show. The creature that had appeared to be so docile was now anything but. It was like a supernova went off as the creature exploded in fury. Energy beams shot from its eyes, which turned the sand into shards of glass everywhere it looked. Similar to the others that had just fled to the sky, it emitted blue plasma energy waves in all directions, knocking even more casing stones from the side of the pyramid. Another blast just missed the Sphinx but blew the reconstructed temple next to it to smithereens.

The thing was pissed, and it seemed to be looking for all who might be responsible for trying to end its time on earth. Then the rage mellowed and it turned toward Grogan, who quickly hunkered behind the slab of granite, breathing hard.

Shit! What the hell can I do now?

That's when he realized there was nothing he could do now except beg for mercy from the unstoppable energy being. He hobbled to an upright position, keeping all his weight on his good leg. The creature was staring right at him.

Grogan tossed the laser-and-scope assembly to the ground, closed his eyes and dropped his head. *I was just doing my job. I didn't want to hurt you. It's just that we're scared of what we don't know.*

It seemed like an eternity that he stood there waiting to meet his maker. He could still feel his heart's rapid beat. He was alive, but for how long? He lifted his head and slowly opened his eyes.

What the ... Where ... where did you go?

The mysterious creature was gone. He dropped his gaze to the laser-scope assembly. All that remained was a pile of dust.

Then he noticed something as he turned to leave. Something was different. He looked around to see what it was and his eyes fell to his feet. He was putting his full weight on both legs.

He reached down and felt his wounded leg. There was no pain when he touched the spot where the bullet had struck his thigh. He put even more weight on his bad leg. It was completely healed.

CHAPTER 66

THE GENERAL HAD TOLD Dan and Selena that HAARP was a go. The unprecedented plan of attack sounded ludicrous at first, but in actuality—according to the staff scientists—it was quite plausible. They said HAARP had the capability to auto-tune to the atomic resonance of anything. If the beam could be held on the target just long enough to trap the atoms of the material within the bandwidth of the frequency, there was a good chance the material could be atomized.

He still had his doubts about such an absurd plan of attack, though, especially since the United States military had the finest weapons in the world to choose from to defend itself. A lot of money had been poured into the defense of the country over the past few years, and it was times like this that made the investment worthwhile.

The general's landline rang only once before he picked it up.

"Yeah? … You saying it's not working? … Jesus, this is just going to make a bigger mess than we already have. Can't say I'm surprised.

Have 'em shut it down and I'll take care of this the way we should have from the get-go. If I were you, I'd get my ass out of there … That's above your pay grade, Grogan. Now do as I say. That's an order!"

Poor bastard. At least he thinks he has a chance. That's not a bad way to go out when serving your country.

The general didn't hesitate before he dialed out. It didn't take long for the party on the other end to answer.

"Is everything ready? … Good. The minute they're all in the same spot again, it's a green light, so get him off the ground now! … Evacuate Cairo? Shit, Colonel, we'd have to evacuate all of Upper Egypt on over to Israel to save everyone in the way. … There's no time for that! … We don't have the time, you imbecile! … I'll worry about any retaliations later. If we try to save those few millions, we might as well wait and evacuate the entire goddamn planet! You saw what they were capable of down in Australia! If we wait, there'll be no stopping them! I'd say it's justifiable! Now get 'em off the ground ASAP! Understand? … Good!"

He slammed down the receiver and stared out the window as a smile began to form on his face.

All right, you sons of bitches, it's time I put you back to sleep—permanently.

In Orbit

Butch was amazed at the power this beam seemed to have over his pursuers. However the hell it worked, he didn't care, but it was obviously going to literally tear these spiritual beings apart. That he was witnessing firsthand.

"Go back to wherever it is you freaks came from."

He was enjoying the moment when the beam stopped. Just stopped.

"Shit! What now?"

The two hundred's energy-packed bodies had enough mass that gravity still had a hold on them. They begin to plummet back to the earth as soon as the beam quit. Butch could sense that they were still quite alive and that this wasn't over by a long shot.

The girl—I gotta get the girl.

Butch was getting the hang of his new body with every experience he had. The thought of being back on the Giza Plateau was enough to instantly transport himself next to Erica in a split second. The time lapse was so quick that the others were still falling to the earth.

She still lay there as if she were stuck in a trance, which was probably for the best, considering the wild nature of the unfolding events. He quickly embraced her in his spiritual grasp just as the first of the two hundred came falling to the ground. From what he could see, they would soon be back to their original stature and strength.

Butch had to get Erica and get the hell out of there. He needed to take her somewhere safe. Someplace he could leave her until the dust had settled from whatever was to come with the fallen ones. The first place that came to mind was where his transformation had taken place. Only a few feet away but hopefully locked up in the ancient vault and undetected by the others. It was worth a shot.

In the blink of an eye, they were deep inside the Great Pyramid. This time, though, it was the King's Chamber that drew this thoughts. Something told him that was the spot, and that's where they materialized.

His luminous body lit up the room when they appeared. What was it that drew him here? There had to be a reason, but what? Then he saw it and everything became clear. The Israelites' gift from God. Their most cherished possession, but better yet the ultimate weapon: the Ark of the Covenant!

The long-sought relic fit perfectly in the coffer as it pulsated with an ominous glow. Almost as though it were alive. Could it be? Might there be a soul locked in the Ark? Even in his new body there was something about the thing that made his hair stand on end—that is, of course, if he still had any. What was it that gave him this feeling?

He laid Erica next to the wall and slowly moved up to the coffer that held the ancient artifact. Being nervous was rare for him even in his physical body, so the fact that he felt as he did now was quite unsettling.

He slowly reached into the coffer and lifted the Ark out and carefully set it on the floor. He then gently picked Erica up and placed her in the empty coffer.

"You should be safe here. I'll be back soon."

He turned and approached the Ark. "All right, Moses, looks like your ace in the hole now belongs to me."

CHAPTER 67

PRINCE SULTAN AIR BASE, SAUDI ARABIA

THE B-2 HAD LIFTED off the ground only moments ago. It was a short flight from the Prince Sultan Air Base in Saudi Arabia, and their mission was clear: drop their payload and continue on to the United States. Everything in Upper Egypt and the surrounding area would be annihilated.

GIZA PLATEAU, EGYPT

ALL OF THE TWO hundred were back on the plateau and had regained complete control of their spiritual bodies. The effects of the sonic-energy beam had come close to ripping their essence apart, but now they were free again to do as they pleased. This time they would do what they needed to get rid of the one who didn't belong.

"Spread out, my comrades," Samyaza said. "It seems being together has put our existence at risk. We must find the newcomer and convince him to join us. If not, he will face the same frozen prison we have endured for centuries. The choice will be his."

"Look, my Lord." Azazyel pointed. "There is the one now, next to the stone feline with the head of a human."

Next to the Sphinx was a familiar blue glowing figure, squared off and staring right at them. It was the newcomer. In front of him was a container of some kind that pulsated with a mysterious aura.

BUTCH STOOD THERE with the Ark placed in front of him. He wasn't sure what the outcome of the near future would be, but the force from within the ancient container now seemed to be flowing through him. If he truly had the ultimate power with the Israelites' legendary weapon from the Creator, he would surely now be unstoppable. And going against the multitude of angels before him, he was going to need all the help he could get.

"Which one of you shall I address?" Butch said to the group.

"It is I, Samyaza. I am the leader of the Watchers. And who is it I am speaking with?"

"Your worst nightmare, asshole! Unless you stay the hell out of my way. There's plenty of room here for all of us, but I sense that's not good enough for you. Am I right?"

"You came seconds away from destroying us once." Samyaza motioned to the others. "I cannot allow that to happen yet again."

Not only had Butch's senses intensified since his transformation, but standing in the vicinity of the Ark made him fully aware of everything. Even of the fact that Azazyel was planning an attack from the rear while he spoke to Samyaza. It was as though he were God himself!

Without turning around, Butch sent a powerful plasma blast directly at Azazyel, which sent him back several hundred feet, immobilizing him for several seconds.

"I was being nice to your friend. Try anything stupid like that again and you'll see what I mean."

Samyaza turned to Butch. "Ah, so you possess the power of the almighty one. How fortunate for you. Tell me, newcomer, what makes you think you can trust the power of the almighty to stay true to you? Even his chosen people were eventually subdued. If you join with us, there will be no doubt of the survival of all of us and our reign on this planet."

"A tempting offer, *friend*. I'll give it some thought. In the meantime, I have some business to attend to."

FORTY-THOUSAND FEET OVER THE GIZA PLATEAU

THE B-2 AND ITS destructive payload were directly over the multitude of energy beings that stood on the plateau below. Major Collins had practiced bombing missions numerous times in training, but this was for real.

"Target acquired, sir." The major flipped open the guarded switch, exposing the point of no return.

"Yes, sir." The major took a deep breath and stiffened his jaw. Then he flipped the switch. "Package has been sent."

THE DISTANT PAST

TY AND GRANT WERE moving at a fast jog and getting ever closer to their destination. Ty was being drawn toward the center of the oasis by a force he couldn't describe. The sensation was almost overwhelming.

The stage they were on now was big, probably the biggest of all. When he had first appeared here only a few days ago, the tranquility of this place was almost indescribable, giving hints as to its location in time and space.

All traces of Ty's memory fog had been extinguished. As they moved closer to their goal, he couldn't help but think of the magnificent setting they were in. One that numerous adventurers had searched for throughout history. The only time on the planet that utopia had ever existed. A true paradise with everything that any living creature could possibly want in order to live an unencumbered life.

Ty slowed to a stop and stared. They were there. The center of God's first gift to his human creations. The Garden of Eden.

The site was something to behold. Ty and Grant stood still with a fixed gaze as though they had been frozen in time.

A small opening in their lush surroundings was what held their attention. Two trees only a few feet apart. Both were very different varieties and not to be found anywhere else in the entire paradise. Neither were full-grown, and they were not much taller than he was. They both emitted a magical glow as though they contained a life force.

Ty broke from his trance-like state and slowly walked around the two magical trees, never taking his eyes off them. They were unlike anything he'd ever seen, and they pulsed ever so slightly, creating the sense that they were much more than ordinary trees. It was as if they possessed a soul trying to escape the confines of their physical host.

"So, you have finally found what you came for ... Son of Jared," the serpent hissed from behind him.

Ty drew his sword without looking, still fixed on the trees. "Call me what you wish, serpent. Your days are numbered, and there's nothing you can do to save your pitiful self now."

"Save myself? I will be in existence for all eternity. That I can assure you of. Even if you succeed with what you intend."

"Oh, I'll succeed, all right. That I promise you."

Ty looked at the two trees. Neither had grown enough to bear fruit. His timing was impeccable, and his mission would soon be complete.

The serpent hissed as he spoke. "Do you not think man will ever sin again if you take down the tree of knowledge? Surely eating the forbidden fruit will not be the one and only time man will disobey the Creator."

"Ah, the great deceiver and his words of wisdom. Tell me, serpent, do you not know you are destined to crawl on your belly for your future actions? Look at this as me doing you a favor. Maybe you should be thanking me."

Ty stepped in with his sword held high and, without hesitation, released all his power into the downward swing with the razor-sharp weapon.

"No! You fool! What are you doing?" The serpent hissed frantically. "You know not what you do, for that is not the tree of knowledge!"

Ty's sword sank deep into the trunk, almost severing it with one blow.

"Do you truly expect me to believe the greatest liar of all time?" Ty said as he pried his weapon from the base of the tree.

The serpent advanced toward Ty as he raised his sword even higher than before. "Your forked tongue will not work on me."

Ty let loose with enough power to finish the job. There was nothing the serpent could do to impede his aim.

"Noooooooooooo!" The serpent frantically hissed. "You fool! You must believe me! That is not the tree of knowledge! It is the tree of li

THE END

EPILOGUE

WHAT REALLY HAPPENED ON top of Mount Hermon all those years ago? Is it possible the story in the Book of Enoch found in the Dead Sea Scrolls is actually true? Numerous legends across the planet tell a similar tale. Might they all have originated with this one event?

Also known as the "forbidden place," Mount Hermon is referred to several times in religious texts. It's even mentioned in the Epic of Gilgamesh, which may be some of the oldest literature on the planet.

In 1869 inside the ancient temple ruins of Qasr Antar on top of Mount Hermon, Sir Charles Warren found a stone with the inscription *According to the command of the greatest and Holy God, those who take an oath proceed from here.* The stone can still be seen today at the British Museum. Author unknown …

Several decades ago, the United Nations constructed an outpost station on the very top of Mount Hermon that remains in operation to this day.